The Public World of Parable Jones

DOMINIC BEHAN

COLLINS
8 Grafton Street, London W1
1989

William Collins Sons & Co. Ltd
London · Glasgow · Sydney · Auckland
Toronto · Johannesburg

First published 1989

BRITISH LIBRARY CATALOGUING IN PUBLICATION DATA
Behan, Dominic
The public world of Parable Jones.
I. Title
823'.914 [F]
ISBN 0 00 223478 5

Photoset in Linotron Ehrhardt at
The Spartan Press Ltd,
Lymington, Hants
Printed and bound in Great Britain by
William Collins Sons and Co Ltd, Glasgow

For Josephine Behan

CHAPTER ONE

Quare Times

Parable Jones was incommoded. His wife incommoded him. His mistress incommoded him. He could put up with it from his mistress. His wife could go and have a mass said for herself. Once again her bad temper had triumphed over the work. Once too often, once again.

Long before the streets were well aired, he had jumped up. Bright and early. With the day, rearing to go. Only yesterday, feeling like Fluther on a dry run, he had passed every pub, looking neither right nor left, but straight in the direction of Terenure, home and beauty. Beneath his oxter he had carried a parcel from Easons 'the stationers'. A ribbon for the portable, and a ream of paper.

This morning he had taken his wife's toothbrush to the typewriter and scrubbed the journalism off each tolerant key. It seemed to make sense – Jeannie had no use for the toothbrush and the *Herald* had little need of Parable Jones. Not since he had written that piece about the 'scrounging rich'. Anyway he had made himself fit and ready to do battle with the blank paper that would be as awkward as a new whore.

Art, in the morning, comes dropping slow. There's no forcing it. Diligent application – the prerequisites of which are peace of mind and isolation. Myles was of the opinion that the promiscuous daughters of Zeus often needed a kick up the jacksi. Milligan swore that part-time celibacy worked. Parable had long ago made up his mind that, if ever he had to choose between art and arse, fornication would win, hands down.

Tolstoy had put all worldly things aside, and found that, to the pure of mind, life is dull, dull, deadly dull, and boring – though, at nearly eighty years of age, remembrance is about the only thing that sex can call its own. Of course long before *Cyclops Erectile Erotica* saw the light, Leo had previously known his Russian Fagin to weep copiously through its only eye over the best part of St Petersburg. Gide too had taken the pledge, but then he had so little to give up it was no great sacrifice. When John Joe Murphy found that his writing wasn't coming, he cut off his cock.

– Only to find, said Parable, that the fault was in his head.

Inextirpable hedonism of the head. How P. J. yearned but to succumb. How frequently he assured himself that of all the emotions temptation is the sublimest of the sublime. Wilde's negative approach to enticement was half-hearted, to say the least. Temptation must be grabbed by both hands and a willing mind. Parable was of the opinion that broad gestures like abstinence should be reserved until a man was *in articulo mortis*.

Writers should be like that. But not those who enjoy doing it – the ones who can't. Shavian pedagogues. Parable had seen them at it more than once. And they all looked the same, whether they were like that clever don who stole *Under Milk Wood* from a drunken poet in Great Portland Street, London, or wiped up Dylan's vomit from his Bayswater basement. Poor sentimental Dylan! What sort of a gesture was it from him to cry, 'Who's afraid of James Augustine' and protest his apostasy in *Portrait of the Artist as a Young Dog*?

Parable had enjoyed his time with the BBC and was sad when the accountants came to claim their heritage.

It was the lowering of standards that P. J. had found unacceptable. Though of course he would never have left had he not been kicked out. It was not the bad writing that had hurt Parable. Bad writing is a graffito you can ignore except in prison or lavatories. Bad writers were the problem: like MacNeice's genii, one rub of the lamp and there they were in the persona of editors and producers.

And they were so sincere. They wore their mediocrity like a badge of arrogant modesty. So goddamn sincere. That pamphleteering earnestness that made Parable Jones long to puke. Even the bloody blank paper is precious to them; palimpsest – almost. And, in so far as castration for literature is concerned, how many times have you heard Parable say:

– That sort of thing went out with adult boy sopranos. Castration? I'd let them cut me balls off first.

Dr Johnson did as much for literature as anybody else. Nor did it matter a tuppenny damn that his intellection was belched out in farts, groans and graceless grunts. He did not like those who saw writing as a discipline, and reading as a duty. He admonished one person for reading a book through, and told another that 'A man ought to read just as inclination leads him; for what he reads as a task will do him little good.' Parable told himself that it was easy enough for Dr Sam, who, like Joyce's publisher, 'had a red-headed Scotchman to keep his book'. But not a great many writers can afford such a life-style now. Even the days of the amanuenses were numbered.

First the Boswells, then the dictaphones, later the Becketts, and then the word processor. Louis B. Mayer had the right idea. P. J. hankered after the world of the long-legged secretaries and Hollywood casting couches.

Dublin is a station of the cross where Jesus falls for the umpteenth time – last chance saloon for the person who believed that pleasure is the chief good. The rest of Ireland is a begrudgery. Sadism and masochism is so much in evidence that folk think Paul took the road to Damascus in the belief that he was on his way to Knock.

For five days a week Humpty Brinsley MacNamara humped dumpy little Miss Brazil who kept goal for Radio Eireann down in Henry Street. On Fridays he would think of Easter Week and hump her on top of the GPO and then dump her outside a confession box in Dominick Street chapel. He would mortify his sins of the flesh and promise never to do it again – until Monday. And it was a good job that Brinsley was half blind, since Miss Brazil of the miraculous middle had a face like a disappointed cripple back from Lourdes. One look at Bernadette Brazil and a really horny Humpy would have worn the condom on his head. But Brinsley was only doing research, experiencing sex second-hand – although even that must have been some improvement on the first-hand stuff he used to get with the Christian Brothers at Clane.

Parable recalled the excitement of the confessional. He remembered as a kid wanking when he felt there wasn't enough sin in his week to earn a proper penance. Didn't want to waste the confessor's time. And then the fascination of the priest's anger. How dare he abuse himself in such a way! But young Parable didn't think of it as self-abuse. He thought he treated himself very well: twice a day and three times on a Friday – because he knew he wouldn't be able to do it again until after mass on Sunday.

And were the Kimmage clergy stone deaf to all the young men going blind in the right hand? Every Friday evening an adolescence of boys would be outscreaming each other in the agony of ecstasy. Behind the wall in Jameson's field and within an ejaculation of the chapel. The place smelled more of fish than did Aberdeen market. All changed now since rationalism had taken all the sin out of masturbation, and the Hierarchy commanded a sublimation of sex. Changed utterly: a terrible beauty was bored.

The 'in' word with publishers that morning was 'picaresque'. It had been in since *Tom Jones*, but because Fielding was signed up by somebody else, most publishers had to wait until the film of the book. Hence the popularity just now of 'picaresque'.

Parable needed a model. Most of the people he knew were rogues, but who in his right mind with even a threatening of honesty, could describe any of them as 'lovable'? Mallarkey did the most outrageous things but always in the manner of the peasant. Paddy Swift had entitled a canvas on the murder of Kevin O'Higgins, 'The Ides Have It', then spoiled the whole effect by claiming to be a 'working-class painter'. Young Martin sat sketching his old man's death throes, and, so preoccupied was he, his father slipped away without the artist noticing. But then the magnificent Shavian disregard for family went for nought when the same young Martin wept at his brother's funeral.

Parable Jones was still looking through his memory for a picaresque model when his wife entered the room. She smiled a crocodile smile as she noticed the satisfied look on her husband's contented face. She knew he was thinking of anybody else. He always was. From the very hour they were married he had brought his fancies to bed with him. The dirty bastard! Talking about what he'd like to do to her sister – or to his own, the pig! God, but his mind was like a sewer.

In the beginning she hadn't minded his outspoken sexual fantasies: it was all manly and above board. She had thoroughly enjoyed it in fact, once. But then, his friends started to drop all sorts of hints, nothing precise, just innuendo. No, they never said anything, just suggested that he might be. Anyway Jeannie started to look at him differently because she could accept a great deal but not that the man she was married to wasn't.

A look of triumph filled Jeannie's eyes as she emptied the contents of the mail-box right under Parable's nose. Letters, the litter of litigation, littered the literator's table. Oh, Mary! Sweet Mother of the Martyred Messiah who died suffering the pain of others! Mariolatry or marine metamorphoses? I'm sunk. Flotsam: jetsam: litoralis. But every man's shore is only so big, and there ain't room here for the two of us, Jeannie! What sadistic postman, Parable pondered, could whistle 'O What A Beautiful Morning' and deliver shit like this?

Bunting for a bailiff's birthday! Bills for gas and bills for rent, life unearned, already spent. With a wry smile Parable looked from the table to his wife, and back to the table:

– Have yeh, by any chance, been borrowing debts from the neighbours? Have yeh been on the knocker, Jeannie?

But, there she was now and her gone. She had stomped out, banging the door in her self-satisfied wake. Parable had raised the window, and, throwing the typewriter into the garden, had screamed after it:

– Grow a book! For jazes sake grow a fuckin' book!

Mrs Dolores O'Kane's cocker spaniel cocked a leg on Parable's typewriter, paused and pissed. It then sniffed a soiled sheet of A4 that was crooked in the platen, but all the dog could read was:

> Careless Mary, quite contrary, went beresk when her little
> lost lamb was rammed by a prick of a prize picaresque.

Parable Jones, patron saint of the second-hand coming, cursed

Christianity, and recited, silently, the Lord's prayer according to Joyce:

– 'O Vague Something behind Everything'. For the love of the Lord Christ, change my curs-o-God state of affairs. Give me, for Christ' sake a pen and ink-bottle and some peace of mind, and then, by the crucified Jaysus, if I don't sharpen that little pen and dip it into fermented ink, and write tiny little sentences about the people who betrayed me send me to hell.

Parable knew how lucky had been the author of *Ulysses*. Reared for Gethsemane, Joyce would have perished in the Garden of Eden. To be born with that magnificent sense of betrayal in the same land, of the same blood, of Dermot McMurrough, Tim Healy, Richard Pigott, and the Catholic Church! Good God, God, was any man ever more in his ancestral element?

Ever since literary conception, Parable, like Larry McHale's dog, Tristram Shandy, had gone a step of each literary road with the anti-Christ. He had lurched toe to toe with Myles when that man expressed his bog jealousy of Joyce a little too rustically. He had applauded James Augustine's thesis that the wet humour and dry wit of the Irish had been responsible for the quicklime in Parnell's eye. He had cursed Dante with Mr Casey and Simon Dedalus. He had prayed for bygmester Finnegan of the stuttering hand.

He had even agreed that the slaying of Brian Boru after the Battle of Clontarf on Good Friday, 1014, was an uncalled-for act. But, when Joyce decreed that we weep for the death of Fionn MaCumhail, Parable Jones said, 'If ever mythology is taken out of the realm of politics, history will have us fucked.'

Now he argued with the all-pervading Joyce because he knew that the very talent of the genius was forbidding. Maybe Myles was right. No man should have to admire his nemesis, and that was about the height of it. And yet, once a Joycean always a Joycean. He couldn't help remembering that all his literary-political disciplines had been imposed on his thinking by the Camac colossus. Over and over again he went over and over in his mind the complaints that had issued from Joyce to his brother Stanislaus. In Trieste he hated the 'damn silly sun that makes men into butter' and was 'glad that soon Sol would be abed'. He was delighted that: 'The damned monotonous summer was over and the rain and soft air made me think of the beautiful (I am serious) climate of Ireland.'

He could be as serious as he liked. In the long run the whole thing was as absurd as the notices Parable had seen in Wandsworth High Street: 'DOGS FOUND FOULING THE FOOTPATH WILL BE FINED'.

First find your Dylan.

As he settled into the middle seat of the Terenure bus, Parable Jones decided that the late James Joyce, late of Trieste, had had a great deal to worry about.

The vibrating bus turned the flesh to gristle and he crossed one leg over the other so as to stem the rising tide. He remembered seeing a vibrator for the first time. Sally had asked him to take some cream from her bedside table and he had come across this torch thing that looked like a plastic penis. When he pressed the switch it led a life of its own, and when he asked Sally what was the precise function of this pen-like object that shed neither literary nor physical light, she had replied simply:

– To help me remain faithful to you, lover.

Afterwards he had felt such a fool.

Across the aisle, and from behind a brown paper bag filled with green vegetables, a bored housewife smiled at him. Parable touched his hat and almost at once crossed himself as the ugly exterior of Harold's Cross Chapel passed by. Two birds with but a single stone – he had been good mannered and, by a simple deception, had given the impression that he believed the middle leg to be for cricket and procreation.

Anyway, he had reservations about cheating on Sally-Anne Millington. If a man is not going to be faithful to his mistress! Well, for fuck sake. Parable Jones believed that a man must be bound by some sort of morality. Besides which, he thought he had seen the woman before:

'Maybe a neighbour of Jeannie's, if the truth be known. Wouldn't like the wife to earn the pity of another woman. Every one a saint until she's a mistress. Nothing worse than one bitch feeling superior to another, "Poor cow, a right randy-Andy she has for a man.

Honestly, missus, if he was mine I'd peel the fornicating fucker like a banana."'

As he opened and closed the quotes round the different dialogues going on in his mind, he wondered if interior monologue had been recognised as such before Joyce and Dujardin. But of course it must have been sensed. 'I exist, therefore I am.' To exist is to be recognised, surely. Precepts of existentialism. Was the world really waiting for Dujardin and Joyce, Virginia Woolf and the stream of consciousness? But then *monologue intérieur* is merely a literary narrative device.

At Harold's Cross Greyhound Racing Stadium, Charles Philpot Robert Emmet Parnell Belton stepped aboard and almost pulled the omnibus to one side like the handle of a can. The laugh and the sag as Belton dragged his huge unwieldy bulk up to the top deck was a signal to abandon the sinking ship of atheism:

– Oh God, thought Parable, let me be like a snowflake in the Sahara.

But as, Belton sat down beside the almost crushed writer, he announced his presence:

– There yeh are, Jones!

To which Parable replied:

– All but, Charlie, all but. And, despondently disclosed to himself, here we go now on Eamon de Valera, playboy of Limerick Junction, and Brough's incestuous contribution to world ignorance.

Reading his friend's mind, Belton observed:

– Wasn't born in Brough at all, yeh know.

Bored God, he was carrying on the interrupted conversation of their last meeting. Belton was only one of many Irish people writing biographies of the Pope, or de Valera, or James Joyce.

Usually, most cunning Celts are into some verbiage or other at onetime, sometime, somewhere, anytime, anywhere. But here, on the edge of Dublin's 1,000th birthday, the children of Anna Livia had at least three ready made subjects. In her millennium, the Holy Trinity was no longer a mystery. No magic trio is Eamon de Valera, James Joyce or Pontiff Paul. Poles apart, this pope was no paraclete. The three had one thing in common, their Irishry. Joyce and de

Valera through blood, with the Pope through religion. Oh, he might never become as Catholic as the rest of the Irish, but they'd never tell him that to his face.

Hand-knitted Dev and Dandy Jim were born in 1882 and the Holy Father had visited Dublin on their hundredth birthday. Not that he'd know who Joyce was from a bar of soap. Maybe Dev, for it is clear now that stupidity is an attitude of mind. Yes, Parable convinced himself that de Valera and the Pope would have been soul-mates.

Irishmen, publishers, and Yankee presidential election agents have lived on anniversaries since the pagan Pliny, the Catholic Kennedy; and the 'Whatever you are yourself' Reagan, showed us where to look for the origins of Christianity. But, long before the 80s, Parable had wondered about that. Were the Essenes the direct ancestors of the same monks who penned the Book of Kells? Was the first pope black? More importantly, was St Peter PLO or Hagannah? One thing was certain, the Dead Sea Scrolls proved that Jesus was a Jew and we have publishers to thank for that, although they'd never make the Irish believe it.

– Who wasn't born in Brough? asked Parable, who would gladly go to hell for the sake of propriety.

Belton's face was as near to P. J.'s ear as distance would permit:

– Dev wasn't. Nor near it. I checked up on it because you were so positive.

– I was positive. Are yeh sure, asked Parable who couldn't believe he had ever been remotely interested in being positive about anything regarding such a boring old bastard as Eamon de Valera.

Nor had it come as a surprise to P. J. that the master of Gandhi's spinning wheel would have been a century had he lived or not until 14th October, 1982. Parable Jones never thought the old chancer had ever been less:

– Of course yeh were, said Belton, d'ye think I'd forget something as important as that? Remember at Paddy Ennis's funeral when 'Long Kelly' and Charlie Joe were wondering who'd go next? From the pit of his gargantuan belly threatened the rumble of a laugh that almost rendered speech impossible. Who'd go next is right! Didn't Kelly take the low road the following week. And Charlie went with

Fergus the week after! But then sure didn't he always do whatever Long Paddy Kelly ever told him? Gave up the ghost, Parable. Though a lot of that may have had to do with the Almighty, for when God has something on His mind He doesn't fuck about, does He, Parable?

As Belton laughed and P. J. was covered in spit there was no knowing which way to turn. Parable would not wipe his face, but neither had he any intention of turning the other cheek. Pretending to scratch his ear he took the opportunity to clean his phyiz with the elbow of his sleeve before responding:

– Maybe God and Macbeth were of like mind, that there's nothing serious in mortality?

Charlie wasn't into things Scottish just then:

– Anyway, you and Charlie Joe and Long Paddy were in the corner of the Brian Boru Bar, if yeh remember?

– I wouldn't doubt yeh, said Parable who didn't give a damn. But Belton persisted.

– You're not goin' to tell me that you've forgotten the remark that Kelly made to the Yank, when that tourist gentleman asked why, in a world of avenues named after Griffiths and Collins, there wasn' a single terrace called in honour of Dev?

Parable was at a loss, but Belton wasn't, for he had, as P. J. was fond of saying, a mind like blotting paper, and just as eclectic:

– Kelly looked nearly through the Yank as he told him bitterly, 'Because, mister, we've never been able to find a street that was long enough or crooked enough to name after the ould fucker!'

Charlie rocked on his laughter to Kelly's quip and the whole bus-load of passengers was affected in like way, so infectious was Belton's laugh and so deep their disappointment with Eamon de Valera.

The bus turned into Camden Street and Belton rose to alight at Kelly's Corner. Still with his eyes streaming, he called from the top of the stairs:

– Lexington Avenue at Fifty-first Street, New York. That's where Dev was born on October 14th, 1882.

From the window of the bus, Parable saw him skip gently into its momentum. For such a huge man he was nimble on his pins. Soon he was swallowed up by the milling throng, big and all as he was.

CHAPTER TWO

Knock Hard

Rumour has it that Harry McGill of McGill and Gill, publishers, cannot read. In a profession where simple accountancy is preferable to a degree in English, illiteracy is not considered to be a great drawback.

Some say, or did say before he became a mogul, that Harry came into books on a hand-out from Eamon de Valera, who required that McGill keep shtoom on how the 'Long Fella' got his hands on the *Irish Press*.

And yet, most mysteries are easily explained. Harry's father and Joe McGrath were known in the old days as Dev's Deadly Devils. They would shoot the odd impediment, but chiefly they were bank robbers for the Republic.

Harry senior and McGrath had long ago decided that the first duty any sensible patriot owes to liberty is to free himself. Together with a chap called Jack O'Sheehan they founded the 'Holy Trinity' of Michael Collins' 'Twelve Apostles'.

Collins sacked Jack O'Sheehan when he caught him with his hand in the ideological till. Then came the 'split' between the 'Long Fella' and the 'Big Fella'. Dev's crowd killed Collins in a shabby ambush while the 'Big Fella' was half drunk. O'Sheehan celebrated the achievement in his song to de Valera, 'Soldiers of the Rearguard'.

Dev, never a man to forget tributes or insults, wondered what he could do for his pet groveller. He gave Jacko the job of directing the Irish Hospitals Sweepstakes. It was the making of O'Sheehan. He was in charge of a goldmine. The 'Sweeps' was a charitable foundation that made rich men out of the wealthy and paupers out of the poor. Charity, thy name is opportunity.

Charlie Belton was thinking this as Harry McGill thumbed his way through Charlie's manuscript. If the publisher couldn't read he was taking a helluva long time looking at the words.

Bulky Belton sat back into the deep hide of the luxurious settee and it made a rude noise that surprised him and made McGill's secretary look questioningly at the big man as she left her boss's office having placed Belton's file in front of her employer.

Charlie coloured and tried, with his eyes, to explain away the sound:

– Wasn't me, miss, honest . . . the leather . . . honest to God. He longed for the brass neck of the actor, Mrs Pat Campbell. She used to go to the wings, piss into a bucket, and return to the persona of Lady Bracknell to examine imperiously the unfortunate Ernest Worthing.

She and Shaw, and them and marriage. He a vegetarian and she who could have eaten the Sacred Heart, stuffed. Imagine the children they could have made together, she had told Shaw. But G. B. S. had reminded her that his Protestant religion owed more to soup than to conviction. Although born in a stable he was not necessarily a horse Protestant.

As Harry McGill perused Belton's manuscript it was clear that he was more interested in which part of his anatomy needed most attention. He bit a finger nail, scoured an ear, picked his nose and scratched his bollocks. If being inscrutable is the nature of enigma, then that is what McGill's face was, inscrutably enigmatic. Neither by frown nor smile did he betray a single emotion. But, sure, how could anybody read about de Valera and smile? Sweet Christ, a person couldn't even think about de Valera and smile.

Like de Gaulle, Dev was as dull as death. Between them, it was said, they could speak in nearly every European language, the wonderful works of God. But they knew of little else. Those tall Gauls had an unhealthy interest in religion. Their belief in the non-existence of matter was such as would have done Bishop Berkeley proud. They assumed that man had been made by God and not the other way round.

Then too, their wives had lived the lives of grass widows, for, while Colombey-Les-Deux-Eglises was company enough for Charles, Eamon found comfort in the singular solitariness of Blackrock chapel.

De Gaulle had gone there to await a nation's call that never came, Dev to escape a call to nationhood that never ceased.

McGill looked up, let his swivel chair fall forward, and placed Belton's manuscript on the desk:

– Now, what sort of biography do we have here? A paean of praise to excuse a great man's indiscretions? The history of a despot made warm for the public good?

Belton wished to protest, if only to escape momentarily the irony implicit in the publisher's tones, but McGill was enjoying himself with all the cruelty of the privileged patron:

– Is it what people might think of as the previously published truth, because, believe me, Charlie, if that is the case I have no intention of buying? Why should I pay good money for the resurrected stuff of newspaper morgues?

Belton, avoiding clarity, mumbled an objection. He couldn't risk saying anything that might jeopardise his chances of a further advance. At times like this his principles were a mixture of mortgages and overdrafts. McGill's interrogation was relentless in its despotism:

– What are we trying to do, Charlie? If this is all I'm going to get, I might as well have hired somebody who 'liked' de Valera!

Belton murmured something about wanting to write an 'objective' work, but McGill hated the 'Long Fella' as subjectively as vengeance could decree. De Valera, for whom the dead held no fear, helped the child of an erstwhile comrade. In a moment of Christian philanthropy he befriended Harry, and the publisher would never forget that selfish act as long as he lived:

– Objective bollocks, Charlie! This shit is no more than a bucket of fucking whitewash!

The condition of the poor is that they have more principles than the rich. Belton could scarcely believe what his mouth was saying:

– Whitewash de Valera! Me! You must be joking, Harry! After what that long bastard did to me at the *Irish Press*!

In 'Old God's' time Belton had been a young reporter for Mr de Valera's newspaper. To Ireland's national stadium he had been sent to cover Ireland since God. A pageant was on display there and it had to do with the faith of the fathers and the saints who had brought the dope to the bog of forebearance. It was the living proof of omnipresence – no sooner had St Patrick gone out one gate but St Brigid came through another. St Brendan had barely discovered America when St Benedict discovered drink, and Charlie discovered a pain in his arse. In Bacchanalian bohemianism he had screamed at the football pitch:

– God bless God! Ah but isn't it He of the upper case is the great fella!

De Valera had been seated in the presidential box during the outburst, and when Charlie got back to the newsroom it was to his cards, money, and the promise that he would never again work for a de Valerian enterprise. That proscription covered a wide range of options. For a while the odd editor let Belton do the occasional bit of stringing, or allowed him to ghost for the more drunken – more talented – by-liners, but always de Valera found out and Charlie had to walk again. Dev's great dedication was held together by the sure and certain knowledge that the world was made up of him and potential enemies. According to Archie Doyle, the 'Long Fella' went down on his knees the evening before Kevin O'Higgins was killed and prayed for the repose of his soul:

– Archie, aren't you the lucky man who has but to carry out the wishes of the cause? I will have to mourn O'Higgins' passing for an eternity. On the death of Collins he said a decade of the Rosary.

McGill hadn't been listening to Charlie's thoughts:

– What about all the shit I gave you on the *Irish Press*? He robbed it man! It's of public interest, Charlie, when a guy steals a whole newspaper. And what about the misgivings he experienced when having first made it with his wife?

Belton said he had tried to deal with Dev's marital relationship tastefully. Good taste and Eamon de Valera were not compatible in McGill's eyes.

– De Valera's biography is no subject for the squeamish, Charlie. Poor Sinead! He led her the life of the damned. No time for misgivings when there was no misgiving in his treatment of her, Charlie. He was a sadistic bastard.

McGill, thought Belton, was worse than Dev because he had the words as well as the inclination. And, like most publishers, Harry had the instinct for a con. He wasn't well-read enough to spot it but, like an animal caught in a web of words, he sensed it:

– Lancelot de Valera! I'm not joking, Charlie – with the cost of printing I can't afford to joke. Have you read what you wrote? I'm serious. Listen to this bit, 'Dev marched towards Boland's Mills at the head of one hundred and thirty men. They were the ones who had answered the nation's call from a possible eight hundred.' His highest paid hack, Jack O'Sheehan, couldn't have written about him better . . .

Belton felt relieved. For a moment he thought that the publisher had actually spotted his sources. Knowing that Harry judged most writing by weight, Charlie had pillaged some of 'The Chief's' many biographers to pad his slim volume:

– Jesus, said McGill, will you just listen to this, 'Dev would not let the women fight. He told one of his staff officers, Captain Malone, to use them only as bearers and provisioners.' Che Guevara isn't in it! For Christ's sake, Charlie will yeh catch yourself on!

Belton believed he must protest:

– I don't want to make him all black, Harry . . .

McGill responded at once:

– Why not? It never did Machiavelli any harm with the world. When the British gunboat the *Helga* is bombarding de Valera's position from the Liffey, this Captain Malone asks 'The Chief', 'What happens if the roof caves in' and de Valera says, 'Let it'! That sounds more like John Wayne than Judas!

Belton protested feebly:

– But that's what he said, Harry . . .

McGill roared and his secretary reassured herself that here was at least one scribe who wouldn't be getting any alms today. Miriam Clandillon hated lowly writers who upset her boss and disturbed the computer:

– I don't give a fuck what he says, unless it demonstrates his selfish arrogance.

Belton averred that if the book was to have any credibility at all then the small truths must be told:

– Don't worry, Harry, the lie he lived later brings him to grief.

But McGill wanted him to come to grief now:

– I'm not paying good money to have that long bastard canonised. You're not going to do his PR man on my dough, Charlie . . .

Forgetting that he was the pipe and not the piper, Belton begged reasonableness:

– Everybody in Ireland knows the history of Eamon de Valera. There's just no way to reveal the rottenness of the man if we ignore his bits of gallantry. The Irish like heroics, Harry, and, having bought the 'gallant Jack' bit, they will have to swallow the vinegar as well . . .

Almost before the words formed his unfortunate speech, Belton realised that he had made a mistake. If Harry McGill knew about any race it was the one from which he sprung:

– You're worried about the likes and the dislikes of the Irish! You poor slob! The Irish don't buy books. The Irish don't even read fucking books – except when they're looking for libel. Don't lose any sleep about what the Irish might believe. The Irish think they are too clever to have to read anything by anybody but themselves. The Irish? That's the rock you'll perish on, ould son!

Belton, feeling that he must defend his race, made muttered responses. But the publisher wasn't listening to anything that wasn't going on in his own mind:

– Miriam Clandillon could tell you that we have a room here filled with the unsolicited manuscripts of the Irish. They don't even question if a thing is worthy of publication. They sit at home making up their royalties. Don't give me the Irish, Charlie, I've had those fuckers all my life!

Belton stood on the pavement outside McGill and Hill's. To stand and stare. From the window of his office, Harry McGill looked down on Charlie who knew not which way to turn. Should he go right into Gardiner's Place for Frederick Street, or go straight down to the Diamond?

McGill killed him a thousand times at every visit. He always felt bollock naked but for the cap in hand. And, yet, this most recent advance would at least keep the building society off his back and leave a little to keep the bank at arm's length. The manager reminded him of the sullen bronze monkey that once stood at Blackrock Railway station, you put three coppers in its mouth and it smiled as it spat out a chocolate bar.

On the other hand, McGill realised the nature of Belton's dilemma almost before Charlie did himself. The draft wasn't worth a light without somebody to cash it, and most of those in a position to so do were people to whom Charlie was already indebted. Belton was caught in the cleft stick of paradox – he couldn't afford the ultimate incest, the luxury of cashing a cheque at his own bank.

Belton was worse off than even Harry knew. He would have to eschew not only his own local but every pub in which he was known. The more he thought of it he was convinced that, like Micawber, the only route home was by the way of the angels.

McGill could have given him cash, but it is no business of business to have contented slaves. Anyway, scribes with full bellies were arrogant bastards. They got the idea that publishers like McGill were there for no other reason than to arrange for the printing and distribution of books. Harry had never forgotten the remark of that cunt, Parable Jones, when he had foolishly extended a hand at a publisher's party:

– Publishers should be over in Lichfield, minding their barrows with the rest of the booksellers.

If Harry could ever help Parable Jones as he went on his way, it would be off the end of a rope. How he longed to tell that sarcastic bastard that nobody in McGill and Hill's would ever be tempted to wipe an arse in a mountain of his manuscripts.

Charlie turned right for Frederick Street and Harry went back to his desk to peruse further the life and times of Eamon de Valera:

> De Valera was quite unmoved by opinions contrary to his own. His motto was, 'A place for everything and everything in its place'. The Chief quoted from himself a lot because he

> was a very ill-read man, except in mathematics, 'a subject', said Professor Tierney, 'in which he had read wrongly'. His Vice-commandant said of him during Easter Week, 'He was able to discuss every detail, even to the places where it would be possible to secure an alternative water supply . . . I cannot remember a query put to him, that he was not able to answer immediately.'

– Shit, said Harry McGill, and flung the manuscript from him in disgust.

CHAPTER THREE

Ould Dog. Hard Road.

Where the Jacobs biscuit factory once stood near the corner of Redmonds Hill, the bus idled in neutral. Folk crossed Aungier Street. Some – hierarchaeologists looking for the anthropomorphic friend they had in Jesus – to mass at Whitefriars Street. The more practical ones on their way to Werburgh Street Labour Exchange. Alighting from the bus, Parable Jones joined the maddened throng. Among two congregations dedicated, one to the misery of poverty, and the other to the poverty of misery, P. J. didn't feel like Marx chastising Proudhon, he felt a fraud. At this hour of the morning a man should be about with purpose in mind. Parable Jones was more idle than unemployed. Nor did he feel any need for invisible means of support.

Hyper-sensitive of his own condition he had all but dismissed himself, when a chap, concluding he had copped a kindred soul, observed:

– It's the pensioners, yeh know. There must be thousands of them. They've used up their own span and begrudge anybody younger an extra go at life. Its a vicious circle, so it is. People like Larkin spend years looking for decent conditions so that folk may live better longer, and for what? So that they can fuck up the rest of us.

Parable didn't know what the hell he was on about, but, judging by the cough and the cigarette drooping from the corner of his mouth, he didn't think that this particular man in the street would be for long a burden on anybody. He inclined an ambiguous nod and the man continued:

– D'ye know that twenty-five per cent of the electorate are old age pensioners? Did yeh know that? Twenty-five per cent! Give the old bastards an extra five shillings a week and they'll sell the country to the highest bidder. Mickey Mouse could be in power, or Donald Duck – for ever. Don't take my word for it, have a look at Britain. That Mrs Attila seems to have been in office since the fuckin' flood. And who's goin' to put her out? That's the question, flower.

Parable asked timidly about the other seventy-five per cent on the voting register, and the shabbily dressed oracle gave him a withering pitying look of disdain:

– Most people make that same mistake. There isn't a hundred per cent, yeh see. There never is. Mostly there are folk who have never found their way on to the register, or there are folk on it who have been dead for two, or three elections and they all vote the party ticket. Emigrants and house confined cripples vote the party ticket and most of the unemployed can't be bothered. D'ye know that most governments are elected by less that forty per cent of the electorate? It's more personation than personality. That's why the government looks after the old. Conservatives. Everybody in the queue for Heaven is a right-winger. Otherwise government would have introduced enthanasia years ago.

They had almost reached the entrance to Werburgh Street unemployment office and the oracle, hosting a guided tour, announced:

– Well, here's us. The other members of the exchange will already have gathered to welcome the chairman. Say a prayer to St Anthony that the state of Wall Street or the Bourse hasn't affected our shares. The hours I spend worrying about Hong Kong.

Parable felt such a fraud as he informed the oracle:

– In fact I don't have any business here, friend. I was on my way somewhere else . . .

The oracle took a step back and looked Parable up and down:

– Yeh mean you're workin'?

Parable nodded:

– More or less.

Anxiously asked the oracle:

– Yer not a snooper?

Parable was at a loss and the man said:

– Oh yer not a snooper. Real bastards are made in bed and heaven, snoopers are all failed polis.

Visibly the oracle's confidence drained, and Parable felt sorry. Suddenly, from loquacious certitude, the man all but dried up. Less than equal, he muttered:

– Well, this won't get the kids fed or the wife washed . . . see yeh round . . . maybe . . . and he was gone with the rest of the anonymous multitude to claim Lloyd George's legacy.

Parable stood for a while to stare in his vanished wake, and realised why he had never noticed the legitimate poor before. Out of sight, out of mind – was that then, the true meaning of evanescence? Unemployment is a statistic, but the unemployed are a reality. Smiles simply played round their lips as they tried to look like anybody else. The haunted, hunted eyes gave the game away. Job-loss too is a statistic, but, when you see men and women in congregated poverty, you know that when the worker becomes as redundant as the job, all hope is lost.

Irony of ironies, looking up he saw that the lane leading to the labour exchange was dominated by a bust of Jonathan Swift. So this is the new redemption, though, even with the second coming, governments would not heed the lessons of Brobdingnag:

> And he gave it for his opinion, that whoever could make two ears of corn or two blades of grass to grow upon a spot of ground where only one grew before, would deserve better of mankind, and do more essential service to his country than the whole race of politicians put together.

Despite the fact that world bankers paid people to grow less food, Parable felt some relief in the knowledge that literature lasts longer than laws. Some day the 'savage indignation' of the Dean will burn the bastards from power and the books of the great will make the meek strong enough to inherit the earth.

Feeling that he had supped his fill of the spirits of adversity, he made his way to Christchurch Cathedral and paused. He couldn't make up his mind whether or not to cross the river. After a pint or two on the South Side he might still feel like getting back home to try again, but a step in the direction of North Dublin was usually irrevocable.

An earnest man, with note-book and pen at the ready, accosted him, peering through heavy spectacles. In an English accent he asked:

– Handel, sir? *The Messiah*. I believe it was first performed quite close to the cathedral?

The English, Ireland's oldest tourists. Something of an innovation these days. Latest novelty since the fall of the dollar. They held on to the six counties but wouldn't be caught dead in Belfast. Reggie Maudling when he was Tory minister for Northern Ireland fled from Belfast in astonished disbelief. Of course then the crowd up there lost no love for the English. If it wasn't for the half-crown the assasananachs could shove the whole crown up the collective anglo arse, such was the ecumenism of those comical north-eastern Christians.

Parable Jones indicated to the tourist a narrow thoroughfare at the corner of the cathedral and told the enquirer that there in Fishamble Street, had the *Messiah* been first performed in 1741. He then made company with himself and proceeded down Wintavern Street hill in the direction of the fruit market. He didn't want to get involved with people who might think that drinking and a glass of stout were synonymous.

P. J. liked familiar but not quite intimate faces with whom to ease himself into the morning. A nod here and a 'There you are' there, was how the day should begin. The idea of dwelling on the life and times of George Frederick Handel did not appeal him to him one whit. (Did he mean to think that word? 'Whit' – the smallest particle or creature imaginable: a 'wight', and not to be confused with Whitsun, which means white.)

As he waited to cross the road at what was once upon a time the 'Irish House' on the corner of Wood Quay, he realised that the Butchers Hall in which the *Messiah* had first been performed was away as well. So evanescence was the countryman's watchword too, only they used it vindictively. They took Synge's *Playboy* literally, and now the mountains came to Mohammed. True to the prophecy of

'Crazy Horse Nolan', the bogs of Ireland were about to be repeated – in the middle of Dublin.

Now he knew to what the trauma of the morning was due. It wasn't the misery of the unemployed on their helpless way to hopelessness, nor even of the opium eaters on the road to Damascus. It was the bits of Dublin represented now by neat ricks of bricks. Aye, it was all peat in a bog; the bastards were laying us out to dry!

They wanted to expunge the very memory of the city. Parable hadn't walked on the South Side in a long time so the culture shock was all the more acute. In previous remembrances most of the city had been intact, but when he had stepped off the bus this morning, Jacobs biscuit factory was a heap of rubble.

Did nothing mean anything to these people? Were we to return to the parish pump and cross roads dancing? Irish flamenco: countrymen with their first boots. To their primitive Irish and illiterate English? Jazes wept!

Parable Jones was no crazy nationalist. Indeed he was as anti-chauvinist as anybody else. But when it came to demolishing places that were the physical embodiment of the renaissance, he found it hard to take. Oh folk may talk about Yeats and his friends, but nobody would persuade Parable that the real Dublin didn't begin with the four Georges and the Wide Street Commissioners.

And, when our rebels made fortresses of the town houses and brought their terrible beauty to gestation, who had a better right? Didn't Dublin stone-masons like Thomas Ivory think them up? Even the tourists, replete with cameras, used to stand in awe of the cheeky few bastards who had come out with sticks and stones to defy the might of Empire. Dublin was Ireland's Gaza, and the Dubliners were the Arabs who refused to wear the second-hand yellow stars.

Time was when the visitors used to read the history of Jacob's garrison from off a board that stood on an island dividing Peter Street and Aungier Street. The commanding officer had been the poet, Thomas MacDonagh, about whom history does not say a great deal more. But nothing was ever quite as it seemed in Ireland. Being Irish was a trick of the imagination. Culture is a country's highest point: its heritage. Culture is a country's history and the Irish, like the Egyptians, were enlightened when England and the rest of Europe were still in the dark ages.

It was not proper that a nation's endeavours should be consigned to the minds of peasants, or her artefacts to a builder's yard. Being Dublin was the highest stage of being Irish. The Dubliner lived. Jesus! Didn't he just! And Christ, did he know his history! God, the dates of the triumphant disasters that made up his mind!

General Maxwell declared martial law and then told the rebels that he would bombard the civilian population unless the nationalists surrendered. And so, to save the people from the wrath of imperialism, MacDonagh's commander and fellow poet, Patrick Henry Pearse, gave in to the English. He ordered MacDonagh to throw in the towel but the latter, on being told by the courier that the rebel C-in-C had given the order from captivity, told the messenger:

– Say to General Pearse that I will not accept orders from a prisoner of war.

A brave line, but more poetic than practical. Before the next month was out, MacDonagh had been shot dead with Pearse and Ceannt and Plunkett, with Clarke, MacDermott, Connolly and Macbride. Four of the eight had been poets so Ireland's culture machine had taken a fair knock. Not to worry, thank God and His Blessed Mother that Willie Yeats had stayed home to mind the shop and to remember the dead leaders, in particular the chap he hated for no other reason than he was husband to the woman he loved:

> . . . This other man I had dreamed
> A drunken vainglorious lout.
>   He had done most bitter wrong
> To some who are near my heart,
>   Yet I number him in the song;
> He, too, has resigned his part
>   In the casual comedy;
> He, too, has been changed in his turn,
>   Transformed utterly:
> A terrible beauty is born.

As he crossed the river to Inns Quay, Parable remembered MacDonagh's boy and the difference between father and son: one a fine poet who was shot for politics, and the other a political judge who should have been shot for writing poetry:

– What's this his name was, thought Parable? Oh yes, Donagh. Donagh MacDonagh, 'A name,' said the poet Kavanagh, 'that, like his poetry, goes on for ever.' First man to call itinerants 'travelling people'. Donagh wrote a play protesting their miseries. Then when a caravan load appeared before him on the bench, he gave them three months apiece, with the admonition that if vagrants wished to share the benefits of the community they must abide by the laws of society. The tinkers were less peripatetic after their meeting with hump-backed Justice Donagh MacDonagh and his blind lady of the well weighed sword.

And yet it was they who laughed loudest as they laughed last. When they looked at the cultured Quasimodo who was sticking them in the nick for their own good, their leader cried:

– Christ! boys, but there's poison in that hump! And the screws, with the laughing, nearly fell from the dock along with their prisoners.

The rebels of Easter Week held out for seven days. Shortage of ammunition and a disregard for their own lives at the expense of their fellow countrymen who had, for the most part, done nothing to deserve such respect, made them surrender. They could have forced a resolution because they were not short of food. The Irish knew about hunger so they had already made provision against being starved into submission. Aye, from the famine queen they had learned all about empty bellies. Victoria had proved a damned good teacher.

Parable smiled as he thought about his father's version of the 'Famine Song' which he sang to the great annoyance of his mother who remembered, daily, every triumphant disaster, every shallow grave, and every coffin-ship that ever set deathly sail from the coasts of Hibernia:

The praties they are small
  over here, over here.
The praties they are small over here.

The praties they are small
And we dig them in the Fall
And they're better than fuckall
over here.

It was from James Gandon's Inns of Chancery that the quay across the Liffey derived its name. The Central Criminal, or Four Courts, as the building was known to Dubliners. It too had been occupied during the 'Troubles' but that was in 1922 when the followers of 'Dev' had gone there to fight against Collins and the truce. The beautiful columns bearing the pistol pockmarks of conflict, bore testimony to the hatred that erstwhile comrades could generate for each other in civil war. De Valera thought that:

– Treason needs no conscience.

Having said which, he began to plan the wholesale slaughter of Free State troops, approaching the task with the same zeal that he found later when dedicating himself to the judicial execution of IRA men throughout the 40s. The Long Fella decreed that it was a crime to be 'legal' during the Rising, the War of Independence, and the Civil War. It was against the law of God to be 'illegal' while Dev ruled the roost. There must have been some justification to it for he was admired by at least five international statesmen – Hitler, Mussolini, Franco, Salazar and Eugene Pacelli.

The 'Big Fella' Collins could be every bit as single-minded in dealing with former comrades, and it surprised nobody when he sent to England for some big cannons that he might blow the 'rebels' out of the Four Courts. Throughout the spring and early summer of 1922, he had resisted Lloyd George's demands that the left-wingers be expelled from the Inns of Chancery. Then the British Premier swore that his Army would go in if the 'Big Fella' didn't. Collins acted on the evening of June 28th and so began the Civil War.

How Gandon's magnificent edifice survived both the British and Irish trigger-happy vandals is something nobody has ever properly explained, but it did, and, with the sun glinting on its beautiful dome and playing on the Wicklow granite, it made you feel grateful that man's eyes for destruction are bigger than his balls.

Parable always lingered longer at the Four Courts. They held a special significance for him. His father had been there under Rory O'Connor and Liam Mellows. Indeed it was around the time of the Four Courts and before Parable was born that he saved his father's life. There had been an interregnum, and while Jones the soldier was at home Parable was conceived. Jones père discovered that making love was every bit as exciting as making war and a damned sight less dangerous. He decided to stay away from the fighting for a while, during which interruption the Fourt Courts garrison surrendered. A little later, O'Connor, Mellows and the other leaders were summarily executed by Collins. Parable frequently told people that he and his father owed their lives to each other.

As P. J. was making his way along Greek Street, he met Bryden MacWilliams coming from and going in the opposite direction. Bryden always walked with his head in the ground, like a child hoping to find sixpence, and he would have passed Parable by without an upward glance had the latter not made his presence known:

– There yeh are, Bryden.

– It's yerself, Parable Jones?

– Or a decent imitation.

– Yer going drinking, I dare say?

– A fair assumption, Bryden.

– I couldn't persuade you to join me at mass in St Adam and Eve's, I suppose.

– How right you are, Bryden. And the tall gaunt figure of Professor MacWilliams shrugged itself down to its normal huddle and contemplated the route to Eve and Adam's where he might, if he so wished, negotiate his way, as Joyce recommended, 'From swerve of shore to bend of bay' and, if he wasn't careful, eventually wind up in Bruno's 'commodius vicus of recirculation'.

Bryden MacWilliams it was who had explained *At Swim Two Birds* as Myles writing a novel about a man writing a novel about a man writing a novel. He had suggested that Parable Jones was the only Irish writer not at present writing a novel about a man writing a novel. Harry McGill's comment on Bryden's thesis had been shocking, if succinct:

– Bleeding writers! If only somebody would invent a fucking

machine! And everybody thought he was thinking of Molly McGee the girl with the dirty name.

Parable wasn't writing a novel at all. Most certainly he wasn't writing anything picaresque. Most definitely he was not writing the definitive novel. That, he believed, had already been written by Jane Austen and the Brontës, by Dickens and Conrad, by Stendhal and Tolstoy and Joyce and Mailer, Virginia Woolf and Mick McGilligan's daughter Mary Anne, not to speak of Henry Miller. Definitive novels were old hat and anybody who hadn't written one by the age of twenty was a genius.

Parable Jones' real ambition was to *hear* the best book ever spoken, and with this end in mind he went from pub to pub with cocked ears. He believed in God the Father and the Son and the Holy Ghost – but only if they believed in him. He believed in the mysteries of Joyce and Virginia Woolf and that they had almost dispensed with writing as the language of literature. Nobody could read either *Finnegans Wake* or *Between the Acts* without the aid of a radio station, a film unit, and a couple of historians.

He agreed with Mrs Woolf that modern writers placed far too much emphasis on reportage and not enough on the art of language. With Joyce she understood that a day in the life of a book is quite enough. She proved in *Orlando* that literary dimensions are not disciplined by place, space, time, or indeed anything but the stream of consciousness. She wrote *Mrs Dalloway* to show what could be lived in a single day. Parable didn't believe that Joyce and Virginia had, between 1922 and 1925, emptied the pot, but he longed for a dialogue that was more talk than speech. No, he wasn't just thinking about oral literature – that sort of thing went out with the seannaice – he thought he was thinking of thought.

One theme he had heard being boozily bandied sought to prove that Fionn was the father of all Dubliners. But mythology has its awkward moments as the author of *Finnegans Wake* discovered. Macumail senior had been killed in the battle of Castleknock, but, in so far as anybody knew, Fionn himself was afterwards caught up in the hunt for Diarmuid, and the subsequent seduction and bedding of Grainne when she had been suitably widowed.

Yet another fella thought to do something on comparative religions. He wanted to show that St Patrick was the most dangerous man in Irish mythology. Patrick had set out to expunge our best pagan leaders from the religious memory. The De Danaans were the ones he really went after. They were the crafty magician gods of old Ireland and Fionn Macumail would have been many's the time in a bad way had he not been able to call on their help.

There was the little Jewish guy 'Anti-Christ' Cohen, who said that Lourdes had been the ruination of us all. The warriors changed their gods and changed the odds. The men of sixteen would never have been vanquished had they not thrown in their lot with the dreary Christians. Lion fodder. Damn all else but lion fodder. Dublin Zoo was the only public building that the republicans hadn't commandeered for a garrison. 'Something mysterious about that,' said 'Anti-Christ' Cohen:

– Pwhat was that, mister? somebody leaving O'Hara's said.

Parable mumbled something about it being a fine morning and the interrogator observed:

– It was, a mhic, for them as was up to see it.

Telling himself that countrymen wore calendars on their wrists, Parable Jones squeezed past the rustic and into the pub. He had barely time to ease himself into a vacant corner when a loud voice announced:

– There yeh are, Parable. Yeh wouldn't believe who I just met and me on me way down Parnell Square!

Without hesitating, P. J. answered:

– Charlie Belton.

– Jazes, yeh must be psychic, said Vincent Van Gogh Keogh, who had been given his last name by the successor to his father, his first one by his mother in honour of St Vincent de Paul, and his two middle ones by a chief superintendent in remembrance of the occasion when he had bitten off part of a police dog's left ear during the commission of a robbery.

– Not really, said Parable, anybody who doesn't meet Charlie Belton at least once each day on the North Side of the City is fortunate. His publisher has a shop over in Gardiner Place.

– That's right, said Vincent. He was telling me that he had been in to make sure they weren't making any changes to his new book on the 'Long Fella'. 'One cut,' he told Harry McGill, 'and I'll find another fucking publisher.' He's a harder man than you'd think, isn't he, Parable?

– Yeh could say that, lied P. J.

– Indeed, said Vincent, you writers are not all nancy boys.

Parable, pretending greater poverty, began to count a pocketful of coins, asking of Vincent as he did so:

– How much is the pint here?

– Oh, one-forty-something, replied Mr Keogh and decided that it might be better to keep himself to himself this morning.

– If it goes up any more, said Parable, we'll need an overdraft to quench a thirst.

– Indeed, yeh could say that again, said Vincent, as he made his way to stand at the bar among the yeomen of old Ireland who had just started on a new crop of fivers and tenners. Parable Jones quietly paid for a pint of stout, and brought it back to his table. He wasn't mean; he just wanted to listen to the day for a while, undisturbed.

Somewhere in the corner somebody was singing about an old woman plucking young nettles and blessing the memory of bold Fenian men. The old woman was Ireland, the nettles were what had given strength to Cuchullian, and the Fenians were the soldiers who had never been able to catch up with Fionn. Maybe, thought Parable, Pearse would:

> I have turned my face
> To this road before me,
> To the deed that I see,
> And the death I shall die.

Parable meditated on the poets and writers who had not died: who had not fought. George (A. E.) Russell sympathised, but could not offer himself on the altar of a 'bourgeois' insurrection. George Moore's brother resigned his commission following the Easter executions. O'Casey waited for a lead from Yeats and when Willie decided to fight the good fight in verse, Sean resolved to put the show on the stage. Joyce had never forgiven his race for betraying Parnell, and the 'bourgeois' revolution was far too socialist for Oliver St John Gogarty.

Over on the 'mainland' where he saw the 'Great Fallen' as a conflict between cousin king and cousin kaiser, Shaw refused to condemn the insurrection as 'unfair'. He told Nancy Astor:

– The only 'unfair' thing about the Rising, are the terrible odds my countrymen have to face.

De Valera had confided to his priest:

– We'll be all right, it's the women who will suffer. The worst they can do is kill us, but the women will have to remain behind to rear the children.

And yet Parable knew that the anti-heroes are always a bit like this – nothing without the corpses of their own imagined consciences. Brutus *sans* Caesar: Macbeth *gan* Duncan. Would Othello have been the same man without Desdemona, or was the whole disaster a projection of Iago's manic humour?

– Was it, wondered Parable, the case with de Valera? A Jape that went wrong?

That the rebels had painted a premature sunset, and that Britain had fallen for the illusion, there could be no doubt. They made an actual hole in the hitherto impregnable shield surrounding the British Empire. But, argued 'Anti-Christ' Cohen, had the Brits gotten at us more than we ever knew? Had they eaten our forebears, De Danaans and all? This crack they'd made in the Empire; what if it was a black hole made infinite by the cloaks of the witches of Cuchullian? Even Erskine Childers had run from glory in Flanders to an inglorious death in Ireland. They had taken everything else, so why not our good gods? After all look at what they had done with a perfectly good Jewish carpenter?

'Haveth Childers Everywhere'? Did Joyce mean that men like Erskine died that Finnegans Wake? Was the betrayal of this most loyal of English Irish republicans tit for tat in Irish self-abuse? Was Parnell fingered so as to give credence to the shopping of Joyce.

Did Dev go bravely to his court martial in the sure and certain knowledge that, as an American citizen, the Brits could never top him? That would be the most sophisticated betrayal of all, the man who offered himself as the sacrifice knowing that he was not eligible!

– Well, of course, Parable told himself, if I knew that the 'Long Fella' was born in America, why the hell would I have told Charlie Belton that he was born in Brough?

Parable experienced an exquisite sense of relief. He didn't want it to be thought by anybody that he would ever, consciously, or willingly, think on Eamon de Valera. For God's sake! It's like sensible people contemplating royalty or the White House. Parable told himself that Charlie always goes off half-cocked:

– The same when his wife wanted to know why he was to-ing and fro-ing between the lavatory and his typewriter, instead of getting on with his *Life of de Valera*. 'I am getting on with it,' he had screamed. 'Not when you're just sittin' and shittin',' she had told him.

– According to Miller, Charlie had retorted, a writer is always writing. 'And would that be Glenn Miller, Mick the Miller or Golden Miller?' the shrew had jeered, while Charlie exploded, 'Henry fucking Miller – he was an American!'

– And did he write about de Valera? his wife had demanded as Charlie came in to land. 'He wrote about the erotic', to which his spouse had commented, 'A damn sight more healthy than writing about Eamon de Valera, yeh queer bastard!'

Mary Belton was an educated woman with a common tongue. No way would her husband ever be a writer and she knew that. Charlie was too good a story-teller to give himself up to anything as dead as words caught between the covers of a book:

– Parable Jones now. There's a completely different kettle of fish. All his words match, and his conversation is the envy of the whole city. He can steal my knickers off the line anytime.

CHAPTER FOUR

riverrun

Bryden MacWilliams paused in the stone porch of Adam and Eve's chapel. Without seemingly realising that mass was imminent, he paused to allow late-comers to bless themselves from the holy water font in front of which he stood. Satisfied that all that were coming to mass were arrived, he unbuttoned his greatcoat. He took from his right-hand inside jacket pocket a right-hand surgical glove into which he placed his right hand. He then dipped his dextrous digits into the holy water font and simulated on his forehead and shoulders the sign of the cross. Removing the rubber sheath, he deposited it carefully in a litter basket set into the wall beneath the font. He walked to the nave of St Adam and Eve's, genuflected to the altar, entered a pew and knelt.

The celebrant, with two serving boys in train, entered from stage right, kissed the altar, went to his chair, turned, stood, and faced the congregation:

– In the name of the Father, and of the Son, and of the Holy Spirit.

– Amen.

– The grace of Our Lord Jesus Christ and the love of God and the comradeship of the Holy Spirit be with you all.

– And also with you.

Bryden MacWilliams knelt through the priest's welcome, heedless of the responses from the congregation. Thoughts of AIDS terrified him. And yet he had been celibate since 1950.

The good old days. When friends used to show each other their chancres and wonder if they got them in the same place. He remembered the 'Ginger Man' boasting that he had as much penicillin in his arse as would have wiped out all the TB in the Third World.

Only it wasn't the Third World then. Even the Israelis were little more than refugees – it would be some time before they could claim to be a master race. The Third World was mostly still the Empire and the Empire was civilised. Vaguely he heard the Entrance Antiphon being chanted, badly: English was no language for the mysteries of the church. English? Father Kurt Fahrt would have pronounced 'The Word' to sound like syphilised and the memory of Myles brought his mind back again to AIDS.

– Sex, said yer man, is no more than a waste of perfectly good press-ups.

Maybe, like the drink, he had given up the ridey-roos too late. God knows but the sublimation of sex was holy, and he enjoyed practising the abstinence. But, there was always the nagging doubt, could Ibsen be right? What if the whole thing was the sins of the father visited upon the son? No, no! That was not the case. What, he had really meant to wonder was, if it was the sins of the past visited upon the present. His past. His sins?

Then the priest in the confessional had posed a question such as should never have been postulated by a priest. What if he was enjoying celibacy for other reasons than being celibate? What if he was a sexual masochist? Sin compounds sin and, while the sin of birth is accidental, the sins of commission and omission are the death of the everlasting soul:

– My brothers and sisters, that we may prepare ourselves to celebrate the sacred mysteries, let us call to mind our sins.

– I confess to Almighty God and to you, my fellows in Christ, that I have sinned. Through my fault . . .

In remigrate reflex Bryden MacWilliams' hand struck his breast, while his mind was still mostly his own. He didn't know anything about the cause of AIDS. Nobody did. And yet he could hardly believe that it derived from men committing unnatural acts with beasts.

Men had been screwing dogs and cats and anything that wouldn't lie down or fight back, since time immemorial. Even pusillanimous Bert Lloyd had been with men and sheep in the outback. Indeed he had often told how he had fallen in love with a Queensland woolly, as a consequence of which he had nearly killed the man who turned it into mutton chops and a sheepskin jacket:

– Lord God, Lamb of God, You who take away the sins of the world, have mercy on us . . .

Thousands of years ago, unnatural acts had spawned VD, but Fleming had come up with a sure-fire cure. Folk had hypothesised that experiments in germ warfare created a biological imbalance. That maybe too had been dismissed by the scientists, and so Bryden MacWilliams was convinced that AIDS is the sins of the past lying dormant.

– *Domine Fili unigenite, Jesu Christe, Domine Deus, Agnus Dei, Filius Patris* . . .

Always the Lamb of God. For ever the sins of the world. The lining of his stomach had perished through drink and his penis had shrivelled through lack of exercise. Now, convinced that the AIDS Man cometh, Professor MacWilliams was a most unhappy penitent.

Somewhere, somewhere-else, Bryden heard the mass as it was, once upon a time. Over and over again his mind reiterated the phrase '*Agnus Dei*'. And he smiled as he remembered how he had slipped into a Glasgow speak-easy chapel to get a Latin fix, Tridentine and pure:

'The Gloria' had then, even with the incredible attempts of the Scots to give the kiss of life to a dead language, brought back the wonderful obscurantism of the mass when he was a child. So much more theatre of the absurd than it could ever claim to be today: but, in mystery, taken much more seriously:

– . . . *Filius Patris, qui tollis peccata mundi, miserere nobis: qui tollis peccata mundi, suscipe deprecationem nostram*. Please accept our prayer! For pity's sake take our prayer! Receive, we beseech Thee, our prayer. But who could reject the magnificence of *Suscipe deprecationem nostram*?

Who but a droll Pole. The Vatican had put its arse in a sling. And it was all the fault of Karol Wojtyla, who had been elected Bishop of Rome on 16th October, 1978.

Bryden didn't trust foreign popes. Latin or nothing he declared. Maybe Italian Roman Catholicism was only second to Irish Roman Catholicism, but it was the next best thing now that all the saints had left Ireland to confuse the world. Had Bryden been consulted by the Holy See, he could have told them where they were going wrong. Had it not been for the archbishop of Dublin at the time, that anti-Christ, John Charles McQuaid, maybe the Vatican would have listened to Professor MacWilliams. Imagine picking a man like Eoin O'Mahony to be a papal count! Extraordinary! Of course the Corkmen have it made.

And now he had the feeling that Harry McGill wanted him to do a snow job on the peripatetic Polish Pontiff. No way. As far as he was concerned John Paul II was no different to Ronald Reagan – an actor playing a part: a Pole in a role. And what a performance! 'Was it not strange,' he had asked the local curate, 'that AIDS was first noticed about the same time that John Paul II got scared of flying?'

– Scared, asked yer man, of flying?

– Well, said Bryden, he's always so grateful to get down safely that he kisses the ground under him. That doesn't show a great deal of faith in the Almighty: much more a belief in what goes up must come down. Apart from which he must be spreading disease from country to country. How many green monkeys cavort around the landing fields of the world's jungles? John Paul kissed them all.

He had researched the lives of thirty-nine anti-popes, from Hippolytus in 217 to Felix V in 1439, and none of them proved to be any worse than Adrian IV or Alexander VI.

Adrian, the only Englishman ever to occupy the papal throne, gave Henry II permission to conquer Ireland in 1156. Of course the modern English scholars argued that the bull 'Laudabiliter' was a Norman forgery, what else would you expect? But Bryden believed that the same Nicholas Breakspear had indeed granted hereditary possession of Ireland to his own king.

Furthermore, and what was much worse, that same 'Laudabiliter' gave Thomas, Lord Wharton, the idea for a song that, according to Gilbert Burnet, bishop of Salisbury, played an important part in driving King James II from the throne in 1688. The gentlemanly Marquess of Wharton mocking the Irish Viceroy's speech defect, said it sounded as if Richard Talbot pronounced the word 'Laudabiliter' as 'Lilliburlero'. So later, in 1724, the equally gracious

Gilbert recalled in his *History of His Own Time*: 'The whole army, and at last the people, both in city and country, were singing it perpetually. And perhaps never had so slight a thing so great an effect.'

The priest on the altar asked Our Lord:

– Almighty God, cleanse my heart and my lips that I may worthily proclaim your gospel. And Bryden MacWilliams prayed, fuck foreign popes for the ratbags that they are.

He also cursed the External Service of the BBC which still insisted on using the anti-Catholic song as its signature tune. But his most vengeful wrath he reserved for the Spanish Borgias, in particular Cardinal Rodrigo who afterwards became Pope Alexander VI. Rodrigo and his mistress Vanozza dei Catanei were parents of Lucrezia and Cesare Borgia. Professor MacWilliams told himself that he could overlook the incestuous relationship that the pope had with his daughter. He could overlook the fact that with Alexander VI's complicity Cesare had murdered his elder brother. He could even ignore Rodrigo's instruction to Cesare to kill Lucrezia's husband, Giovanni.

– But how reprehensible the act of Pope Alexander VI to annul Giovanni's marriage to Lucrezia on the grounds of nonconsummation. The seeds of the Reformation were sown in the profligacy of that papacy.

He had been outraged when Harry McGill had told him to go back and think again:

– For Christ's sake, Professor MacWilliams, I chose you because I thought you would do a favourable life of the Holy Father! You can't tell innocent Catholics that the papacy was a breeding place for incestuous murderous whoremasters. I want to sleep safely at night without the feeling that righteous children of the Lamb of God are going to consecrate me in bed with hatchets and bicycle chains. Don't you realise we are a Catholic country where Pope John Paul II is almost as popular as John F. Kennedy?

And yet there were folk who had not seen this side of Bryden MacWilliams. He was thought of as an intellectual Matt Talbot. Matt had been found dead, wrapped in chains after a lifetime of drunkenness. He had been an industrial supergrass. A blackleg who had made scabbing grounds for beatification. Professor MacWilliams saw himself as a fading Howard Hughes, an ageing Paul Getty. Parable Jones thought that Bryden was more like Mr Duffy in Joyce's 'A Painful Case':

> Love between man and man is impossible because there must not be sexual intercourse, and friendship between man and woman is impossible because there must be sexual intercourse.

Bryden MacWilliams wouldn't give a fuck now if it was to save his life or create another.

Myles had jeered Joyce for that remark; 'Trite shite!' he had called it. Yet Joyce had declared his intentions. In the same paragraph he indicates that two of the volumes on Mr Duffy's shelves are by Nietzsche: *Thus Spake Zarathustra* and *The Gay Science*:

– Couldn't call a book that now, thought Bryden MacWilliams. *The Gay Science*! Crazy brother of a crazy sister who's real claim to fame was that she was an unashamed admirer of Adolf Hitler and widow of an anti-semite. 'You try to reconcile opposites,' her brother had told her in 1890, for which remark she had her revenge after Nietzsche's death by calling herself Forster-Nietzsche after her brother and her racist husband.

With his head in his hands on the top of the pew, Bryden dwelt on his knees. He was not conscious of God's presence, nor of the priest or the congregation. He didn't notice when the multitude shuffled to stand or to kneel. He heard not the tinkle of the bells nor witnessed the fishlike responses. He did not even hear the spoken confessions:

– Lord, Jesus Christ, you said to your apostles: 'I leave you peace, my peace I give you.' Look not on our sins, but on the faith of your church, and grant us the peace and unity of your kingdom where you live for ever and ever.

– Amen.

Bryden remembered that Nietzsche had become an ascetic after contracting syphilis during his student days, eventually to die from GPI: General paralysis of the insane. Mr Duffy didn't have VD to excuse his actions to Mrs Sinico. Or did he? Was that what Joyce was indicating? If not, why the books by Fred Nietzsche? Above all why *Thus Spake Zarathustra*? In his academic mind the academic said, 'Compare':

– Love between man and woman . . . etc. And *Thus Spake Zarathustra*: 'One still loves one's neighbour and rubs against him for one needs warmth'.

Was this then from where Mr Duffy sprung, the nihilism of Nietzsche? Or did Nietzsche, Joyce and Mr Duffy owe everything to Castiglione? Was he the progenitor of all that barren thought which sprang from the mouths of two ascetics and the mind of an anti-Christ? Compare then what Castiglione writes in *The Courtier*:

> I have spent a long time wondering, my dear Alfonzo, which of two things was the more difficult for me: either to refuse what you have asked me so often and so insistently, or to do it.

Mrs Sinico's love had been dismissed with the same sophistry when she asked Mr Duffy why he did not write out his thoughts:

– For what? he asked her with careful scorn. To compete with phrasemongers, incapable of thinking consecutively for thirty seconds?

The priest, looking at his watch, was racing to a finish. Maybe he had a few funerals waiting, or a couple of weddings:

– Then in your kingdom, freed from the corruption of sin and death, we shall sing Your glory with every creature through Christ Our Lord, through whom you give us everything that is good . . .

Bryden MacWilliams told himself that he was different from Mr Duffy. The celebrants and congregation prayed a while in silence with the priest giving anxious looks from his watch to the door of the presbytery and back to his watch. Then:

– The Lord be with you.

– And also with you.

– May Almighty God bless you, the Father, and the Son, and the Holy Spirit.

– Amen.

The congregation shuffled past the kneeling penitent and many wished themselves as devout as he. They shuffled past him and out through the doors and shielded the eyes of their little ones from what appeared to be five condoms sticking through the litter basket under the holy water font in the porch. 'God', thought some, 'works in mysterious ways; how incredible that He should use AIDS to bring contraception to holy Ireland.'

CHAPTER FIVE

Alas Poor Yeats

Charlie Belton paused at the corner of North Frederick Street and Gardiner Place. Martin Walton's Music Publishers was getting a wash and a varnish. Jet-black, flat and copal. A bit like Martin himself – looking for all the world like a long yard of stout. Gold on the facia, spared. A bit like Martin himself – all hair and no head.

– Aye, Martin Walton was the man for ever in the van. That'll be the very whale. Swore he wouldn't visit a barber until Ireland was free. Used to go round Dublin dressed all in black – every last inch of his six feet two. Like a high-class undertaker longing for a high-class corpse. According to Parable Jones the competition for the job of burying the dead Archbishop, John Charles McQuaid, was very keen indeed, with morticians falling prostrate over each other to get the contract. 'The lowest tender need not necessarily be accepted.' I suppose the fellas who plant popes are made up for life.

– Peadar Kearney and Seamus Heaney, who wrote the Irish national anthem, wouldn't hear a word said against Walton: 'Did his bit for the country when the country needed him'. Aye, that'll be the day.

– Played the violin for his fellow prisoners at Ballykinlar internment camp, and, later on, the fiddle for Ireland. A prison impresario, who, when the truce came, had a ready-made music business to soften the pain of eighteen months' incarceration for the ould sod. Kearney and Heaney perished in poverty while still comparatively young, but Walton learned that the secret to longevity was to be hirsute and rich.

Across the road, on the north side of Parnell Square, the secondary object of Yeats' poem, 'To a Wealthy Man who Promised a Second Subscription to the Municipal Gallery if it Were Proved the People Wanted Pictures'.

Well, of course people wanted pictures. Ever since Joyce opened the first British movie house in Mary Street, people had wanted pictures. Charlie's parents had pawned the last remnants of respectability to hear the first talkie.

But seriously:

– Seriously me arse! How the hell would people know whether they wanted pictures or not until they had seen a few? It was like asking the poor if they wanted food, without realising that, among large sections of the population, eating is an acquired taste.

It was nearly seventy years since Yeats put the wealthy man down, and still very few folk had seen any pictures. Galleries are such forbidding places where officious officials officiate only to that part of the public that looks at home among canvas and plaster. Parable Jones held that unsophisticated mortals get little change from the minders of the nation's heritage:

– They must have just cut it from the frame, sir.

– Was it a valuable piece, my man?

– God sir, it was one of the biggest in the gallery.

To prove to the world that he hadn't been talking to himself, Charlie whistled, and, almost at once, went back inside his own head:

– They blame the poor for being ignorant as well: and how the hell could they be otherwise? Austin Clarke believed that the whole world of culture was somehow diminished because the working class refused to recognise art as something anybody should have time for except outside working hours.

– The same Austin said a lot more than his prayers. Down in Gerry Dwyer's he was, one night, telling the company that Yeats, a Sligo man, had a more Dublin accent than James Joyce – said that the creator of Anna Livia spoke like somebody up for the match. And he said that there wasn't a great deal of originality in Joyce when it came to the creative end of the market. But Austin had his arse both ways. Yeats was born in Sandymount and there's nothing more Dublin than that unless you want to swim across to the Pigeon House. And Joyce was more unique than original sin.

– Poor ould Austin! God, but Dubliners hate the idea that accomplished people, the image of themselves, can be markedly different.

Parable was the only one who didn't hunt with the pack. Unconcerned, he observed from a fit and proper distance. He saw the begrudgers from the corner of his mind and dismissed them, all wrapped up and finished in pith.

To describe Myles, he had paraphrased that old French geriatric nymphomaniac, 'Speech,' he said, 'was never his language'.

– Of course it was all very well for Patrick Joseph Jones; he did it all by cracked mirrors in the roads. Anybody could write anything if they read as many books.

– Not all artists shared Austin Clarke's views on the plain man's cultural condition. Arthur Dooley didn't. He had worked in Liverpool Art Gallery because he couldn't afford the fees to attend it; and he had learned to resent the 'official' attitude to art as public property outwith the jurisdiction of the public:

– 'Ere then, wot are you abaht! Stop touching that statcha! Think it wus made so that you could leave yer sticky fingerprints all over it! That's art that is, an' you just show it proper respect!

– Dooley, a wonderful sculptor, made wondrous pieces and placed them all round Liverpool. He wanted to show the need to *feel* a shape. Tactile is as touching does.

– And of course he was right. We live where art galleries are no better than museums; the whispered tones; the hands off the figures and the freezing of giggles at the surprise of a bare-arsed Adonis.

– And yet the poor innocent Yeats thought the wealthy man unreasonable. Willie may have known about art, but he had a helluva lot to learn about the art of being wealthy. What was it that Kavanagh told Parable about friends in high places?

– When you make up the account at the end of a lifetime, you'll soon discover that, poor as yeh were, you spent a helluva lot more than any of the rich.

The poet's belief; Paddy's belief: that a man can trust the closed fist of his betters more than the clenched fist of his liberators. Yeats, all poetry and not a political conclusion in his head; tilting at windmills with his bare mind:

Your open hand but shows our loss,
For he knew better how to live.
Let Paudeens play at pitch and toss
Look up in the Sun's eyes and give
What the exultant heart calls good
That some new day may breed the best
Because you gave, not what they would,
But the right twigs for an eagle's nest.

Parable pitied 'poor Yeats and his crazy ideas about economics, about how the rich stay rich'. But, God, how great a poet must a poet be to escape from the horrible consequences of the Protestant ethic? He should have told the rich man to shove his money up his arse. Of course then, according to MacNeice, such vulgarity about wealth was nothing more than the product of apostasy. Protestantism was – that is.

'No religion for a gentleman,' said Charles II. And how could it be? Were not all the right-footers so called because that was the digging side of the spade? Even if all they had in their tight little world was the cutting of turf, they had that great Protestant faith in the work ethic. It's their word for all seasons – works of God and sales of work; work hard and God'll love yeh. He will in his arse. God help the permanent and pensionable Protestants who never learned how to surrender.

Having in fear and trepidation demanded that Ulster be contraceived, they could no longer enjoy sex. Yerra, God help them, if they could at least find satisfaction in frustration and French letters. And yet, yeh'd be surprised at their dourness, and them spawned by King Billy, a monarch who was as gay as a two-arsed monk.

The Catholics were, thank God, a feckless lot. And just as reckless with their faith. The same Austin Clarke had spoken the unthinkable feelings, the unspeakable anti-clericalism:

And yet I tremble lest she may deceive me
And leave me in this land where every
  woman's son
Must carry his own coffin and believe,
In dread, all that the clergy teach
  the young.

A shout from the direction of the Rotunda caused Belton to think of the day abroad:

– There yeh are, Charlie.

– Jazes! That's all I need. Some of these fuckers can smell the few shillings through a chap's trouser pockets.

Vincent Van Gogh Keogh crossed the road and reflected the smile of Charlie Belton who felt fit to be tied:

– God, yeh were well into yerself comin' down the square. The very picture of contemplation. I felt like offering yeh a penny for them.

– Yeh'd be wildly extravagant, ould son. I was thinking about the question of movement.

– Movement?

– Yeh know when Mr Micawber goes home across London's rooftops?

– Aye, 'by the way of the angels', he says.

– Actually, I was just wondering if maybe the brazen approach was not the best way to outwit a creditor.

– How d'ye mean 'actually'?

Inwardly Belton cursed himself for having used the meaningless adverb – 'this carping fucker will dine off the remark . . .' Aloud he said:

– Well, who's goin' to expect debtors like us to walk openly through the main thoroughfares of Dublin.

– Yeh could have a point there, ould son, said Vincent Van Gogh Keogh, and at once decided to see if prospects were any better in the markets area. See yeh around, Charlie, I have a man who wants me to do a little job for him down in Capel Street. Eh, yer not goin' that way, I suppose?

– No, Vincent, I'm determined to meet my fate in the fullness of the public view. Head on: that's the only way to greet adversity.

'Thanks be to jazes, for that,' Vincent Van Gogh Keogh told himself, 'I'd a lucky escape there.' Aloud he told Belton 'goodbye' and scuttled off down Parnell Street in the direction of the bona fides.

– Jesus, Belton thought, there but for the grace of jayzes goes the makings of a spoilt drunk.

A black coat on a bicycle flew past going towards the Gresham, and Belton recognised the back of Father Michael Clery, the 'Singing Priest':

– The Blanchardstown wit. His old man used to own a pub and greyhounds. On television introducing the pope to the multitude, no less. There he was with John Paul's bodyguard, Marcincus, that stand-in for Al Capone who looks as if he could go fifteen rounds with the best.

– Strange tale that. First of all, the Pope's banker Roberto Calvi hangs himself underneath Blackfriars Bridge, with his hands tied behind his back. Then Licio Gelli, John Paul's financial adviser and head of the Vatican mafia, scarpers to Switzerland, and defies calls for his extradition. After which Marcincus couldn't go into Rome without fear of arrest, and the Italian police couldn't go into the Vatican for fear of being mugged by the Pope's Masonic Lodge, P2.

– It makes you realise when you hear all those rumours about Dr Paisley's friends making bum-boys of the young men of Northern Ireland Borstals, that Christianity is in a bad way without Christ. But surely even the skulduggery of them both must make grounds for ecumenism? As things stand they're just giving atheists like Parable Jones a field day.

– Be consecrated by the likes of them? said P. J. Jazes I'd rather receive absolution from the Kray twins. Between the Pole in the Vatican having his enemies dried out under bridges, and the Kennedy brothers sending Marilyn on ahead to keep a bed in Heaven warm for the ménage à trois! John the Robber and John the Murderer and there's the two of them grinning over every sacred heart lamp that ever darkened an Irish tenement room. Sacred icons? There was more piety in Burke and Hare!

Belton wondered if any of the literary crowd had ever trusted a live clergyman? Kavanagh offered his soul as an old horse at twenty fairs, and warned that the clergy would form a ring and eventually get it for nothing, 'With the winkers thrown in':

– Imagine, not being able to sell your own soul to your own pastor, without fear of being done on the deal. Simon Dedalus swore that none of them would ever put his feet under his mahogany. Mother

Church could take your soul with all the style of a plump Mephistopheles. And, if you complained, she could excommunicate you with the back of her hand. Still, she can scare who she likes, who's afraid of the Holy Ghost?

Charlie, squeezing the cheque in his trouser pocket, felt fine and told himself that if ever he had security he'd never say another prayer. Only poverty prevented him becoming a twenty carat atheist.

Tommy, the commissionaire, from the steps of the Gresham shouted to 'Mr B' that 'himself was in last night':

– Himself?

– Aye, Mr Jones.

– And did he float home, or did you send him in a chariot?

– Oh, he was game ball when he was leavin' here, sir, a bit on the Kildare side, but, sure every cripple has his own way of walkin', I always say.

Belton warned himself that he was thinking like Parable again:

– I haven't even read some of the books I think about: second-hand opinions from Parable Jones.

And P. J.'s anti-chauvinism. His mockery of what he liked to call the 'Patriot Game'. At the same time he went around claiming every important person in the world as Irish. The Swifts and Sternes and Congreves and Goldsmiths and . . .

– Sure not one of them would have thanked you for saying that they were born here. Christ, there was more fame to be had in coming from Newgate prison. But Parable could tell you that the Yeats crowd were also the Pollexfens and that 'Sweet Auburn' was in reality Goldsmith's hungry village of Lissoy, 'More Celt than Cleric, so he was', so Parable Jones said.

– His latest recruit was that Yankee fella, Gore-Vidal, who, according to P. J., comes from the Gore-Booths, Con and Eva about whom Yeats said that one was, 'A gazelle'. The same Vidal had the same sarcastic sense of humour as Parable: but with more money to speak his mind. He must be wealthy indeed. The Yanks hadn't put him in prison for saying that American welfare lagged behind the West because money could fetch such a price in the morals market:

– The result is a unique society in which we have free enterprise for the poor and socialism for the rich.

Belton, angry with himself again for thinking like Parable Jones, gave his feet a treat and jumped into a waiting taxi at Eden Quay:

– The Castle Bar.

– It's not time yet, Mr B, only the Market pubs . . . plenty of them . . . they've been open since seven.

– OK, take us across to Slattery's.

– Righto, boss.

They turned right around and almost retraced the route taken by Belton that morning. At North Frederick Street, Belton still angry at his imagined inferiority to Parable Jones, looked the taxi-driver full in the face and asked:

– You're a Dubliner, right?

– Born and bred, Mr B, from Granby Row to Dorset Street, and never stepped in cowshite in me life.

– And yeh still don't know your fucking way around the town.

– Indeed, bejazes there's not an inch of it that I don't remember; every pisshouse and pothole.

– Then why the fuck are you trying to get to Slattery's pub via Belfast!

– What the fuck else can I do, Mr B? Since the Department of Transport was taken over by the Kerrymen, every street in Dublin is one fucking way and that one way only leads in one direction – to the fucking bog! I'm trying to save yeh money Mr B, but unless I was to be driving a fucking helicopter . . .

Belton apologised for his bad tempered remarks and sat quietly as he was whisked through Bolton and Capel Street, to the corner of Little Britain Street where they saw the swaggering back of Vincent Van Gogh Keogh who was making his way to O'Hara's. As the cab drew up outside Slattery's, Belton knew he was going to have a good day:

– Christ, am I steeped! Avoiding Keogh twice in the one morning! I wonder what the odds against that are?

CHAPTER SIX

Ipsissima Verba

Jeannie Jones rang Mary Belton most mornings and then dropped in for coffee. As usual, the subject was Parable, and this day was no exception. Parable Jones and God were her obsessions.

Mary Belton could read her husband like a book and she frequently told him so, but never told anybody else:

– True as jazes, Charlie Belton, but I could read you like a bloody book.

Did she like him? It was neither a question of like or dislike; she was used to him. She made it her business to use the lavatory before he rose, and, with elongated finger-tips she picked his smalls from the bedroom floor, and it was as if on tongs she transferred them to the washing machine: but, on the whole, she could put up with his habits.

He was kind and gentle and courteous in his own way – an awkward way. He broke wind in her presence only involuntarily – red with embarrassment when he farted. True enough he scratched his crotch incessantly and picked his nose, but these were mannerisms born of nervousness: he was in no way unclean. In any event his lack of personal etiquette was irrelevant now; she was too old to start breaking in somebody else; besides which, age makes men a better bargain.

His sexual proclivities – or priorities as he liked to call them – usually meant her going without. But she had learned to feign sophistication; folk may say what they like about girls' boarding schools but most of their old girls were well able to bring themselves on without help from any outside agency.

Anyway, it took the poor big bastard all his time to do his thing.

She could mind her own needs whenever the occasion demanded. Oh aye, she was fair of face, with a trim figure, and a hankering after youth – not her own for she was quite satisfied to be her age, as long as she didn't have to act it. For a while now she had felt more than a passing fancy for the young boy who had been delivering the milk: when she was busy with herself it was his face on which she fantasised, on his tight little bum like a young snooker player leaning over the table. His name she repeated over and over, until, in a torrent of ecstasy, the turgescence subsided:

– Terry!

And then she had changed his name to Tom because 'Terry' made her laugh and laughter frustrated the orgasm. The first Terry she had known had tried to make love to her on the edge of a hill and he had kept slipping down the side. This Terry with the pleasing bump and the double-meaning smile seemed to her to be a randy little devil with a generosity of spirit ulterior in the extreme:

– Need any cream today, Mrs B? My boss says that he has given more cream to the women in Terenure, than anywhere else on the round.

The way he looked at her each morning caused her to contemplate letting her dressing gown fall accidently open when he stood talking on the doorstep. She deliberately encouraged his childish *doubles entendres* and felt weak and wet whenever she felt he was going to make a pass.

Most young men are horny little buggers, rearing, romping, and randy. It was how he would talk of it later that prevented her from making the first move. Tales of milkmen are well told. And God, in this scheme, scandal was far more popular than prayer!

She could not recall the first time with Charlie, and she felt . . . no, not guilty . . . a little sad, maybe. She remembered well enough when she first came with him, or – to be more precise – without him. He had walked her home and they had stood to kiss and feel each other in the hallway. The light had gone on in the master bedroom and her father, with gentle parental regard, had shouted:

– When the fuck are you getting to bed, Mary?

Charlie had just about gotten his trousers open before he had to quickly close them again. It was the first of the zipped flies and, in his haste to do them up, he had pinched his cock. Talk about coitus interruptus! while she moaned in satisfaction from her almost conjunction, Charlie's anguish could be heard all around the parish:

– Oh, jazesfuckinchrist! Me poor cock is in bleedin' bits!

The one man she'd really pop her cork for was Parable Jones. She fancied him so much that the yearning became a physical pain. But he behaved as if she didn't exist outside of her husband. Hints were to no avail, indeed Parable Jones would have ignored her overtures had they been composed for a forty piece brass band. He was a twisted bastard, and that was the truth.

And Charlie! Whenever he recounted some of Parable's clever comments, made about 'this fella', or to 'that fella', or about 'the other fella', Mary Belton felt like screaming. Charlie even tried to imitate his voice and his gestures. Christ it was pathetic! Nobody could impersonate Parable Jones. That was the real trouble; the fucker was unique.

He even got at you from the pages of the newspaper. Like the morning he parodied one of Yeats' poems: 'Married Women May Go Mad' was his paraphrase, and he went on to write about the loneliness that could drive a housebound woman round the bend when the husband and kids had been packed off to work and school. She could have written between the lines; only the day before, she had nearly mounted him when he had come to see Charlie. Parable, pretending not to notice, had kissed her in a brotherly way on the cheek, left his regards to her husband, and left: leaving her fretful, frail and frustrated. Was there any truth in what Jeannie had said – only his mind was up to it; sober he won't, and drunk he can't?

But wives are not in the business of telling the truth about their husbands – that's the surest way to wind up at the end of a queue of your own creation. Capable or not, Parable was a more human class of creature with a few jars taken; a woman might get the pants off him then. But, if you were to believe Jeannie, it would be winkle-picking with a pin to find Percy. No, the John Peel treatment was best: ply him with drink the night before and let him rise with his horn in the morning.

The intermediate stages were the worst; when Parable was half-drunk he was offensive and vain: fond of blowing his own trumpet and boasting that he could write any other into a cocked hat. But just before he passed out!

Christ, could he insult folk! Her sister – the failed nun. When she had been a novitiate. When she was sent home so as to make up her mind about life in the convent. When she eventually jilted God, practically on the altar, it was all Parable's fault – or the fault of his tongue.

But Mary blamed her husband, for Charlie was a natural atheist – not like poor Parable who inwardly bowed his head every time anybody took the Lord's name in vain. Parable Jones anti-religious? Some hope. Anti-clerical maybe, but he wouldn't argue with the Boss: Parable Jones wouldn't go two rounds with God the Father on less than five pints. But then, oh Christ, didn't the words lose their temper!

Poor Annie! The more hysterically holy she got, the more hatefully witty Parable became. 'Mother Teresa and her fight for the health of the world! And who,' might he ask, 'created disease in the first place. Was her God schizophrenic? Was He getting too old for the job? Maybe they needed a few redundancies up there. Should He call up Mrs Thatcher? Oh, if only He would.'

On and on, relentless and without let-up. 'Why the hell was she so intent on marrying a God who helped the Nazis to exterminate large chunks of humanity, or made the Israelis forget the Israelites? Why was it necessary to ask Him not to lead us into temptation? Was He a mental defective? Honest to Christ there must be some reasonable explanation for His behaviour unless religion was but a rigmarole.'

There was no way that anybody was going to stop Parable Jones that night. n and on he went as though he, and not Annie, was on some sort of religious crusade.

Maybe it was time for God to turn it in. He'd had a good innings and now He must be as old as tea – if history was anything to go by. Not that history had anything to do with God; religion had made up its own history as it went along just the same as history had made up religion.

Annie protested the purity of her Christian faith and beliefs, and Parable told her 'not to be talking shit'. Lovely language for a novice nun and small wonder that she found that she and God weren't suited after all. Parable had cited 'the converted Aztecs whose idolatry the Spaniards had incorporated into their South American version of Catholicism. Not that Montezuma was much of a loss, the cruel bastard, but, did one civilised barbarity cancel out the other? Jesus Christ, Annie, it must have been the terrified Inca saw the first horse.'

That night Charlie was in his element and, whenever Parable's criticism of the deity seemed on the point of petering out, Mary's husband stirred the fire into flames. He hated religion and it was his great joy to sow another doubt in a sea of mistrust. Parable, yielding to encouragement, in no time at all was rearing to go:

Did Annie really believe that crap about St Brigid begging land for a convent from the pagan High King? As much as her cloak might cover was the witty monarch's response. It was well known that nuns' habits covered a multitude but did Annie really believe that St Brigid's cloak covered the whole Curragh of Kildare?

Parable didn't want her to get him wrong: he had nothing against God as long as folk remembered that each man made his own. It was the 'wills' of God to which Parable objected.

The wills of God were too handy for manipulating people and, Parable said, it had all got to stop. His own God was totally anti-Christian and violently anti-religious. He was a fun God of Falstaffian proportions, and, when Annie asked what he meant, Parable sank to the floor, looked up Annie's clothes and told her that his God said that there was a paradise between her legs that she was aiming to let rust:

– Don't knock it until you've tried it, honey. It's better than sadism, Catholicism, masochism, Judaism or Presbyterianism. It killed John Knox but only to put a smile on the old reprobate's face for the very first time, 'I'm coming, Jesus', he cried, and Jesus did he come. In fact he came at the same moment that he went and left his wife of sixteen years with a penis erectus petrified in rigor mortis, and that brought a smile to her face too.

Parable was not a man to get himself out of trouble if the only escape was to leave somebody with a sore heart. Mary was fully aware, therefore, that it was not the religion of her sister that he was intent on degrading but that of his wife. Jeannie wouldn't listen, so Parable Jones shouted at other women.

Mary Belton knew the score. Ever since what she called the men-pause Jeannie had carried on a war of attrition against men in general and her husband in particular. By the time the last flush had fled, men would be no more than the wild oats of her youth. Mary was sorry that Jeannie would find no romantic autumn to crown her tatty life. She had never been keen on literature, and her husband was the author of dirty books. She took consolation in the words of Father Jesmond, who had told her that she must pray that her husband came back to the path of righteousness:

– A lost soul, my child, and it is all too easy to mistake pornography for art.

Path of righteousness indeed! Wild horses wouldn't have dragged him in that direction. Anyway he wouldn't have known what the priest was talking about. He had his own righteousness, just the same as he had his own good and bad language. The priest was right, Parable Jones was a dirty man – it was as simple as that.

Parable had called the priest 'a bollocks', but that changed absolutely nothing. Mary knew that the trouble with Jeannie was that she had never liked herself very much and she had never been able to believe that anybody able to do anything well would have had anything to do with her:

– If he's as clever as people make out, what would he be wanting from me, Mary?

– Affection?

– Aye, that'll be right. One cuddle and his true nature comes out. His eye is always on the main chance: and at our age!

Jeannie's ignorance shocked Mary Belton. But the very idea that she had never told her husband about Father Jesmond's invective shocked her even more. She hadn't even told Parable about the priest's visits. Jeannie had the pure mind; the unspoiled mind: the sort of mind that is closed against its own thoughts. Mary couldn't believe that anybody could live peacefully in a head liked Jeannie Jones'; to the pure of mind all things are immoral – or as Parable says, 'how the hell can you clean something that was never soiled?'

Parable was the butt of everybody's opinion. They all 'knew' how he treated his wife. They were all 'aware' of what she had to put up with. They didn't have to be told about a 'man like Parable Jones'. Mary knew how gentle he was without the protection of his tongue. She knew how inhibited he was when the wine wasn't red. She knew that he never criticised his wife – although he had plenty of reason to do so. There was the time when she found him kneeling desperately over the fire, his fingers black as he tried in vain to rescue one of his dirty manuscripts that Jeannie had consigned to Satan. But all he said on seeing Mary was:

– We hope to be able to afford coal shortly.

There was the day that Jeannie had boasted of how she had burned her husband's copy of *Ulysses* because she had heard him and the Pope O'Reilly talk about Molly Bloom comparing the sizes of men's 'things'. And that was something else; Jeannie would never articulate the particularised: of penis and vagina she never spoke: indeed all the nouns, vernacular or foreign, used to describe the male sex organ, offended her.

Not that she wasn't completely au fait. She just knew that penis, cock, dick, champer, langer, plonker and 'yer man in the red hat' were all dirty descriptions of the external male organ. The one and only time Parable had asked her to take his 'prick' in her mouth she had slapped him across the face and ran from his penis as if it was a red-hot poker.

She complained to Mary that P. J. referred to his weapon as if it was an old friend; he'd say to her:

– 'Shake hands with poor ould one-eyed Fagin, and wipe away his tears of love.' A dirty ugly looking brute that he refers to as 'yer man' when he's not talking about 'Custer's Last Stand'.

Mary hardly knew where to look when Jeannie recounted – in the usual strictest confidence – the happenings on her wedding night. She had gone to bed fully dressed. Then Parable handed her the night shirt that she had put in her bottom drawer twelve months before. Article by article her travelling clothes were carefully removed and replaced by her night attire. Nocturnal metamorphosis! Prestidigitation! All her husband saw was the movement of the bedclothes:

– D'ye know, Jeannie, the only time I ever saw your bare arse was when you came out of Blacrock swimming pool having split your bathing suit, and then I was only one of hundreds.

Aye, Jeannie knew that she had had a lot to put up with. If only Mary understood the whole of it. She had borne the embarrassment of his love-making with hardly a complaint; but afterwards, when he asked her to 'stroke poor Fagin, for it's plain to see that he has come over all funny and him lying there on me leg, sorely in need of artificial respiration', Jeannie knew that she was married to a dirty beast.

To Mary, Jeannie had a mind like a sewer so it came as no surprise to learn that she had deliberately interrupted the work on Parable's book. It didn't come as less of a shock, but, well, as she said, it came as no surprise:

– Oh God, if only he was mine! I'd work my fingers to the bone to keep a man like Parable Jones happy. He'd never have another worry in the world. Get on with the work and I'll find the rent.

CHAPTER SEVEN

The Waters of Finn

Jeannie Jones was pleased to see the back of her husband and it boarding the Terenure bus. It was a bit of a bonus; absence mightn't make the heart grow any fonder, but it made life bearable. She had been to Houliuhans and purchased two herring, half a pound of rashers cut at two-and-a-half – she liked the bacon sliced thin, to be grilled crisp – a quarter of mushrooms and a fresh batch loaf. She would cook a good breakfast for herself and Parable Jones could get as drunk as the mood took him:

– Was I on the knocker indeed! Still, it was a bit much, I suppose, dumping all those bills on his desk. But it serves him right; coming home at all hours of night and smelling either like a rose garden or a brewery. Anyway the bills have got to be paid and the sooner he gets back to journalism the better. Literature will never put bread on the table. Literature how are yeh; the aristocrats of print are newspapermen!

As she made her way along Kildimo Avenue, she pondered Parable Jones. Why did he have so little to say to her these days? Why was it that the most uncontroversial conversation always ended in bitter recrimination? Why did he seldom bring his friends home now? Home? he hardly hung his hat there, now.

She heard the rattle of an aluminium ladder and, without looking towards her house, she knew that the window cleaner was on his rounds:

– Two pounds he'll want. Nor was he paid last time! I haven't got four pounds to pay him. All I have is a fiver to manage on. Jesus Mary and Holy St Joseph, is it not a terrible thing that I can't even look a window cleaner straight in the face. Its all the fault of that bloody literature.

She'd ring Mary Belton from the phone box at the corner of the street and call in for an hour:

– I was looking forward to a nice breakfast. But sure hunger is good sauce and it'll do my diet no harm to wait an hour or so. Diet! me! that's a joke! The other fella says I'm a walking advertisement for anorexia. 'One communion wafer is hardly enough, love, to do a healthy day's kneeling.' That Paddy Jones and his blasphemous tongue!

She called him 'Paddy' and was a bit put out if she heard other people refer to him thus. Some folk addressed him as 'P. J.' and she didn't mind that, but 'Paddy' was her name for him and that was as much as she shared of Parable Jones. Little enough – too much.

Her feelings for him were very confused, or mixed – she never knew which. They had been torn asunder a long time ago and, although she remembered when the break came, she never knew why. He accused religion, in the shape of the clergy, of coming between them, 'Maybe I should be feeling complimented to have God as a rival.' He demanded that she be at home to look after the three of them, and when she innocently asked who he meant he had said, 'You, me, and Fagin'.

He said she was either at mass or benediction, confession or communion, when she wasn't doing the seven chapels she was on some sort of religious retreat:

– It's like trying to copulate with an angel, Mary, and I'm no puffin; I can't fuck on the wing.

One spiteful remark had borrowed another until nowadays all was invective. And he told her nothing now, nothing at all. He didn't even discuss work in progress. No, that least of all. She longed for them to talk but he inevitably brought the subject round to sex – to 'screwing, humping, riding, and fucking the arse off of her'. It was all so degrading and he'd blow up and say, 'The trouble about your idea of talk is that it's not conversation you know about, it's fucking gossip!'

In the beginning it had been different. In the beginning? ah sure, when all's said and done, the beginning was the start of nothing.

– He belligerently denies that he's writing a 'Life of James Joyce' and yet I've seen all the books open and ready. Dozens of them:

Richard Ellmann; Herbert Gorman and . . . Paddy says that for every word written by Joyce, a thousand were written about him. But how he hates that one by Padraic and Mary Colum, *Our Friend, James Joyce*. The language out of him when he read it. God, he must have sworn for days without repeating himself, 'If those bog bastards were Joyce's friends, Brutus was Julius Caesar's protector'.

But, when she asked Parable if he had accepted the commission all he had said was that 'Mr Joyce was well able to write books about himself, without any help from the likes of me. Indeed, if the truth be told, he seldom wrote about any-bloody-body else. Anyway I agree with Synge, who swore that he followed Goethe's golden rule never to explain his work or talk about what he was doing.'

She rang Mary who stood dripping wet to answer the phone:

– I'll be expecting you, then . . . look, Jeannie, I'll have to go, I've left the bath running.

Jeannie took the long way round to Mary Belton's. She wanted to get there in Charlie's wake. He always left the house around eight o'clock and walked to the top of Leinster Road before taking the bus the rest of the way into town. His 'morning constitutional' he called it, and, Lord, to see the weight he carries around with him, he needs more than a morning walk.

Poor Charlie was a big bulky boast of a human being, as red in the face as a flush of tomatoes in a carpet of greens. But Mary never went short: Charlie was a great provider: wherever he knocks it down, he never leaves his wife without. Of course then he was really nothing more than a hack; Mary said that herself, 'You're very lucky that you're married to a real one, Jeannie'. 'Christ! why should I have all the luck?'

Jeannie couldn't make up her mind about Mary. The two were the best of friends but 'friendship,' said Paddy, 'claims more victims than hate', and while she didn't understand what her husband had said, she felt that she knew what he meant:

– Everything is so bloody profound. You couldn't say that it was a nice day without Wordsmith greeting it with 'A host of golden daffodils' or Shakespeare comparing you to a summer's day.

When her mother died of cancer of the stomach he recalled every detail about the death of Mrs Dedalus. Christmas was celebrated by most folk but remembered by the literati. If he was half drunk he'd read the Christmas Dinner from *Portrait of the Artist as a Young Man* just to attack Father Jesmond; hopelessly pissed, he wept his way through *A Christmas Carol*. By wishing somebody something as simple as a 'Happy Christmas' you were in danger of creating a literary incident.

Was Mary Belton trying to make a play for Paddy the last time we were both around there together? Do I care? Yes, I think I do. Of course she thinks that if everything in the world was equal she should have Paddy and I'd be ideal for Charlie. Oh God no, better Paddy Joseph drunk than Charlie Belton sober any day of the week.

– Nor is that to deny the correctness of what she was saying. Mary Belton is definitely into literature. And it had her brain addled. She was quoting things to me there that nobody would ever put into print. Nor was it of recent origin! Indeed not, she was forever on about that Chaucer and the dirty things he used to make up. Good God, the man had a mind like a sewer. Between hot pokers up . . . Lord, I couldn't even repeat it.

– And then real monks put their noses to the spokes of a wheel while the Abbot puts his bum to the race so as each got his fair share of a fart. Imagine the mind of a man who could think up the likes of that. Father Jesmond was right, literature became degraded when books were taken out of the province of the clergy.

– And, of course, the proof of the pudding is in the eating: where would you get anything like the works of the Four Masters? Where would you get anybody to create the likes of the Book of Kells? And there's no publication that sells as many copies as the Bible. Aye, Father Jesmond was right.

Mary Belton felt the hot bath water in and around her excited and swollen vulva; she was almost ready and in a second she would reach a tumultuous and satisfying climax. She had locked the bathroom door and now with her vagina almost buried in soap cream she would succumb to her morning orgasm. She would like to have stayed longer in the bath but she knew that Jeannie would be coming up the garden path at any moment.

She thought of Parable Jones and came. Ever since her schooldays she had been attracted to writers. Their aggressiveness to each other, sometimes culminating in physical violence; the heady atmosphere as they threw names of authors around. The language they used – almost ciphered. Yes, that was it, they spoke in code.

Mary had used poor Charlie. He had been her passport to this fascinating world of the word. She supposed that the Pearl Bar and the Palace were still open and busy. Charlie used to take her to those places when he was young, and new on the *Times*. It was in the Palace that Smiley, the editor, used to hold court.

Paddy Kavanagh, always the worse for drink, came in when he was working for the *Catholic Standard*. His name was almost as common to Dublin walls as was the demand to 'Release Frank Ryan or Else': 'Read P. K.'s Reviews in the *Catholic Standard*'. Kavanagh, battered poet under a battered hat – from the head of a peasant spoke the mind of a colossus.

Mary remembered the 'mild-mannered, modest spoken Austin Clarke' who didn't really hold with drink but would take a drop of whatever anybody was buying. There was the randy red-haired Yankee, Gainor Crist, about whom all the girls had been thankfully warned, so that wives, mothers, and daughters tossed up to see who'd be last away from him. Lord, he was the most handsome of men, though she never thought much of his bear-like friend, Donleavy, who followed the Ginger Man everywhere, pen and notebook in hand, the poor man's Boswell, ready to write down whatever might fall from the lips of the tall, good-looking American.

There was Myles, or Flann O'Brien, or Brian O'Nolan, who was forever leaving bits of himself in various government departments, hid in every pseudonymous persona, away from the prying eyes of his civil service masters. When not being excessively secretory, he would expose himself in the columns of the *Irish Times*; that was when he was not passing snide remarks about Mr James Augustine Joyce who, once upon a time, had praised Myle's talent as the most comic in Ireland.

Parable thought that Myles might have been more at home in the Phoenix Park looking for that soldier who, completing the mystery of metamorphosis, rose at the behest of God, Bram Stoker or James Joyce, in the persona of 'Humphrey Chimpden Earwicker', 'Bygmester Finnegan', or 'Oh Mr Porter'.

There too, remembered Mary, was Brinsley MacNamara who had written *The Valley of the Squinting Windows*: for which he was exiled for ever from the villages of Clane and Straffan. *Clochmerle* could teach the Kildare lechers little of lewdness, looseness, licentiousness, lasciviousness or plain old-fashioned lust.

'Ah,' said Parable, 'had Brinsley been a better reader, he might not have bothered his arse chancing his arm at the writing, because the whole thing was all there, word for word, years before in a book by Douglas Brown called *The House with the Green Shutters*.'

– Lord! I'll never forget how they beat each other up and down the length of the bar. It was in the Palace that Parable had imparted that knowledge to Brinsley and all his lionisers, and Tommy told them to take their literary arguments elsewhere as his was a respectable public house.

As a student she felt that it was the Pearl and the Palace, McDaid's and The Tower that put back the life into the books that the university professors took out. Later yet, she told herself that if she could have had a hand in one book by Parable Jones, she wouldn't have called the queen her aunt:

– To get away from Charlie and de Valera! Imagine! when the books about Joyce and all were being mooted for his centenary, P. J. had told them all to shove their commissions up their respective arses. He told them that it was hard enough to find some of Dublin to write about, without putting more in that monster's way. And, in some respects he wasn't far out; the way they're destroying the town, it might, as Joyce foresaw, have to be reconstructed from the pages of *Ulysses*.

Mary dressed slowly and deliberately. She brought her brassiere straps to the front of her chest, fastened the ends, twisted the under-garment right round, and felt some satisfaction as the cups slipped over her shapely bosom. In her student days she had burnt her bra with the rest, but she was never happy because her breasts needed support, so she secretly got back into harness because there was nothing worse than tortured tits.

She hitched her pants high round her waist because sometimes the top band of the tights dug into her belly so that she was all the time wanting to scratch. Just before she pulled the pants up she slipped a paper towel round her vuvla so that the pants would not dig into the lips of her vagina:

– God, but men have it made! Just slip into their y-fronts and then zip up their trousers.

Mary remembered that she had left her shoes in Charlie's 'cell', as he liked to call his den. She had paused to look at a copy of *Playboy* that her husband must have been wanking to and had forgotten to put away:

– Charlie and his fantasies! They're more real to him than reality! The time he told me that he always regretted being an only child, 'Oh, Mary, if I could have screwed a sister – it must feel like being inside yourself.'

She found her shoes under Charlie's desk where she had left them on the previous evening; she shoved the copy of *Playboy* into the back of his filing cabinet along with his other porn, and paused for a moment to read the newest pages of *Eamon de Valera*.

The Rising was nearing its end and the diplomatic General Maxwell was presenting the surrender terms to the insurgents, 'Give in or we will shell the civilian population of Dublin':

> From the General Post Office, Pearse ordered the republicans to lay down their arms, admiring them, 'During the last four days they had been writing, with fire and steel, the most glorious chapter in the history of Ireland . . . They have redeemed Dublin from many shames, and made her name splendid among the names of cities . . .'
>
> He spoke of the officer commanding the Dublin Division, the Scots-born James Connolly, 'He lies wounded, but is still the guiding brain of our resistance.'

Mary scoffed and told herself that the English had only been second to the Pope in asking for Connolly's blood. Not that Charlie Belton would ever mention that. Oh, God, no! Her husband was far too good a newspaperman to be controversial about people who count. Good reporters know what makes news – press barons and prime ministers. Charlie had learned this lesson well, and his *Life of Eamon de Valera* would cause few ripples. The gentlemen of the press know when to conceal their true feelings – it's called 'being objective'.

And yet she must hand it to her husband. His style was pure Fleet Street. No literary allusions to disturb the readers' digestion; and yet with a few meaningless phrases he could make holy communion exciting. It was this 'man eats God' instead of 'man bites hand' with which every ragman learned to replace meaningful communication:

> Connolly, reporting from a hospital stretcher, on the republican losses, mentioned the one redoubt remaining, 'Commandant de Valera stretches in a position from the gas-works to Westland Row, holding Boland's Bakery, Boland's Mills, Dublin South-West Railway Works, and dominating Merrion Square'. But, as Pearse was surrendering to General Maxwell, de Valera's ammunition was all but spent.

A 'Captain Hitzen' was sent from the Vice-Regal Lodge to demand Dev's surrender, and told the 'Long Fella' how sad it was that the rebels had not been fighting with the British against the Germans: '"We had our ideals," Commandant de Valera had replied.'

Mary thought:

– That must have been before the long bastard learned the true value of money.

She wondered if Captain Hitzen had ever returned to visit the Phoenix Park when Dev took up residence in the Vice-Regal Lodge:

– Phoenix Park, where Parable says that all modern life began with *Finnegans Wake*. Even in my rusty Irish the name has nothing to do with the mythical bird. The English who have made it their imperial business to speak everything from Sanskrit to Esperanto would never pronounce the Irish words because they thought that we, in our stupidity, were trying to say 'Phoenix'. How conceited is the arrogance of the ignorant. Aye, Joyce was right to reset the universe there, where Finn's father had been killed at the 'Battle of Castleknock', for that's where it all began, Finn's Town, Finn's City, like all human life everywhere it came from Finn Uisce, the Waters of Finn.

The crunch of feet on gravel disturbed her reverie:

– That'll be Jeannie going round the back, I'd better put the kettle on.

CHAPTER EIGHT

The Black on the White

Harry McGill lay back in his swivel chair and contemplated the nicotine-stained office ceiling. The centrepiece was set in ovals, which were, in turn, a feature of painted panels and delicate scrolls. A deep cornice with defined reglets bore testimony to the fact that the plaster-work was eighteenth-century and in the style of Robert Adams. Georgian Dublin had learned, through Adams and the Italian Renaissance architects, the glory that was once Pompeii.

From the polished roll-top desk, to the polished book-cases, to the lower corner rail with its fans and hanging garlands, the room – certainly the upper part of the room – was much the same now, as when some lord's bastard had lived in town to get away from the monotony of the Irish countryside with its unpleasant peasantry who refused either to be rack-rented, evicted, transported or hanged without fighting back.

In this house of exquisite Georgian proportions a writer could write and a painter could paint; ready-made for the sculptor, it could lift the heart of the composer. The ceiling was more than just something overhead; in its own unostentatious way it was more eloquent than any Sistine Chapel. It was a celebration of all that was good about man, and it was obviously proper that a publisher of books should work here. And yet it did not overawe Harry McGill, who was thinking to himself:

– I wonder how many sheets of hardboard it would take to cover up that dust-trap?

Writers were a mystery to Harry McGill. They didn't fascinate him – only wheeling and dealing did that. They puzzled him; for people who were often quite literate, they were mostly dumb bastards when it came to percentages. If he had been a writer – which God forbid – he would have bought a calculator first and the dictionary could come later. He had never heard of anybody losing money because they couldn't spell, but the bankruptcy courts were overflowing with insolvents who couldn't count.

McGill had the reputation of being 'a decent ould skin who would never see a chap stuck'; he was 'rough in his talk' and 'pretended illiteracy' in conversation. But, 'behind all the bluff was a man who knew what he wanted'. The pubs were filled with writers who 'had scored off Harry McGill'. Writers had themselves invented the fiction; Harry only lived up to it – talk is cheap, so cheap that it costs nothing.

The intercom buzzed and Harry brought his chair swiftly to earth, flicked the switch on the communicator, and heard his secretary, Miriam Clandillon's voice, to which he responded:

– Yes, Miriam, what is it?

– It's Sean Daly, Mr McGill.

A poet looking for money: an advance on royalties. They were a bloody nuisance to the book trade. Publishers always had trouble from writers, but poets were the worst of the lot; mendacious mendicant monsters who thought they must be as poor as church mice to write, and as rich as Jeffrey Archer to live. Mostly they lived in hope of being libelled, though no lie about them could be more defamatory than the truth. The hell with them the scrounging bastards. Business is business. Do these beggars never read contracts? Of course not – some of them never even read what they write.

Harry loved the feeling of righteousness that power gave him. Parable Jones said he smiled at his enemies and gushed on everybody else; friendship never entered the reckoning since Harry never made friends.

He removed his finger from the intercom switch and it reverted to the off-position. He sat back to consider himself. Miriam Clandillon smiled at Sean Daly and the poet remarked:

– He's taking his time, is he not?

– He's very busy, Mr Daly.

– Aye, like the fox in the bush.
– Pardon?
– Wonderin' if he loses or gains by coming out of the long grass.
– I don't follow you, Mr Daly.
– No need to, *asthore*, there's no escape for him.
– What in heaven's name do you mean, Mr Daly?
– Well, there's only the one way out, and unless he's going to jump sixty feet to the ground he has to come through here.

Poet and protector bore the silence in patient unease, until Daly asked:

– Fond of your job, Miss Clandillon?
– It's a job, Mr Daly, like any other job. Mr McGill is a good boss.
– Is that so, now? Parable Jones says that Mr McGill would have betrayed Anne Frank to Hitler for the rights to publish her diaries.

Miss Clandillon busied herself with papers. She knew that her employer took such insults in the name of Mammon; after all's said and done, the picaresque Parable Joneses of this world sold literature, while respectable men like Harry McGill sold books. Miriam might have been reading her employer's mind as he told himself:

– A man has to be firm, or the literati would walk on him. No advances. No advances at all. Every quarter the royalty statements were distributed. Unless of course a chap is successful. Successful writers can have money any time they asked for it. Shakespeare, now he had the right idea, 'Put money in thy purse'; there's meaningful literature.

It was better that way. Better for them and better for Harry. The fact that successful writers seldom needed money before royalties were due had not escaped his notice or attention. Better still, each year he increased the royalty period; when he first went into business the company paid every quarter, now it was every six months, and even that could be extended by blaming delay on the computer. It must have been some hard nosed publisher who coined the phrase, 'every mickle makes a muckle' – for every penny he could keep in the bank for any little while longer, the more pounds he could screw out of the hated writer. Harry McGill basked in the admiration of the business community, the people who counted. He had been named 'businessman of the year' by the chamber of commerce.

He switched the intercom on again:

– Miriam, say I'm getting ready to fly to London . . . that I'll get back to him before I leave . . . if I get the opportunity.

– I think, sir, that it might be better to see Mr Daly . . .

– Between you and me, Miriam, I will decide who I see.

– But, Harry . . . I mean, Mr McGill, you don't quite understand . . .

– But me no buts, Miriam.

Almost before he finished speaking, Harry heard, through the door, the shrill voice of his secretary protesting:

– You just can't go in there, Mr Daly. Mr McGill is at a conference.

– Conference my fucking arse, said the Clare accent of the gargantuan Sean Daly: poet, novelist, gaelic football player and celebrated wild man of French letters.

He almost leaped at the startled publisher as he bounded into the office. Harry all but disappeared behind a pale, painted smile, as the man mountain stood towering above him:

– As I thought, McGill! In conference is it? Pullin' your fuckin' wire more likely! Have you any idea – cretin that you are – how hard it is to work when four children are cryin' from the hunger? I've a good mind to hang you, by the hasp of your arse, from the window of your beautiful Georgian office.

Harry McGill managed a thin smile:

– If it's not yourself, Sean! Miriam! he shouted at the intercom. Why didn't you tell me that Sean Daly was waiting to see me!

Shaking his head sadly to and fro, for the benefit of the poet, he told his secretary, in the voice of a man deeply hurt:

– Christ, Miriam, have I not always told you that when Sean, or one of the other important writers, wants to see me, you were never to stand on ceremony? Show them straight in is what I've always told you.

He confided to the big man:

– To be fair to the poor woman, she's just trying to protect me.

Looking round, as if for strangers in the gallery, he informed the poet in a near whisper:

– There are some people I just have to avoid, of course. You know, Sean, ould son, some folk could bore the arse off a politician. Life is too short for that class of thing. Ah, sure what's the use of talkin'! All I can do is beg your pardon and hope for your forgiveness.

Daly assured him that since no offence was intended, none was taken. If only he could have an advance to pay the grocer and the rent, and a few other bills . . . Harry wouldn't listen to another word:

– Say no more, me old mate. Not another word. Your very security is my future. Could a publisher get along without his scribe? Could a bird fly on one wing? Just spell out your needs, Sean; my time is yours. To prove which, he shouted to his secretary:

– Miriam! I'm in conference with Mr Daly. I don't want to be disturbed – for any reason. If that call that I'm expecting from London comes through in the next few minutes, just tell them to hang on until I've finished. Oh, and Miriam, bring in my cheque book on the number five account, please. Now, Sean, I'm all yours.

Daly was fascinated by the insolence of the man. And yet he was not unamused by the businessman's naivety. He knew what the next move would be, even before McGill made it. The publisher would give the cheque book a flourish – would twenty pounds cover the poet's needs? Then, with a devil-may-care gesture:

– Ah the hell with it, sure it's only money! Twenty quid goes nowhere these days . . . I'll make it fifty wha'?

This was known as the 'subvert the supplicant' move. It made the normal chap feel too embarrassed to ask for more. Unfortunately for Mr McGill, Daly was in his Oliver Twist mood. Before Harry could make out the cheque in the amount of his choice, the poet told him in tones intended to coerce:

– I've worked out what I'll need to keep ink in me pen until my royalties fall due. Two hundred and fifty notes, Harry, and that's cuttin' everything to the bone.

McGill could feel the blood draining from his face. The figures engraved themselves on his ulcer, and he was all the more sick because he was trying to smile through premature rigor mortis:

– Two hundred and fifty pounds, eh?

He forced his hand to write the cheque, and quipped as he handed it over:

– Are yeh sure you took your first thoughts away, Sean?

The poet held the draft briefly; folded it carefully, and put it in an inside pocket:

– Tis true what the world and Garret Reilly says of you, Harry – you're as generous as an orchard in a storm.

Miriam Clandillon shouted through the intercom that London was calling, and, rising to his full stature, Daly grasped the publisher's hand warmly and told him:

– Don't let me hold the wheels of progress back, Harry, me ould flower. Sure if you don't keep in with the English we'll all be waiting on the potato, and God knows, a cara, them same spuds is a poor dependence. Push the frontiers of art as far as you can, Harry, the world of literature is depending on you.

He was gone and still Miriam Clandillon was screaming about London being on the other end of the phone. Infuriated, McGill bellowed through the intercom:

– Fuck London, and its friends in America! Christ Almighty, Miriam, what's the point in telling me that when the big bog bastard is away!

If only he could write, and print, and distribute. Oh, to be able to do the lot yourself. Surely, when penniless picaroons can put words together, it can't be all that difficult to put the black on the white?

CHAPTER NINE

The Great Hunger

Parable thought a mutton pie might be in order. Joe Hughes took one from a glass case with a flapping lid and popped it into the micro. He went off to serve folk at the end of the bar before returning to the oven. A paper napkin was placed in front of P. J. and Joe went to scrape the heads of a row of filling pints before topping them and setting them in front of their owners. To one customer he said:

– Credit card, Tommy? Only if you've stolen somebody else's.

He opened the microwave oven, removed the repast, and placed in front of Parable Jones a plastic knife, a plastic fork, and a plastic pie on a plastic plate. Parable took a bite from the pastry and asked for sauce. Joe stood with his back to the gantry and addressed the pub:

– Would yeh credit it! He wants sauce! Is this a public house or the penny dinners! And, where will it all end, that's what I want to know? First it's condiments and the next thing you know it'll be *café au lait*! What was the point of serving five years to the bar trade when I could have been a fucking waiter in five minutes! Why d'ye want sauce, Parable?

Without taking his eyes from Joe Hughes, P. J. told him:

– To disguise the taste of the fucking pie, yeh ignorant bollocks!

A jingling of car keys at Parable's elbow told him that the husband of his mistress was ready to chauffeur him to his assignation. Jack Millington told P. J. that he was a bloody hard man to find:

– I've been everywhere, from O'Hara's to Slattery's. Why the hell d'ye keep changing pubs?

– Because, the drunker I get, the more obnoxious becomes the publican.

– D'ye not think that the amount you drink might account for some of their hostility? Still, for somebody whose been gargling all day, you seem to be strangely sober, ould son.

– Well, don't let Joe Hughes bank on it, because, in a minute I'd shove that mutton pie up his arse.

– Not now, Parable, publicans are very quick to send for the polis, and if I don't get you there on time to meet the missus she'll blame me.

There were those who thought that the relationship between the Millingtons and Parable Jones was a *ménage a trois*, but such was not the case – as might have been clear to anybody listening to the two men as they made their way to Jack's car:

– Yer a lucky man, P. J.; that woman thinks that the sun shines through your arse. Had she thought as much of me, I might never have run off with her brother. Still, I don't know though, with all due respect, he has a better-looking arse.

He looked anxiously from his watch to P. J.

– We'd better shift if we're to get to Dawson Street by six.

– Six? Is it six? The last time I remember noticing today was the Angelus ringing out twelve. I must have slept in Joe Hughes' for the whole afternoon. No wonder the poor shit was being sarcastic about me turning his pub into a café – he might well have accused me of using it as a lodging house.

Jack Millington dropped his wife's lover off at the corner of Anne Street, and it was with relief that he heard the evening Angelus ringing from behind him at Clarendon Street. Millington was gone with a wave, and P. J. paused for a second to steady the buffs and shake off the muzzy feeling that always followed a sudden conscious emergence into daylight.

He bumped into a man and was surprised to hear the man apologise. The last time that happened in this street was in *Ulysses* when Mr Bloom knocked against the blind stripling who swore at him and said he could see more than Bloom, blind and all as he was. Then followed all that bit about closing eyes to see what it's like, not being able to see, but sure the stripling had made it all clear – blindness is the most diabolical infliction ever imposed by God.

Parable thought of Joyce's use of the word 'parallax' and closing his eyes briefly to change his position so as to cause a change in the position of St Anne's, when he opened them again it was Sally-Anne Millington he saw. She was clinging to the railings of what used to be H. Sibthorpe, Painters and Decorators. Seeing her lover at the same time, Sally-Anne gave a shy, girlish wave, over-balanced, and fell, flat on her face:

– Ah Christ! Pissed out of her mind, and the evening is hardly in it!

Sally-Anne is the daughter of a monumental mason who refers to Henry Moore as 'Polo Mint' and swears that the English sculptor is not out of the womb yet. He hated everybody with the name Moore – particularly the ones with whom he was acquaint. Henry, because in art school they spoke of little else, and George because he had failed English by not liing *Esther Waters*. He had been beaten by a teacher called John Moore for not knowing the capital of Outer Mongolia; he still didn't know the capital of Outer Mongolia and if anybody ever told him the capital of Outer Mongolia he'd get a firm chisel up the Khyber.

His name was Michael Aidan O'Reilly and he was known as the 'Pope' because of his necrographic encounters with the clergy. He was a well-avoided man and his sense of vulgarity was purely for the sake of obscenity. At one time he was known by the Gaelic Athletic Association as 'The Alien' because of an essay, 'French Letters Destroyed Irish Literature', which even more narrow-minded folk construed as an unwarranted attack on Samuel Beckett.

Most people reacted favourably to his sense of humour, with the possible exception of clergymen, policemen, publicans, prostitutes, politicians, and his family. Sally-Anne told her paramour:

– His wit is no bloody joke when you're on the other end of it. He's the most unpleasant old fucker that any person could be a child of. Do you know that I used to come home at the end of term and go down on my knees in front of my mother begging her to say that I was a bastard. Even in the graveyard of his mind the old reprobate lets nobody rest in peace.

When a memorial to Sally's mother was unveiled it was seen to be in the form of a gigantic penis pointing to her grave and the inscription along the shaft read, 'I come! I come! My heart's delight!' When the cemetery company told the 'Pope' to remove it from their necropolis with all possible haste, he took the opportunity to call into question every tender memorial placed by every grief-stricken mourner in the graveyard:

– God dammit, are you not ashamed to exhibit some of the dreary artefacts that are placed here! Death is not the end, it is the beginning. I rejoice in mortality as the beginning of something new. Death is a celebration, man! Celebrate!

The director said he didn't care if the memorials were artistic or not – just as long as they didn't have foreskins. This infuriated the 'Pope':

– Dammit all, man, how the hell do you expect us to have resurrection without erection. Penis erectus for ever!

Really, it was, according to Sally-Anne's father, the 'symmetery of the cemetery' that was really *de trop*. He warned the clergy about art that was not 'scrotumtightening', and begged them to heed Epstein's plea for 'sculpture with balls'. When the clergy sent for the police, the 'Pope' spoke about 'priestish prejudice, hierarchical hypocrisy', and 'clerical claptrap'. He told his daughter:

– When *in articulo mortis* the curtain of life is removed, you will see, lurking in the shadows, at least one meddlesome priest.

The 'Pope's' close friend was a hospital porter called Johnny Carey. Younger than Sally-Anne's father, what he lacked in years, he made up for in dogged indifference to religion. 'Ah yes', the 'Pope' was fond of saying, 'Johnny Carey is worth a battalion of mealy-mouthed agnostics'. His job he kept because a deaf registrar thought he was saying that his favourite interest was in diagnostics.

He and the 'Pope' shared one achievement in common – Carey was a master of dog Latin. Indeed, it might be true to say that, in so far as tridentine fervour counted, there was only Carey, the 'Pope', Bryden MacWilliams, and Archbishop Lefebvre.

The fight against the other pope – the Polish one – was quite a personal thing; Carey, like Bryden MacWilliams, had only distinguished himself in the tridentine mass; he could neither sing nor dance, but Christ, had he mastered the responses! Johnny Carey was the first and only man to be barred from the pro-Cathedral for yodelling the *mea culpa*.

That he was a real fourteen-carat atheist did not seem to the 'Pope' to contravene his own Christian agnosticism. With the slightest adjustment, Sally-Anne's father could have made his irreligious convictions as sound as Johnny Carey's. Of one thing he was quite certain – Carey was right when he predicted about hokum preached in a language that the majority of churchgoers couldn't understand. The way matters stood now, anybody, from a Protestant minister to a rabbi could be a Catholic. If John Paul the Pole was allowed to carry on, Rome would be as undistinguished as every little born-again Christian in every little born-again hamlet, from Ballymena to Ballyporeen.

The 'Pope' O'Reilly supported the cause of Johnny Carey because he saw in its anti-clericalism the vindication of his forefathers. But, tradition smedition! The 'Pope' didn't care if they said mass in Shavian Esperanto attended by communist cuties in Marxist tights. 'Let the mistakes of the past take care of the past', was his motto. But he would not give up his greatest love, this vindictive hatred of religion.

Graveyards were his domain, and, when men in black cassocks told him how to remember the dead, the 'Pope' O'Reilly would tell them where to get off. He had composed a simple aid to mourning, in which he pointed out that it was much more pleasant to remember a loved one when he was coming than when he was going. The cemetery company refused to handle copies, and the 'Pope' said he was not surprised that they should try to stop him earning a living since they had already persuaded mourners that dying was the end of life.

Oh yes! Sally-Anne remembered Johnny Carey, all right! A younger edition of her father, and in, roughly, the same business. The 'Pope' O'Reilly had met him during one of his visits to the Hospice of The Next World, where Carey worked as a porter in the mortuary. He had written this disgusting thesis about necrophiliacs being the outlawed of society – they were the neglected minority who couldn't come until the other person had gone.

Johnny Carey had been hand-made for Sally's father. Any self-respecting hedonist would be put off by the 'Pope' O'Reilly; all his vices were of the senses: but it didn't stop there. He didn't drink because it made him impotent and he didn't smoke because he had met a chap with emphysema who didn't have enough breath to fulfil his potential. He needed no phoney stimulus because he was always confident that, like Herne the Hunter, his horn would always rise to the occasion.

Not that he held anything against those who needed aphrodisiacs to complete the hunt. He had admired Hemingway, but not as a hunter – it was the courage with which he committed the supreme sexual act of taking his own life; oh God, the excitement of coming like that must have made necrophilia seem tame indeed. Then too, according to himself, Ernest had killed a man, just as Buck Mulligan had saved one. Well, the 'Pope' O'Reilly had killed a man.

As Sally-Anne had heard it told, it happened in the Australian Bush. The man had buggered the 'Pope's' horse. When Parable had asked Sally-Anne's father whether there was any truth in the story, the 'Pope' had put neither cap nor cloak on it:

– The guy had tried to alienate my horse's affections. That sort of thing is frowned on in the Bush. How would you like some bastard to screw your horse?

– I don't have a horse.

– You haven't lived, son.

He didn't have any feelings of guilt in the matter. It was a simple crime of passion, and anybody can understand how a guy feels when he has been cuckolded by a snake and a horse:

– How would you feel if you came home to find some smart ass in bed with one you loved?

Parable was about to make light of the question, but, at the time, what with a lump hammer in his hand, and a serious look upon his face, it didn't seem as if the 'Pope' was being funny. He decided to play a straight bat:

– It was a filly, I suppose?

– Well, of course it was! What the hell d'ye take me for – a bloody queer?

CHAPTER TEN

A Church Not Without Religion

As Charlie Belton was saying and him leaving Grogan's, Castle Bar:

– Bryden MacWilliams, Johnny Carey, and the 'Pope' O'Reilly? There's a Trinity that's a real mystery.

But Joe Starkey couldn't disagree more or care less. He disregarded the Church in the hope of redemption:

– Natural allies, surely? Basically they're three reactionaries, one agnostic, one atheist, and one Catholic traditionalist.

Starkey was respected on matters clerical – he was a spoiled priest, unfrocked for God knows what, but heterosexuality is any good man's fault, and, in so far as the other is concerned, the Church has only itself to blame for leading men into temptation:

– Marcel Lefebvre? He's a sweet thing in a child's frock, believe you me, but he's only one of many bishops, archbishops, and princes of the Church who are opposed to the new religion.

– He's not alone then? asked a man behind Charlie Belton's back.

– Don't be kiddin' yerself. There are three cardinals in particular, so much to the right of Lefebvre that if politics were mathematics, they'd damn near emerge on the left; and if the clergy was subject to the same laws as the laity, they'd all be in jail . . .

– I really thought that Archbishop Lefebvre was a loner, I must admit, said the man behind Charlie Belton's back, but Joe Starkey blinded him with statistics:

– A loner? He is in my arse! For example there's a city in northern Italy called Piacenza, and nearly everybody in it is a supporter of Cardinal Silvio Oddi's mafia.

– 'Piacenza'! There's a great sound of Italian names, said Charlie Belton, all ice-cream and opera:

– Piacenza is teeming with Catholics who are 'anti-Jan Pawel'. And Oddi is not the only dissident cardinal round there: Opilio Rossi and Antonio Samore are two more who have thrown their red hats into the ring along with Lefebvre.

– And this is just a protest against the loss of the tridentine mass? said Charlie. I find that very hard to accept.

– Bollocks, retorted Joe Starkey, they couldn't hope to care less if the mass was to be celebrated in Swahili – you could say it in deaf and dumb and they wouldn't give a fuck.

– But I always thought, began the man behind Charlie Belton's back, but another man said that he shouldn't be in the conversation since he was off the drink for Lent. Joe Starkey ignored all the interruptions:

– These old curias are like the Orange Lodgers of Ireland; any change they see as unconditional surrender.

– They live back in an age when anti-communism got grants from the US treasury. The Piacenza mafia never could get used to the idea of the Pope coming down from Mount Olympus and leaving the Vatican; they didn't like it when John XXIII did it. Most of all, they can't stand being upstaged by an actor who hugs communist mayors and fascist politicians. Like every other thespian he probably calls them 'darling' as well.

– Yer not suggestin', said the man behind Charlie Belton's back, that he's one of 'them'?

– If he is, said Starkey, I'd be most surprised because, according to everybody, he's very fond of a bit of the other.

– Well, Joe, said Charlie Belton, fascinating as is the Vatican intrigue, it's time for me to catch the missus with the coalman.

He was quite relaxed as he left Grogan's by the side door and made his way to Neary's of Chatham Street. His inside pocket was well lined with fivers and oncers. Paddy O'Brien, that decent man, had cashed his cheque without complaint. Now he could go to the other place without fear of having to pay anything off his tick bill.

There was a new production at the Gaiety that would make a few lines for one of the 'Sundays'. Tonight was dress rehearsal and most of the actors would be hanging on to their boiling half-pints. Three or four judiciously spent pounds would open the mouths of an entire company. Most journalists eschewed 'stringing', but Charlie wasn't proud.

In Neary's, John Burke and John the 'Robber' Burke informed Belton that they had, just a moment previously, seen Parable Jones and a lady in some distress, lean in a taxi queue at St Stephen's Green:

– That'll be Sally-Anne, said Belton, the 'Pope' O'Reilly's daughter.

– You could well be right, said John Burke. But I would not swear to it, for we could not see the lady's face.

– But it was her, said John the Robber, for, without a doubt, Sally-Anne Millington has the finest and most distinctive arse of any woman in Dublin.

Poor Parable Jones had dragged Sally-Anne to the taxi rank on the corner of the Green. She draped around, rather than clung to his neck and P. J. prayed that a herd of hackneys would arrive soon, and vacant. The smell of drink from his loved one was fast making him sick. John Burke and John the Robber Burke passed by on their way to Grogan's Castle Bar:

– Is she still on the multi-slurps? quipped John the Robber, and a murmur rumoured round the queue about the 'poor dear having multi-sclerosis'.

A considerate news-vendor, from the railings of the park, taking the bull by the horns, asked gently and loudly:

– Is the poor woman a cripple, sir?

P. J. squeezed up a tear, before replying:

– She is, God help her; a severe case of ebriosis perpetuus. And I have carried her all the way from Westland Row Chapel, because we couldn't get on a bus after her wheelchair was stolen.

A gasp of horrified indignation went through the queue, and Parable – not a writer for nothing – went on with the story. But then there was no way he could have stopped. When Parable Jones gets into the stride of a lie there is no power on earth that could prevent him from completing the fiction:

– This, as you know, is the year of the disabled. Well, we went into the chapel so that she could say a prayer for those worse off than herself. We couldn't have been on our knees for more than an hour, and, out we came, to find our wheelchair no longer in the place where we left it – there it was, sir, and it gone!

All together, like a well rehearsed decade of the Rosary, the queue intoned:

– Well, Jesus, Mary, and Holy St Joseph, is there nothin' in this country that's sacred any more?

When at last a taxi did arrive, the paper-seller came to Parable's assistance, and, with cries of:

– Make way for the paralysed lady! the queue parted like the Red Sea.

Deep in the inebriation of her unconscious, Sally-Anne heard something like somebody ordering more drink, so her mouth demanded:

– Another Blue Lady, Mr Eh . . . and, because of her slurred words, two old ladies in the queue thought that Sally-Anne was praying to Our Blue Lady of Perpetual Succour, and they were thrilled that a young crippled woman should show such great love for Our Lord's Blessed Mother, and her in such dire straits herself. It was surely enough to make any person of hale health feel ashamed. With tears in their eyes, they touched the hem of Sally-Anne's saintly skirt and she farted loudly in their faces. But, knowing well the incontinence of cripples, undeterred they whispered faithfully:

– God and His Blessed Mother and all the saints be with you, child. Never doubt it! We will all pray to Our Blue Lady for you, and the queue knelt in the street.

As the taxi sped off in the direction of the Bridge Bar, the driver took a long look at the kneeling throng, who were now well into their fourth 'Hail Mary', and being joined by casual passing Christians, and said:

– Yeh know, Parable, this place has gone out of its tiny collective mind since the Pope's visit. Mass hysteria! Between James Joyce, Karol Wojtyla, and Eamon de Valera, the country is without a titter of sense. And it's all without rhyme or reason.

Parable assured the cabby that such a change would be all for the best; no way would the people of Ireland have given their place up for a cripple before the Pope came or before Eamon de Valera was a hundred years old:

– It's the new Irishry that is a thing of beauty and a joy for ever. Beauty doesn't need a reason. What is it Schiller says: 'The beautiful is that which pleases universally without the intervention of a concept.'

– Schiller never said that. That was coined by that cunning old cunt Kant.

– Look, you be the intellectual and I'll handle the hack – who needs a clever fucking taxi-man?

– Yes, but don't you think that discussing things like beauty are more important than shooting the shit? Old Hegel now when talking about beauty believed in the 'sensuous appearance of the idea'.

– Yes, but isn't that contradicted by Goethe who maintained that 'beauty can never become aware of itself'.

– Does it, d'ye think?

– Why ask me? You're the fucking taxi-man.

With one arm around Sally-Anne's neck to protect her head from the front seat, and his other hand gripping the door catch, for fear he should lurch forward on top of her, Sally-Anne must have looked an extraordinary sight in the driver's rear-view mirror:

– Jazes, Parable, it's no wonder they think she's a cripple! I know real paralytics who can stand straighter than she can. Thank God it's Reivey's we're aiming for because no decent dram shop would let her into its lower depths.

Sally belched as Parable realised that the hackney-driver had mentioned two of Zola's works in the same line – probably unconsciously, he hoped. She rifted again and the driver asked:

– Do me a favour, mate, if she acts like she's goin' to be sick, shove her head out the winda, will yeh? I can't afford to take a shift off to have the cab cleaned.

Suddenly the wind from Sally-Anne changed direction, and the cabby pleaded as the emission sounded, long, loud and all to the same air:

– On second thoughts, flower, maybe yeh should just stick her arse through the door.

Holding his nose high, Parable looked into the driver's eyes which were staring at him from the rear-view mirror:

– It's hardly the act of a gentleman to remark on a lady's indiscretion, when that particular lady is non-compos-mentis.

– How d'ye mean, ould stock?

– You were suggesting, Paddy, that Sally-Anne farted.

– Well, P. J., may God turn me into a bed-ridden fairy if such words ever entered my mind! She might play a tune on her beautiful instrument, but, far be it from me to imply that a lady with one like that would ever fart through it. Ladies break wind.

– For Christ's sake, Paddy, when did flatulation have its own etiquette? Everybody knows that a person can't break wind without farting.

Paddy the Cab was still shaking his head in disbelief as Parable Jones searched for the fare:

– Jases, Parable, but yer an awful man. If it wasn't that everybody knows that yer a genius we'd all swear that you were goin' around with a screw loose.

– Do you believe I'm a genius, Paddy?

– D'ye think I'd let an ordinary lunatic misquote the classics in me own cab the way you do if yeh weren't?

– And what is a genius, d'ye think?

– Jazes, now yer askin'! I suppose it's what I'm not. Eh, will yeh be able to manage her nibs into the boozer?

Parable nodded:

– I'd give yeh a hand, but I daren't desert the ould waggon – couldn't leave a thing unattended round here unless yeh welded the wheels to the chassis. He looked at the tall graceful lamp-posts reflected in the Liffey and said:

– With a favourable wind the stink of the river will take away the smell of me taxi. Have a good night, Parable, though I think it'll take yeh all yer time.

He let down the hand-brake, slipped from neutral through first, into second gear, and was gone.

The cab driver was from South Dublin and the natives on that side of the river can be very scathing about the frontier pubs which line the north quays. To the Monto man, it's the last outpost, but, to the guy from the Liberties, its the gateway to the South. To Joyce it was Finn MaCumaill, senior, lying in state beside lovely Anna Livia Plurabelle, and marking the history of the world as it flowed inexorably down to the sea to be shared by the rest of the world.

A panda car cruised slowly by and Parable barely had time to pull Sally-Anne into a shop doorway, stand her straightish and simulate the sex act – policemen new from the farm didn't know about indecent exposure, but they hated Dublin drunks – especially when they themselves had to stay sober.

Sally felt her boy-friend pressing into her and through a woolly mouth she said thickly:

– Ah, Parable, honey, honest to jazes, I wouldn't be able.

CHAPTER ELEVEN

Dublin is Myles Better

Tom Reivey was not the most kissed man in Ireland. His face seemed as if it belonged in someone else's head. For that again, maybe the head was the least of his worries – he hadn't wanted to see a great deal of it since contracting alopecia while still quite young. His real trouble was athlete's foot, from which he suffered ever since John-Joe Sheehy threw the hammer at a sports meeting in Tralee. Anyone walking behind Reivey would vouch for the fact that John-Joe's hammer landing on Reivey's foot did little to improve his gait. Worse still, however, was the way the incident drove him from the Mother Church. It was an innocent enough remark of Father Keane's that started the rot:

– You are a lucky man, Tom Reivey, for it is the mercy of God that it was not the javelin that John-Joe was flinging that day.

– If you had my fuckin' foot, yeh wouldn't think it such a laughing matter.

And, of course you couldn't talk to a priest like that and expect to get away with it. True enough, since the death of Cardinal Logue, they no longer had the power to put horns on you, but they could still make life difficult for dissident dale-dwellers, so Tom defected to the B'la Cliats. What's the point in being a countryman if you have no country?

So it was that Reivey decided to abandon the rustic state, and seek citizenship. On arrival in Dublin, he paid eight shillings and sixpence for *Dangers in Demography – The Cunning of The Bog Intellect*, by P. J. Jones. It became Reivey's bedside reading, and now, after much application, he felt he was beginning to get into the mind of the Dubliner:

– The Plain People of Ireland have been the victims of Myles na Gopaleen's invective for many years. It was he who proved that there was life after Joyce, and demanded as his reward the total and unquestioning allegiance of the PPI. Happily, Dublin has always been exempt from such intellectual bondage, and it is for that reason the countryside has been partly denuded of its indigenes. Peasants pour into the Metropolis hoping for a head transplant, an idioplasm transfusion, or, failing all that, an exchange of ideas.

And just as well, because there was no way that anybody would willingly exchange heads with Tom Reivey. The exterior was in such a dreadful state. And yet, once inside, the difference was amazing; it was the very seat of mind, thought, intellect and imagination. It didn't think like a country head; it was open to ideas. Oh, it must have been a dangerous thing to have been carrying about in the days of the bog when bachelors were gay and ploughboys merry.

Were his premises not contiguous to the river, it would not matter if Tom Reivey was blessed with the head of Adonis and the feet of David. Parable Jones' favourite innkeeper suffered from something that could have smelled death to a publican – osmidrosis. Despite the stink of the Liffey, it is said that, in this hostelry – so close to the Dublin vegetable markets – that farmers up from the country, and up to their elbows in cowshite, have been known to complain about the smell from Tom Reivey. 'By the grace of God and His Blessed Mother,' said the 'Pope' O'Reilly, 'it is the fine wide counter that separates Tom Reivey from his customers.'

With his back to the gantry and his arms folded, mine host was listening as Special Branch Detective, George Matthews, recalled the glorious days, when, as a bobby on the beat, he arrested Myles for drunkenness:

– He even wrote about it afterwards in the papers just to make fun of me. Said he was bailed for a quid.

– And was he? asked Tom.

– Yerra jazes, he was not! sure I couldn't get the bastard to court with all the influence he was able to exert. This writin' business runs deep in Dublin, you know. Indeed I remember three justices, two high court judges, and one State Prosecutor who wrote under their own names! Sure didn't the 'Hump' MacDonagh write poetry between sentences.

– 'Poetry between sentences'? said Reivey, now that really is something.

– And what excuse did they give for not charging the fucker? asked a Sligo man in potatoes.

– They told me that Myles na Gopaleen was not his proper name. And I brought them a copy of the *Irish Times*, and there it was as bold as brass and they said that I was a great eejit and did I not realise that this was his cinnamon.

A Galway-man in cattle said:

– Arrah, sure every gosson knows full well that 'Gopaleen' means 'the little horse'; you surely didn't really believe that any self-respecting priest christened any man that?

– And why not? Jesus Christ, man, sure was it not in the papers!

– But you don't believe all that you read in the papers?

– Not now, but I did then, because I wasn't long up, and, in my part of the country we always knew everybody whose name appeared in *The Bogside Broadside*, and there was no such things as cinnamons or anything like that in the country; it wouldn't be allowed.

Much to the annoyance of Det. Matthews, Tom Reivey read aloud Myles na Gopaleen's own account of the case:

– The justice said that the defendant could now leave the court without a stain on his character . . .

– But it's all lies, Tom. I tell you the case never got to court . . .

– It's all here in his book . . .

– I don't give a fuck if it's in the Bible . . .

– Maybe he appeared in his cinnamon and you didn't recognise him . . .

– Tis a terrible thing, Tom Reivey, that ever since you gave up your nationality you're forever making fun of your own.

People didn't get to the Bridge Bar by accident; only the committed ever find their way there. Few folk ever go to discuss business and the only work ever really talked about is the length and the price of a short time. Heavy crooks come to watch writers and artists at play. Actors come to bask or praise or damn in the wake of a curtain. In the early hours, burglars drop in to buy the addresses of worthwhile gaffs from the thirsty police.

The police didn't worry about the crooks and the relationship was a genuine vice versa, it was a question of you scratch my back and I'll watch yours – and mark your card.

One of the patrons that the police especially didn't worry about was Mr Mousey Duggan. He was a head banner-person; a pimp's shop steward. He struck the rate for the job and woe betide anybody who worked under it. He made no exceptions – except on the grounds of age or infirmity – thus Bridie MacMahon who had lost her legs while working in the back of a crashed black taxi came cheap, because the customer had to have her in the hanging position.

Mousey gave the police the odd tip and they in turn charged him less for protection. They had much in common – the entire Phoenix Park, to be precise. It was there in the Garda Siochana depot that policemen had been made for years and many a shekooney made many a woman in the same place – or many of the other sort depending on the sexual persuasion of the police, 'and were the shekooneys not the boys to do the persuading,' as Mousey has so often said. But no, the Garda were not afraid of Mr Mousey Duggan.

Det. George Matthews was not afraid of Parable Jones, and this he had told Tom Reivey in confidence. But they were hearing things about an anarchist named Charlie Belton:

– A big, awkward looking fucker who might be mistaken for a decent bogman, until he opens his jackeen mouth.

– And what on earth has he done, if it's not a secret?

– Tis hell-bent he is on destroying the reputation of our late President de Valera. But we Garda Siochana will ensure that the name of Eamon – or, as he was known to us, Ned of the Hill – will remain evergreen in the hearts of place-seekers for all time to come.

A man with a sore head in the corner of the pub told himself that he hoped this tall man in the blue trousers and bicycle clips was not about to sing. He need not have worried, Reivey had Matthews' emotions well in hand:

– And why would he want to sully Dev's reputation?

– What do you mean 'sully'?
– Tarnish: denigrate . . .
– He doesn't want to deni whatever you said his reputation, he wishes to destroy it, man!
– But for what reason?
– For money, what else?
– And who would want to pay for that?
– The English, the Ayatollie, Col. Quadaffi, or, and he lowered his voice to a confidential shout, the fucking Spaniards!
– The Spaniards? What axe would they have to grind?
– Well, yeh know how Dev is supposed to be one of them though he's the spitting image of his mother's brother?
– Jazes, yer right. His uncle Ned Coll could have been his father! They looked like twins . . . more so, I think, when Dev was born with the same old face, later Ned looked younger.
– There's a bit in this bucko's book where he says that Dev's mother was already pregnant when she met Juan Vivion – that was Dev's father on the Spanish side. And of course you know what that would mean?
– Aye, incest.
– It would mean that Dev's mother was a virgin! And God knows but you wouldn't get folk to believe in immaculate conception twice.
'Nor fucking once', thought Tom Reivey, but he said nothing, it was not a publican's job to upset his customers.
George Matthews is a proud if stupid man. He knows that there is far more in a police cadet's knapsack than an 'Evenin' All', and that the average guardian of the law can tell more than the time. On a clear night, in the old days, the voices of command could be heard from the training depot in the Park, teaching the rookies how to walk as if there wasn't a herd of prime beef in front of them. And then they closed down the depot. It was no longer in the 'Finn's Water' that the 'peat-feet' were introduced to footwear for the first time.
The Park was in the past. Close contact with urbanity had put the most valuable asset of the force at risk; stupidity was under threat and drastic steps had to be taken. Time was when a man giving evidence would ask for permission to refer to his notebook; then

there was a rash of rash Garda wishing 'to advert to memory'! Before long they would be wanting to think – and, indeed thinking did actually take place on one memorable occasion.

A chap called Sullivan, straight up from the Blaskets, was found to have concealed a mind under a welter of Irish. Outrage of outrages! He had not alone read a book he had bloody well written one! Worse than that, *Twenty Years A-Growing* was regarded by the English as a modern Irish classic.

Well, Matthews needn't tell you, Sullivan wasn't going to get away with that sort of thing. The Commissioner told somebody who could communicate with the writer, to order him back to the bog. No sooner there than he's sent to intimidate some Galway strikers; and, God help us, if the blaggard doesn't join the picket line!

In Sullivan's wake there was a spate of pen-pols, and, after much research, it was clear that the Phoenix Park was contaminated; the 'Waters of Finn' were corrupting the innocent shekooneys.

Recruits are now trained in the arsehole of Ireland. There they are kept until each mind is as petrified as a sod of peat and there is no danger of extraneous thought filtering through. There will be no more Maurice O'Sullivans if Templemore Police Training College can guard the Garda against them.

Situated on the main Dublin road between Ballybrophy and Thurles, Templemore is justice rewarded – neither the Dublin Jackeens nor the Cork drisheens would ever lay their filthy minds on the new thick blue line.

Following closely in the wake of their English counterparts, the Garda shekooney saw the terrible damage that could be done by words. Each man was shown a picture of a book, and taught how to recognise the folk who make them. In Templemore the collective noun for a gang of literati is 'a suspicion of writers'. They were to be watched closely for they are 'clever-clever fuckers' to whom nothing is sacred; who treat the most reverenced institutions with derision.

The true shekooney learns to hold the penmen up to ridicule; to scoff at their clothes and their effeminate ways: they should mock those who would use one 'jawbreaker' where ten little words would suffice. Most important of all, there were laws against scribes dating back to the Statutes of Kilkenny which had been left on the republican statute book in case the Censorship of Publications Board should prove to be ineffective.

The best writers constituted no real threat to the ignorance of the masses because they were not very widely read, but it was as well to know who they were, in case, through British television, like Durex, they became fashionable. In that eventuality there were ways of dealing with the Shaws, Synges and O'Caseys – who were Protestant bastards anyway. Yeats was an old sod who believed in ghosts, and Wilde was a fucking queer. Joyce and Myles were not to be feared because their work was inexplicable and if any Garda knew the meaning of that word he was to be sent back to the bog for de-thought immediately – de time, de place and de opportunity.

Ah yes, the new training depot at Templemore was to be the cornerstone of the State. The modern shekooney would extirpate intelligence wherever it showed its jeering face. Stomp on the wordsmith was the thing. Have a 'kick the writer' week fifty-two times a year. Scribes are dangerous bastards because people remembered them. Very few policemen are quoted in school so very few policemen are remembered – apart from the fictional ones who are the creations of communists like Simenon and Dashiell Hammett. And Hammett was a case in point; a truly bad lot; a policeman gone good.

– What was that? asked Tom.

– What was 'what'? asked Matthews.

– I don't know; it was you who said it.

– Said what?

– Ah, forget it.

– I said nothin', Tom. I'm one of the closest mouthed men in the force. I took a course in learning how to say nothing.

– It's of no importance. Don't worry about it.

– Don't worry about what, Tom? What's of no importance?

'This guy is an obessional fucking nut', Tom told himself, and decided to change the subject:

– I was just thinking about that fellow Belton you were talking about . . . he doesn't come in here, does he?

– No, you're clean – so far.

– What the fuck d'ye mean 'I'm clean – so far'?

– Well, we've nothing on you; oh, I suppose you could be done for serving after hours, keeping a disorderly house. We could do you for anything, really, but you don't encourage anti-state or anti-religious activities.

– Anti-state? Anti-religious? You're not serious?

– You really are a big baby when it comes to worldly things, Tom. Lord God, man, for years now the British secret service and the American CIA have been warning us about the international plot to promote awareness.

– Is that not good; to make people aware, I mean?

– But, aware of what, Tom, that is the question. We have psychologists in Templemore and they insist that the best thing for the world is to let sleeping dogs lie.

– There's some deep thinking behind that.

– You'd better believe it, Tom. A chap, got sixteen years for making people aware of Israel's nuclear armament potential. And, ever since the ordinary American started to demand freedom of information nearly every state secret is public knowledge.

– Is that bad?

– It means that there can be a fault in the government that might never be put right because you see many a man has an . . .

– Achilles heel?

– What made you say that, Mr Reivey?

– Why did you call me 'Mr Reivey' all of a sudden?

– Why did you start jeering my countrymen's feet?

– I never mentioned your fucking countrymen!

– You did, you spoke about our heels. I'm an Achill man myself and our feet are as good as anybody else's. True enough there are them that say our boots are worn on one side but that's because most of our bogs are on the side of a hill and we have to walk like that.

– My dear man, you have me all wrong! Achilles was a man who suffered from a bad heel ever since childhood when his mother dipped him in the river Styx.

– And the river was polluted and gave him a bad foot? The stupid cow!

– No, no, the heel was the only part of him that didn't get wet and so it remained weak.

– It was holy water, like Lourdes?

– More or less, but quite mythological. Achilles was a Greek.

– Is that so? Oh well, fuck them ignorant foreign bastards.

Two ladies, inebriated and discussing protocol, stood and fought handbag to handbag, over the Galwayman who was singing a radio commercial jingle:

Remember the damage that mastitis can do to your cattle.

Detective George Matthews fled to the lavatory because he didn't want either his cover or his nose broken, and, as Parable Jones entered with Sally-Anne draped around his neck, Tom Reivey stood, his arms folded, in front of the gantry, laughing to himself that there was never a policeman about when one was wanted.

CHAPTER TWELVE

Wholly Holy Father

The evening Angelus had barely finished ringing, confessions had just started, when a pair of pious Glaswegians whispered their first '*Ave*' at the first station of the Way of the Cross in the Church of the Unprofessed Monks, Inchicore. The Albans who, in Scotland, take their religion personally, consider that the oblation of southern Irish Catholics leaves much to be desired. The first North-British penitent threw himself prostrate in front of the Christian-looking Jesus who is – according to the title:

Condemned to Death

> *Consider how the Lord Jesus, having been scourged and crowned with thorns, was unjustly condemned by Pontius Pilate to crucifixion . . .*

The Scotch piety being disturbed, the couple found difficulty in concentrating their sorrow for the tribulations of Jesus, because there was an unholy row coming from the confession box of the deaf Father Lazarian, who was saying, rather loudly, to somebody unseen, and as yet unheard:

– The clergy reserves the right to refuse absolution to any man, woman or child, as the case may be, and, I tell you, Mr MacWilliams, there is no penance suited to your sin of commission. Recant, you wicked man, or live in sin!

– I will not recant. You are duty bound to absolve me; you cannot say to what I must confess.

– Don't you tell me who I can or cannot forgive! Until you

undertake a proper act of mortification, I will not acquit you of your guilt.

– You have no right to define sin!

Jesus Receives the Cross

Consider how Jesus, while making the journey with the cross on His shoulders, did forsake all thought of Himself, and offered for our redemption, to His own Father, His own mortal life . . .

– I cannae hear masel pray, Isobel.

– Dae the best ye can, Andrew, dae the best ye can.

Bryden MacWilliams said that what he wrote in an English newspaper should not be held against him in an Irish confession box:

– You said that Pope John Paul I was murdered by the Vatican Council, and that his present Holiness, Pope John Paul II, was involved in the crime!

– I said no such thing! I merely quoted what was said by the paper *Corriere della Sera* which demanded that an autopsy be carried out on the dead Pope.

– A communist newspaper ready to do the bidding of the anti-Christs!

– It's a conservative bloody newspaper!

– Don't you swear in my confession box and don't you dare contradict your pastor. The Vatican made it clear that there was no need for a post mortem. And that should have been that . . .

Jesus Falls the First Time

Consider the first fall of Jesus under His Cross. His flesh scourged, His head crowned with thorns . . .

– It's nae use, Isobel, I cannae concentrate.

– I never heard the likes . . . look at all the folk earwiggin' a ben the box, Andrew.

Two pews of penitents were listening to the argument between Father Lazarian and Bryden MacWilliams, and neither Father Alphonso nor Father Bonaventure had any customers; instead, each in his respective dark was straining to miss none of the disagreeable shriving-time of the loud priest who retreated into dogma, and the shrill penitent who demanded to be heard:

– Pray now to God for the forgiveness of your sins . . .

– Nowhere have I transgressed against the commandments.

– and that He may grant you the grace of a true change of heart . . .

– God Himself knows that there is no sin in defending the sanctity of the office of Christ's Vicar on earth.

– and of a genuine determination to live your life according to our Lord's word . . .

– The question raised was, 'If Pope John Paul I was perfectly healthy one day, how come he's dead the next?'

– But he wasn't healthy . . . he was dying.

– Who said so?

– He died, didn't he?

– Jesuit!

Jesus is Met by His Blessed Mother

Consider this meeting of the Son and the Mother, the soldiers strike Jesus and He falls several times . . .

– Isobel, I'm in nae fit state fer the Stations o' the Cross, I'm a nervous wreck, so I am, and it's no way tae contemplate oor Lord . . . I think a wee pint is ca'd fer . . .

– We've cam a' this way tae Holy Ireland to dae the Stations we oor very ain an' dae the stations we wull, Andrew.

– Och, mebbe so, Isobel, mebbe so, but the queues are growin' longer and longer roon yon confession box.

Four pews were now filled with sinners wanting to confess their sins to Father Lazarian, and neither Fathers Alphonso or Bonaventure had any takers as yet:

– And why, man, would anybody want to do away with Pope John Paul I, if your crazy allegations were ever to be taken seriously?

– Because he spoke easily of God and threw away the ostentatious trappings of the papacy. He rejected the crown and the throne . . . and wanted us all to be the same . . .

– And you think that Catholics kill each other because of that? Such is the way of Christ, or don't you know anything at all?

– Dissent is no sin.

– Now, be reasonable, Bryden, my son, I know how dedicated you are, but, you must see the Church's side in all matters relevant and pertaining religiously to a pastor's flock . . .

– I will not be guilty of the sin of commission by committing the sin of omission.

– My child . . . no, my friend . . . you know the rules. The formula is simple enough: confess and then I can absolve you, with the words, 'The Lord has freed you from your sins, go in peace.'

– Say it, then.

– I cannot until you recognise the enormity of your transgression! Don't you bloody fanatics know anything!

The Cross is Laid upon Simon of Cyrene

> *Consider how His cruel tormentors, wanting to prolong His agony, constrained Simon of Cyrene to carry the Cross behind Our Lord . . .*

A multitude was congregating in the chapel, and few folk could remember so many of the faithful gathered in prayer on a weekday evening except, maybe, for benediction:

– Will ye look at the crowd, Isobel.

– It's nane o' yer business, Andrew, carry on wi' yer prayers.

– That's easier said, Isobel, but yeh could nearly sell tickets fer whit's goin' on ower 'ere.

Seven pews were now filled round Father Lazarian's confessional, and still the faithful were gathering:

– The Will of God is not to be questioned, nor is the word of the

Holy Father on Doctrine. It was the Will of God to take a good man after the shortest papacy in history.

– It wasn't the shortest, Pope Urban VII ruled for only twelve days, Pope John Paul I was Pontiff for thirty-three . . .

– I don't care if he lasted for six months, you are still not getting absolution from me!

Veronica Wipes the Face of Jesus

> *Consider how Veronica, the holy woman, seeing Jesus so ill-used, wiped His face with a towel, on which was left the impression of His holy countenance . . .*

– Aw, c'mon, Andrew, an' we'll try an' find a quiet pub, there must surely be some place wi' mair solitude than this ravin' nut-hoose.

– But I've finished oney hauf o' the stations, Isobel.

– Ye can dae the rest when we're daein' the seven chapels. If we stay oney longer, Andrew, I'd be afeart o' losin' ma faith.

As Andrew and Isobel left to find consolation in some quiet hostelry they heard Bryden MacWilliams declare in a strident voice:

– Pope John Paul I wasn't acceptable to the right-wing Curia because he spoke about the maternal love of God . . .

– And why should that worry anybody?

– Because he shook the Establishment to the core by declaring that God was not necessarily a man!

– And you think that his Holiness was killed for that?

– I think we are entitled to answers! Do you know that there are those who say that the Vatican newspaper *L'Osservatore Romano* was on the streets of Rome with a big black band around it almost at the same time that he died?

– And, what is that supposed to signify?

– That somebody was expecting him to die.

– Don't you know that Catholics are always ready for everlasting life? It is obligatory to be prepared for death.

– And are they also to be prepared for murder?

– How dare you! Get out of my confession box, and, take it from me, hell will freeze over before you ever get absolution.

– I'll get it elsewhere, then.

– Not while I'm conscious! I'll have you blacked in every chapel in Ireland.

– Then I'll have it done in England.

– Aye, I have not the slightest doubt that that is what you and your likes have in mind; but, while you're there, remember what happened to Roberto Calvi.

Isobel and Andrew paused just long enough to see the strained back of Bryden MacWilliams stooping hurriedly from the chapel, with Father Lazarian screaming in his wake:

– *With anti-Christs like you, who needs Protestants?*

Andrew shook his head in disbelief and asked Isobel:

– Did ye hear how the big man was talkin' aboot the Holy Father?

– Aye, an' this is the Catholic end o' Ireland.

– It's easier being a Catholic back hame, Isobel, there's nane o' these deep theosophical discussions tae take yer mind frae God.

CHAPTER THIRTEEN

Where No Man Has Gone

TV in pubs. Dreadful invasion of man's public privacy. To boldly go where no man, woman, child, or animal has gone before. 'To boldly go . . .' Charlie Belton repeated the phrase, over and over, and then reminded himself that he was behaving like Parable's medium again:

– I really must watch that. Be myself. Mary says I do be acting the goat . . . maybe she's right . . . Jesus! The sudden silence in this place is deafening. Have I been talking to myself again.

But the noise had subsided because of a shared anxiety as to whether Captain Kirk would materialise now that the transporter room had been all but demolished by earth's enemies in space, the Klingons.

When Kirk was himself again a man in a donkey jacket and with honest ingrained dirt, said, apropos of nothing but nearness:

– Ballyfermot.

– What about it?

– The housin' scheme, I mean.

– Yes, I know what Ballyfermot is.

– Don't yeh think it would be the ideal setting for their outer space locations? Though, on the other hand it might be too bare – Ballyfermot, I mean.

They do that in Dublin; out of the blue they address you like long lost friends. And, not just in the pubs: anywhere, on a bus or a train . . . in the middle of the street. Friendly, some folk think, but Parable believes that it's an infringement of a man's civil liberties; thinks everybody should tell cheerful strangers to 'fuck off'. I don't know that I'd like to do that, and especially with all the headcases on drugs and all:

– There yeh are, mac.

– Fuck off!

No, Charlie thought that politeness was still the better part of etiquette; especially when dealing with hard men.

The man in the donkey jacket said again:

– D'ye know, there are people in Ballyfermot, mister, who would have died years ago, had their relations been able to afford to bury them . . .

Belton knew that he was thinking about the new death benefits payable by the State:

– Thirty-four pounds! Sure what person could afford to die on that? And they talk about the cost of livin' . . .

Radio and television! Christ, everybody is suddenly a pundit. God be with the days when folk were innocently illiterate and kept their ignorance to themselves. Charlie contributed:

– There's not a lot we can do about it, one way or the other. We're all dyin' since the day we were born. It's quite natural . . .

– More natural, mister, for some than others; yeh don't see the rich leapin' to get into the great hereafter . . .

– But even they have to go, eventually.

– Yeah, but they take their time about it, don't they?

– Yeh could be right.

– There's Reagan now, all faith and father-in-heaven, but he'd dearly love to postpone the inevitable. They all would. I mean few people could have been on better terms with God than Pius XII, but even he hung on – d'ye know he had a dozen physicians round him at the knockin's? Didn't want to go where no man had come back from ever before.

The man in the donkey jacket was called back to the bar by a friend who had ordered another drink now that the starship *Enterprise* was safe on earth, and a bit more excitement was generated when a man straight off the Inchicore bus told the company how a lunatic had attacked old deaf Father Lazarian in a confession box:

– An argument about Pope John Paul I. This religious nut said that the Holy Father had been poisoned by the Polish Catholics in the Vatican.

– Go way!
– And that everybody was in on it.
– Go way!
– Then Father Lazarian said that if this freak really believed what he was saying then he should remember what happened to Roberto Calvi.
– Who's he when he's at home?
– He was one of the Pope's bankers and he ran off to London, forgetting to unpack about forty million quid that he had taken with him from the Banco Ambrosiano for safe-keeping.
– A tidy sum.
– They found him hanging under Blackfriars Bridge in London.
– And did Father Lazarian threaten this geezer that the same might happen to him?
– Well, not in so many words.
– And what did yer man say?
– He turned at the door of the chapel and told Father Lazarian, 'In time to come, you lot will realise that Blackfriars was a bridge too far'.
– Jazes, yeh'd never know what was goin' on, would yeh? Still, as long as the Pope is not mixed up in it.

Charlie was nicely nourished and he had Mary's money safely stowed. In all the pubs he had visited today he had found a bit for the book:

– That tale from the big Mayo man, Matthews, about Dev being the son of his mother's brother was worth the day in itself. No wonder his uncle Ned Coll had felt such responsibility for the boy. Spanish, indeed! As 'Spanish' as the name 'Valencia' in county Kerry. All those crazy people telling the tourists that it derived from the 'Spanish Kingdom of Valencia; third largest city in Spain'! Spain, how are yeh! That English scholar put them all to shame when he told them that it was just the Kerryman's way of saying, 'Beal-na-h-inse' – the mouth to the islands.

Belton was down here on Wellington Quay, not because he was slumming: he didn't feel at ease in the middle-class pubs frequented by broadcasters who talked about other peoples' books over what was still euphemistically called 'the wireless'.

Parable said that they were a strange band of folk, these denizens of Montrose. Every Sunday morning, while most rational people were in avoiding Jesus, this crowd of citizens spoke from the radio – mostly about what they had read. They formed a sort of animated Readers' Digest.

Parable couldn't understand why Cronin and Kiely and Durkin wasted good writing time on it:

– Yeh know, Parable had said to him, a chap could be strolling innocently abroad, when out of some reckless house or handbag, would issue forth the strains of *Miscellany*, and, if you weren't fleet of foot, you could find yourself the victim of the most awful mixture of pining, opining, and opinionated shit.

'Ah fuck Parable Jones,' thought Charlie Belton and ordered himself another drink.

In the working-class drinking-houses the poor felt happy that the bar staff talked to them as equals. There was in general a paucity of preference. Belton felt more at home here because he hadn't read the same books that the broadcasters hadn't read. In the 'floating ballrooms' of this town Charlie Belton could be a big fish, and the customers went out of their way to defer to a man, who despite the fact that he had obviously never been in a betting shop in his life, carried a fountain pen in his breast pocket. They'd walk up to him with a silly grin and a knowing look:

– Are you not usually with that nutcase, Parable Jones?

Every snug had its own memories of Parable; mostly apocryphal and none the more extraordinary because of that. They thought they had seen P. J.'s uncle walking round Dublin with a nodding head – the result, it was said, of a Protestant bullet received in the 1965 defence of the Catholic Bogside. Jesus, the things people say. That ould uncle's whole body nodded – DT's!

And when it came to Parable himself, it was clear to everyone that he had worked at everything with everybody from John-Joe in McAlpine's, to Dylan Thomas at the BBC. All lies of course, or were they? Nobody knew everything about the picaroon Parable. And all the books? Where the hell did he ever find time to read them? In the nick, was it? Prison librarian for years? Read them he did because

Mary said that even her professors spoke in awe of Parable Jones' reading. They were still, in cloisters, talking of his put-down of Jordan Hutch in Doheny and Nisbetts:

– From Schiller and Goethe, my dear Jordan, came Buck Milligan's inclination to Hellenise Dublin. But, provincial poets like yourself will understand the same expression that was embodied in *Hermann and Dorothea*. Schiller called it 'Goethe's attempt to produce Greece from within'. Did you know that, Jordan?

The insistent use of Hutch's first name must have sounded like the tolling of John Donne's diminishing bell:

– And, when I came in here tonight sober and unable to contemplate your ignorance, Jordan, I heard you and your friends agree that it was Schiller who said 'There is no beautiful rose without thorns'. Maybe John-Joe Schiller from Ballydehob said that, but certainly the poet Friedrich didn't. That is the remark of an old German peasant filled with piss and platitudes. Oh, no, Jordan, bog ignorance is not the exclusive preserve of the bog Irish.

The victims always flushed with anger beneath their tight knuckles white, but they wouldn't take Parable on – nobody in his right mind would:

– What Schiller did say, regarding people like yourself, Jordan, you would do well to remember each time you refused to libate your betters, 'A blessing on those who honour their forebears and a curse upon those who don't'.

It was an old trick of Parable's: call a chap by his first name and you could be as abusive as you liked. Myles had used it because his speech was never up to his writing; the 'Ginger Man' did so because it was American. Parable called a man by his christian name to get under his skin:

– By accident, Jordan, sheer accident, did the so-called Dublin literati hit on the key to Joyce. Not the Greeks, Jordan, but the German poets' teaching of the Greeks. D'ye not believe me, Jordan? No? Then what about Joyce's recourse to Heine? Was it not from him that Joyce and Gogarty learned how not to trust anybody with an axe for grinding in the patriot game? Even Nietzsche accepted that there was nothing after the Greeks – the German Greeks. But then,

Jordan, you will surely answer that since Freddie believed there would be nothing after him, maybe Nietzsche shouldn't be taken too seriously?

Parable Jones was a payer of bad debts. The crowd in Doheny and Nisbetts had tried to belittle the poetry of his friend MacNeice and P. J. spent a life-time making them regret their impertinence. And, if he was vindictive enough while talking generally about writers, it was when he turned on them their own personalities that Parable Jones was at his most vicious: he never let a man get away from himself:

– You were all so much better than Kavanagh or MacNeice. Post-mortem bastards every one of you! But you've all tried to steal a bit of Kavanagh's or Louis' minds sinced they ceased to think. That was why Louis warned us that, 'Goethe captured the Greek spirit so successfully that if translated into Attic Greek it might well pass for a lost fragment of the Athenian stage'. The little college boys who felt so superior to Kavanagh because he wiped his arse with a cabbage leaf. Pity for you, Jordan, that he didn't take time off to wipe your mind with a fucking book!

As Charlie Belton left the pub and walked by Adam and Eve's on the south side of the Liffey, he knew that, think as he might, real thought was in another dimension altogether. He and anybody who had ever longed to put one word after another would have to contend always with that spectre that haunted Dublin. No, Parable Jones was not going to go away anytime somebody waved a crucifix or invoked the name of their lord: this omnipotent bastard had been there before anybody and would surely be there when everybody else was waiting for the last tram to the last pub on the last evening.

At Winetavern Street Bridge, Charlie crossed to Inns Quay and made his way by Arran Quay, Ellis Quay, and Wolfe Tone Quay, to the Bridge Bar, outside of which, a gang of school-kids were hustling a few shillings:

– Want to have one of us for a quid, or two for one-fifty? Ah, g'wan, mister, wanta fuck about for fifty pence?

And, when Charlie ignored their offers, they shouted after him:

– Yeh stupid ould fucker! If yeh talk to yerself yeh probably play with yerself as well.

Charlie knew that paedophiles would have some argument to excuse such infant prostitution, but he could only think that there must be something wrong in a world where childhood was in danger from old age and AIDS. He put the problem to the back of his mind and entered, for the first time, Tom Reivey's gluepot. To boldly go where nobody gave a fuck who split the first infinitive.

CHAPTER FOURTEEN

At Swim, Two Drunks

– I'll leave Sally-Anne here in the window seat, if you don't mind, Tom, said Parable Jones.

– If yeh must, I suppose yeh must; though, to be quite honest, Parable, I'm not short of drunks – am I, Mousey?

– Yeh must have the best collection in town, my friend.

Parable told Mousey that he wasn't easily amused tonight:

– I'm at the end of me bloody tether, so I am. Yeh know, Tom, there's very few things worse in this life than a drunken woman.

– Yer talkin' to the converted, mate.

– I've come all the way from the Green and the drink running from her like shit through a goose or the Tans through Kerry.

Mousey was feeling charitable:

– Give the decent man a drink . . . try a ball of malt, Parable?

– I'd kill for a large ball of malt, Mousey.

– Who the fuck said anything about size? Give him a small whiskey in a large glass, Tom, and let him use that great imagination of his.

The publican served a third of a gill anyway, and remarked:

– Have that one on the house.

– You should rename this health clinic Lourdes, Mr Landlord. Well, here's the first today.

– And God knows yeh need it.

– Never a truer word was ever said in jest, Mousey. D'ye know, one minit more in that cab and I would have been up for wife beating.

– But, you're not married to her, Parable . . .

– Does it matter whose wife a chap beats up? We may not be churched, ould son, but, well, the poor girl is somebody's wife.

– I'd hardly call Jack Millington 'somebody', P. J.

Reivey said:

– Have I met the man?

– Yeh must have . . . tall, good-looking in a pretty sort of way . . .

– I don't think I've had the pleasure.

– If you haven't then yeh'll be one of the few . . . he's one of them, isn't he, Parable?

– There are those, Mousey, who swear he's one of the other. But he's not the worst; at least Sally-Anne can boast that she's one of the only women in Dublin who understands her husband, and that must be something.

– Is he odd, then, P. J?

– Odd? The poor cunt is queer enough, Tom, without expecting him to be odd as well. Put up another drink will you?

– How did Sally-Anne discover what sex he was, Parable?

– Jazes, Mousey! She'd need to be blind! He's more hair than Martin Walton.

– Don't be sarcastic, Parable, yeh know what I mean: how did she find out that he was a bum boy?

– I imagine she didn't know which way to turn on the first night.

Tom confessed:

– I don't know, all the same, P. J., did you never try the tradesman's entrance? My Fidelma, for example, used to tell me about the things her first husband got up to . . .

– Ah, but Jazes, Tom, the poor man could have been forgiven for that, sure your Fidelma has one o'clock shadow even after a good shave.

– Well, aren't they choice things to be saying about the woman a man loves.

– You love Fidelma, Tom?

– Don't be disgusting, Parable, but her father did – indeed he got eighteen months for it. Of course she was young then.

– Ah, sure, we have to be saying something, Tom, and that's the truth. By the way, you might ring that drunk-driving taxi of yours later.

– Why didn't you arrange for the one that brought you to come back?

– Come back, Mousey? For me? For her? He didn't want to drive us in the first place. 'Parable', he says to me, 'I have a dog, and if it smelled as evil as her, I'd have the fucker shot.'

– My first missus used to fart like a man, and that's what turned me to drink. I couldn't believe that this angelic-looking girl could behave like a docker on pints and peas.

– I didn't know you were married before, Tom.

– Aye, Miss Ballybunion 195 . . . oh, I don't even remember the year now. Left me because I was impotent with the gargle, and it was the mercy of God that the Church, minding the nation's morals, refused to allow divorce.

– You still hoped for a reconciliation?

– Me arse! I was hoping for her insurance. She had no sooner left the marital home to say a prayer to Our Lady of Knock, when, through the intervention of God, she was knocked down by Father Horan's collecting van, and it just blessed minutes before.

Tom looked all round the walls of the Bridge Bar before telling them:

– It's as if she's in every brick of this boozer. Thirty grand I had the good lady backed for, God bless her.

– I never knew a woman to leave a man because he was impudent, Tom.

Parable laughed and said:

– He didn't say 'impudent', Mousey.

– No?

– The word is 'impotent', he means he can't come with a drink taken.

– He wouldn't be the only one like that, ould son. Some of my girls tell me that quite a few of the blokes suffer in the same way, and it also makes them as impudent as fuck. One fella I had to take a hammer to because he slapped one of the staff across the face.

Parable looked across at the sleeping Sally-Anne and declared:

– I wouldn't fancy slapping her across the face. She's one of the O'Reillys, and a tough lot they are.

Tom put P. J.'s fiver into the till, took out the change and placed it on the counter in front of Parable:

– She's the 'Pope's' daughter, I believe?
– Yeh believe the truth.
– He's one rum fucker.
– Is that the 'Pope' O'Reilly you're talkin' about?
– For Christ's sake, Mousey, how many Popes are there – outside the Vatican?
– Well, Tom, I know of at least one other. What about the fella on Radio Eireann who used to tell people where they came from?
– The 'Pope' O'Mahoney, yeh mean?
– The very one.

Tom said:
– Used to be a solicitor?
– And what a mouthpiece he was; yeh'd stand a better chance of gettin' off with somebody out of the Deaf and Dumb Institute defendin' yeh.
– He was that bad, was he?
– He was worse than bad . . . he got poor ould Bobo down there a stretch for somethin' he didn't do – am I right, Bobo?
– Yer right, me lovely son. It was during the emergency when the IRA was all the go and I was up before the 'Hump' MacDonagh for a bit of thievin'. Jasez didn't the 'Pope' get me mixed up with another fella who was political . . .

Mousey getting all caught up in the anticipated humour of what Bobo was about to reveal kept up a constant stream of like interpolations:
– Jazes! Wait'll yis hear this; it'll fuckin' kill yis! Go on, Bobo, and I'm sorry for interruptin' yer discourse.
– So the 'Pope' turns to the 'Hump' and says, 'my client, your honour, following in the glorious tradition of Pearse and Connolly refuses to recognise the right of this court to do England's foul bidding . . .'
– Go on, Bobo, tell them what yeh thought about Pearse and Connolly.
– Well, at the time, I thought that the 'Pope' was talkin' about the Pearses and Connollys from Sean MacDermott Street who were always doin' time for the heavy stuff, and I kept pullin' the 'Pope's'

jacket and sayin' 'but I'm not like them, I'm only nicked for a bit of thievin'.'

– And what happened, Bobo?

This entire conversation is carried on from one end of the bar to the other and to the great interest of most of the other customers:

– The 'Pope' totally ignored me and went on about Irish judges doing England's dirty work and the way the 'Hump' was lookin' down at me I just knew he was raging that he didn't have a black cap. I kept saying to myself, if he doesn't stop that carry on, the 'Hump' is goin' to burst a fuckin' blood vessel.

– And did he stop? asked Parable:

– Did he fuck! The 'Hump' nearly screams at him, 'Is your client refusing to recognise this court of law?' 'He is,' said the 'Pope'. 'I'm not,' said I . . .

– And what happened? asked Mousey:

– Well, you know the law, Mousey; in the courts wigs only speak to wigs, nobody listens to poor fuckin' me.

– But surely you could have spoken up?

– The last guy to speak up before the 'Hump' MacDonagh got six months for contempt, Parable.

– And, what was the outcome? asked Tom Reivey.

– I was sent before the military tribunal and the 'Hanger' Joyce sent me to the Curragh for the remainder of the war. Oh aye, keep away from the 'Pope' O'Mahoney if yer into a bit of honest thievin'.

– He's dead, Bobo, gone to that Circuit Court up in the sky.

– Best place for him too, and not before his time . . .

When the laughing stopped, Parable sent a pint down to Bobo and Tom Reivey resumed his discourse on the 'Pope' O'Reilly:

– Yeh know he made a memorial for my first wife's grave, Parable?

– Not a prick, for God's sake?

– A prick? Why should he want my wife to be remembered by a prick?

– Oh, don't let it interrupt yeh, Tom, it's too involved and not important.

– No, it was a marble praying stool with a prayer on the cross-bar of a crucifix and he had chiseled a message, 'Sacred Heart of Jesus, with all *thy* faults I still love thee.' It was so beautifully done that I didn't have the heart to tell him that he had put thy instead of my.

– And you think he made a mistake?

– Oh aye, he admitted as much to the sister when she pointed it out to him; said it was a throw-back to the time he was a Muslim . . .

– A Muslim? Him? The 'Pope' O'Reilly?

– Said that according to his faith, only Allah was perfect.

– Well, the cunning old celt, that fucker would get out of hell.

– Muslims? Is that what the Ayatollah's crowd are?

– More or less.

– And they wear those baggy pants that the missus calls shite-catchers?

– Some of them do I guess, said Parable:

– Jasez, the wife flipped over them.

– How so? asked Parable.

– We went to see this picture at the Mayro called *The Thief of Baghdad* and she does her nut over this bald-headed guy who was takin' the lead.

– Yul Brynner, was it?

– Oh, I don't know, Tom, but, anyway, when we got home and I was ridin' away into the sunset, the quare wan asks me to have me head shaved . . .

– You're kiddin'.

– Straight up, Parable; but she had her arse, and I told her so, 'Darlin',' says I, 'yeh have yer bleedin' arse'!

Tom ran his right hand over his head from brow to crown:

– I often think that hair is over-rated.

– And so you should, Tom, since all you can do with your head is polish it; but for those of us who still have a thatch, hair is very important.

– Well, now, Mousey, don't be so smug. I saw the two days, if yeh want to know. In fact I saw the three days – if you count the red toupee I used to wear . . .

– A jig, Tom, an Irish jig? I can't see yeh in one . . .

– A hair-piece, Parable . . . though, I suppose, since I didn't even have the conventional frieze, it was properly called a wig.

– And why d'ye not wear it now?

– Oh, Mousey, they're more bother than they're worth. I was with this bird one night and she had a terrier; the wig was stuck down with stuff that the salesman said would keep it on in a hurricane . . .

– Anybody could claim that – sure when did we ever have a hurricane in Ireland?

– Will yeh stop interruptin' the sceal, Mousey.

– Well there was me and this wan gettin' into it on the sofa . . . we were comin' into the last furlong and about to enter the straight when this fuckin' terrier dives at me head, grabs the rug, and makes off through the french windows and into the garden – hold on till I get this man a drink . . . what'll it be, sir?

The deranger ordered two pints of stout, Tom pulled them while impatient Mousey muttered 'for fuck sake!' Tom scraped the heads, finished the pints under the drop, charged the man, put the money in the till, gave the man his change, and returned without further prevarication to the story:

– The dog is shakin' me Barnet fair like he'd shake a rat and I run out after him in me bare arse, and there I am in nothin' only me shirt in the middle of the day in the middle of the garden, and this wan starin' at me in astonishment and laughin' her tits off, 'Jazes, Tom, I can't help it, did yeh realise that yeh've got more hair on yer arse?' With all her laughin', poor ould Fagin slipped back into his shell while the fuckin' dog is back layin' the wig at me feet and waggin' its tail for me to throw it so as he can fetch it.

– God help yeh, Tom, but that sorta thing shouldn't happen to a dog.

– And that was the end of you and the bird was it?

– Yerra, God help yer sense, Mousey, to think that grass ever grew on a busy street. I jumped back into the saddle and rode a beautiful finish, with her screamin' 'you lovely randy, baldy, sexy ould bastard'!

– And more power to your stamina, Tom.

– Just remembered what me father said when I fell off me first bike, 'Get back into that saddle, son, or yeh'll never ride again.'

– It's the very same with swimmin', Mr Reivey.

– What's that, Bobo?

Parable told him to come down to their end of the bar:

– If yeh stay up there, we'll need a bloody loud hailer to keep in touch.

Bobo joined Tom and Mousey and Parable and said:

– I was just saying that getting back on a bike is the same as goin' back into the water when yeh've nearly drownded.

– I wouldn't have taken you for a swimmer, Bobo.

– And yeh'd be right, Parable, but the day we were released from the Curragh we got drunk at the thirteenth lock and I fell into the canal and one of the fellas was telling me that that was how Johnny Weismuller became a great swimmer . . .

– The Tarzan fella? He didn't swim in the thirteenth lock, did he?

– Use yer fuckin' head, Mousey, but he had to get back into the water after nearly drownin' as a kid.

– If yeh don't mind me asking, Bobo, what changes did internment make to your life?

– Ruined me whole career. Gave me principles. Sure after doin' five years for Ireland I could hardly go out and do six months for meself, could I?

– God help yeh, Bobo.

– And amen to that, Parable. The day was when it took me all me time to free meself, now I must stick me neck out to liberate a shower of fuckers most of whom I don't even know nor like.

– Maybe yer at the wrong end of politics, Bobo. Maybe yeh should be like the ones that are liberating Guinness from the landed gentry, and the nationalised industries from the people. Maybe yeh should be patriotic like Dev and Mrs Thatcher.

– I've looked at it that way, too, Parable, but, yeh see, the two of them had countries to sell while all poor fuckers like me have are principles, and politics is always a buyer's market.

– Yeh've it all worked out, Bobo.

– Well, I had all of five years to do it, Mousey. Now I can't get over the fact that I must live by my ideals. That humpy-backed fucker turned me into a patriot.

– And what do your old friends think of that?

– They think I'm bleedin' mad, Parable. When I said I wasn't into petty thievin' any more, they asked what the fuck I was lookin' for. I said I wanted nothin' less than the whole country, and they told me, 'Yeh don't want fuckin' much, do yeh?'

CHAPTER FIFTEEN

The Man Who Broke the Bank

Sean Daly was on his way to his bank when he met Sean MacBride emerging from a solicitor's office in the same building to wave a rolled umbrella at hired taxis. MacBride was one of those decent men who had always given his services free to serve some vague humanity. True enough his ego had deranged many a cause, and his politics had more in common with Kafka than Marx; but, he had always meant well, and Daly supposed that was something. His expensive French finishing school lisp could barely cope with his felicity on seeing the big poet:

– Daly, my dear man, what brings you to this neck of the woods – and, in a collar and tie? Not going to see Con, I trust?

Con was the universal solicitor and anybody seen even pausing in Ormond Quay was thought of as 'being in trouble':

– My bank is here in the same block.

'My bank! Jesus, the language of effete businessmen. My bank! nothing could be farther from the truth':

– Ah, banks, Mr Daly, the source of hunger's woe.

– I only use them in an emergency.

– Indeed, Mr Daly, if only we could keep our money elsewhere . . .

'Keep his money elsewhere! Jesus, I have to go in backwards so as to pretend to the manager that I'm comin' out.'

MacBride asked him if he knew that much of Third World poverty was a direct result of interest charges and Daly suddenly remembered that this was the great barrister's forte. Onetime chief of staff of the IRA he nowadays thought himself too big for Ireland alone; he was an international politician, and had the distinction of having at least one piece of universal legislation named after him, 'The MacBride Principles':

– I've never enjoyed worrying about how to keep my money safe, Sean.

– Ah, you poets were forever faced with that dilemma. And how is the work, if I may make so bold?

– Like pulling teeth . . .

– Ah yes, Mr Yeats felt like that most of the time. Poor, poor, lonely poets, I always think.

– It's not the loneliness that worries us, Sean.

He had this fondness for Yeats, and Daly wondered why. After all, the great poet had described MacBride's father as 'a drunken vainglorious lout' and chased his mother, Maud Gonne, with the lines:

> An intellectual hatred is the worst,
> So let her think opinions are accursed.
> Have I now seen the loveliest woman born
> Out of the mouth of Plenty's horn,
> Because of her opinionated mind
> Barter that horn and every good
> By quiet natures understood
> For an old bellows full of angry wind?

The horny old bastard – and the son's upper-class poise! Surely any decent man would hate his father's traducer even a little bit?

MacBride was saying:

– Oh, by the way, you still with that fellow McGill?

– With is hardly the operative word but he is publishing my next collection.

– You might inform him that Con is being inundated with potential litigants all hoping to sue for libel over three of his forthcoming publications.

– Jesus, to the Irish libel is better than the pools.

– And cheaper, Mr Daly! Of course none of them, in my opinion, stands any chance of succeeding since two of the subjects are dead and the third would be highly unlikely to sue . . .

– Oh, you're referring to Bryden MacWilliams' proposed *Life of the Pope* and Charlie Belton's *De Valera*? But who the hell is the third one?

– Parable Jones, they believe, is writing a new book on Joyce.

– Oh, you can take it from me that the last one is a non-starter; Parable wouldn't be caught dead in the same street as Harry McGill: and, as for writing a book about Joyce! He'd be far more likely to do a biography of Maria Monk.

– That is not the story being told in informed places.

– You can take it from me that if Parable is writing anything, it is to do with himself and nobody else.

– Well, just as long as you are aware, Mr Daly; after all, the old alliance of wig and pen is stronger than ink.

Having said which he jumped into a waiting cab. Daly waved the taxi out of sight and, turning to the bank, sighed. He wished the ground would swallow up the manager. Having deemed open-neck unseemly to a practising monetarist, he had arrived garbed in the attire of the supplicant, the unnatural tie of which, was, he told himself:

– Cuttin' the fuckin' neck offa me.

What would he say to this Thatcherite mountebank at all, at all? Maybe he'd say nothing. Maybe he would just speak words. 'Words,' said Swift, 'are the clothing of our thoughts'. A likely story; Jesus, if we said even half of what we mean half of the time, we'd all be arrested.

It was a new manager from whom he was to supplicate and he wondered if he would be of the old school. The lugubrious type? The new breed – witty about money? No sense of humour when it came to gale day and a hurricane of lawyer's letters. 'Gale day'? Yeats' windy bellows?

He had met with the born-again banking fraternity in an 'Irish' bank in Glasgow. His appeal for understanding had fallen on deaf ears. The brash jackeen manager's display of piss and importance had left Daly with a loathing for the smart ass. Worse than that, it had left him with a feeling of embarrassment for Dublin, from whence the poltroon had originated.

This new man he knew only by threat:

Dear sir . . . to hear from you . . . earliest convenience . . . In the meantime, issue no more, for, until funds have been . . . thus far shalt thou go and no further. Now that the fee had gone up it was 'Die dog or shite the licence!'

And the illegible signature in case you hit the fucker a smack in the face . . . MacBride's 'place to keep his money . . .' they probably genuflect whenever he enters – takes them all their time to be civil to me . . .

He knew that his records would have preceded him. Banks, like police stations. 'Jesus, if they pass on the Loxene legacy, I'll be rightly Shanghaied. Destroyed entirely. Ah, but sure nobody would be bad enough to retail a story like that – would they? The old manager had dined out on it, and more than once. Oh fuck, I'll be the laughin' stock of the whole place . . . and this tie is fuckin' killin' me.'

At the time, Daly had been looking for the loan of three hundred pounds. Mr Smith had been the manager. It was a long time ago, when, as Mr Smith was fond of repeating, 'a pound was a pound'. The meeting had been fixed for the afternoon and Sean had drunk a few pints, left his hair steeping in Loxene and fallen asleep. Forgetting about the setting shampoo, he awoke and hurried to the bank. He had been living in Baggot Street at the time and he was passing Fletcher's and Philipson's when the rain started.

Because he was in such a hurry he hadn't paid a great deal of attention to the laughing passers-by. Anyhow, every countryman knows that them Dublin jackeens will laugh at fuck-all. Then he looked into Donaghue's window and saw his head reflected in the whiskey mirror. Jesus Christ! He couldn't believe it! He was like something straight out of Millais. 'Bubbles', with an ageing face!

To the Green he had run, as fast as his long legs could carry him. The whole of the city it seemed had stopped to stand and stare at him – even in the pissing rain. They stared and they pointed. They laughed. They stopped and they stared and they pointed and laughed.

In the duck pond he had stuck his head, and, as he was staring at himself, his reflection was ghosted by a second face looking at his face. He peered, to make sure, but it was no optical illusion, it was the face of his bank manager staring back at him in disbelief. He looked up in horror to hear Mr Smith say:

– Loan three hundred pounds to you, Mr Daly? Stephen's Green may well seem corroboration of your esteem as a poet, but few banks will accept your eccentric ablutary-water holes as reasonable collateral.

When money-talk came round, Daly feigned boredom. In truth he was ashamed. Every time some ignorant cabog of a publican or shopkeeper called him 'mister' he recognised an implied threat. And they always seemed to confide in stage whispers:

– If yeh have a minit, Mr Eh . . . It's about our little understanding.

And that was them being nice! As if anybody understood a creditor. How very like a whale. If only we could all be like the 'Ginger Man'. The time ould Mac told him – in a blaze of secrecy – that one of his cheques had been returned. The old bastard's 'whisper' could have been heard in Hong Kong:

– I know very well that it's an oversight, Mr Eh . . . but if yeh'd like to attend to the little matter . . .

The 'Ginger Man' had not prevaricated:

– 'Oversight', Mr McDaid? Are you trying to imply that you are the only publican in Dublin in possession of one of my bouncing kites? Gainor Crist makes no favourites among whores, whoremasters or publicans.

However wanly, McDaid had actually smiled and said:

– Well, when you can put your mind to it, Mr Eh . . .

– Highly unlikely, Mr McDaid, for today I leave Ireland for Ireland's good, and, by the time I return, you will, in all probability, be as dead as your debt. Until then, I wish you a long life, and would you like to give us a round for the road?

McDaid had retreated upstairs to say a decade of the rosary for the repose of the soul of Gainor's cheque, and the 'Ginger Man' swore that he had gone to turn poteen into whiskey:

– That my friends is the only transubstantiation they know about on Tory Island.

Poor McDaid! One meeting with the 'Ginger Man' and it was

enough to send him to sit by his living-room window, a bottle of Bushmill's by the tail, and a pair of binoculars to his eyes, through which he looked for the nuns in Clarendon Row Convent changing from their greater habits into their night attire. John McDaid, for a religious man, was a devotional deviant.

The sound of the midday Angelus from Arran Quay chapel told Daly that it was time for his appointment. A female voice asked:

– Next please?

Daly went to her position, and, because the Angelus was still chiming, most of the employees were crossing themselves and fishmouthing the 'Hail Mary'. Nobody actually stopped work to pray, for nobody rings bells for Mammon. Daly heard himself ask the young teller:

– Is the manager in?

And, as she went to confirm his appointment, he knew that he had behaved just as the actors do in the bank ad he so despised.

CHAPTER SIXTEEN

Bridge Over the River Liffey

But, before we were so rudely interrupted. On the previous evening, while Tom Reivey served a demanding drunk drink, Parable Jones tried to rouse his mistress from her drunken stupor. Snoring like a pig, and farting like a brand new leather suite, Sally-Anne Millington lay, an unlikely lady, in the window seat of the Bridge Bar.

Her face was waxen, her shoulders rigid; it would have been easier to raise Lazarus. Parable Jones gave it up as a bad job. He ordered a large ball of malt in a bid to quell the terror that was building inside his breast. Tempus was fugitive. It was already past closing time, and the real pubs would be disgorging their bowels all over Dublin. Very shortly, the Bridge Bar would be maudlin – men kissing each other in drink who wouldn't be found near each other in death. Parable was going to be caught like a rat in a trap. It was so unfair. The Bridge Bar was his pub. Now every unpublishable wanker of a word warper in the city would be here. Bohemians for a night 'Ah, fuck it', he thought, and Mousey asked:

– What?

– I said, 'Fuck it'.

– Well, said Tom, you've more chance of fuckin' it than her. Hold on a minit till I see what's goin' on over there.

– It's the provo, Ructions, in his beret, trench-coat, and gloves – d'ye need a hand?

– For that shadow of a gunman, Mousey? Yeh must be jokin'. I'd beat him with Fidelma's rosary beads.

He walked straight into the argument till he was facing the whites of the patriot's crazy eyes, and grabbed him roughly by his moveable shoulders:

– Now look, Ructions, you and me are goin' to have a serious falling-out unless you keep your head down and your mouth shut.

– But you don't understand, Tom . . . yeh weren't listening to the discussion.

– 'Discussion'? Is that what yeh call that ranting and raving? To me it was a shouting match that must have been heard up on the Falls Road.

– I didn't think I was upsetting anybody . . .

– No? That guy there is a practising Roman Catholic and you don't think he's going to be upset when he hears you talking about the 'fuckin'' Pope?

– It wasn't the present Pope I was referring to.

– Past or present, dead or alive, Popes are Popes . . . even the one you were saying gave Ireland to Henry II in 1170 . . .

– He was an English bastard!

– There yeh go again; this is no place to question the Holy Father's race, or otherwise legitimacy: just knock it off, Ructions, old son.

– Do you know what I'm going to tell you about Pope Adrian?

– I know what you're not going to tell me about the man; not even if you refer to him in his maiden name of Nicolas Breakspear. All I want you to tell me is that you're not going to upset my ready-money customers. Understood?

The republican wanted to prevaricate but the publican was getting a mad look in his narrowing eyes, so Ructions contented himself with muttering:

– Well, I don't want to upset anybody, anyway.

– Good lad, now you get back to your drink and I'll have mine before it gets too cold.

And then it was large balls of malt all the way. More so; when Parable saw out of the corner of his mind, Joe Wilmot, thespian, enter by the side-door, he started to drink double-large whiskeys double-quick. Only arrogance would face down the pansophy parasites and their culture club, and P. J.'s arrogance could be released by none but Bacchus himself. The only defence was invisibility – get pissed out of my mind:

– Mine, Tom, mine, the costly anodyne, pour the anaesthetic until I'm paralytic.

– That's all I needed, Mousey, a fuckin' poet.

Wilmot talked through a man in a tweed suit about what he had said to Larry and John and Ralphie, back in the fifties. His familiar was obviously a likely candidate for such guff, since, besides the tweed suit, he was also wearing tweed socks, a tweed shirt, and a tweed hat – it was probably his great sorrow that nobody made tweed shoes. Nevertheless, such a costume was bound to be impressed by such eloquently expressed contiguity with knightly stars.

Although Wilmot's remarks were made loudly, in the hope that Parable might react, the picaroon Jones wasn't having any. 'One raising of an eyebrow, and all will be lost. Interlopers will squat in your mind at the drop of a *pardon*? Lock up your head and think on occasional people.

'Kavanagh was an occasional person. He used to stalk Pembroke Road like a kulak in search of a czar. At one time a rustic in the shadow of a bog; when he learned that peasantry was a state of mind, he changed his mind, and changed the state of poetry in Ireland. He wasn't even born when he left Mucker, for no place outside Dublin could have conceived a thought like him.

'The same Dublin had screwed up a few folk in her thousand years. That same city of *genteel dastards*. She had driven Joyce round the bend, and Beckett into exile. But, maybe Sam's mind had always been a little on the Kildare side. One learns to be wary of poor Dublin Protestants who are neither full-Friday nor pisces.

'Ever since Milton had rejected his grandfather's Catholicism in favour of his father's money, rich Christians, facing the dilemma of a denominational dichotomy, lived with a foot in either camp; like the Sheehy-Skeffingtons and Guinnesses, they could cross themselves with both hands. No Limbo for the ambidextrous who could get each other paroled from hell.

'The Plunketts were an object lesson in ubiquitous Christianity. The half who kissed the arse of Henry VIII looked after the ones who had kissed the arse of Clement VII. Poor Protestant trash like

Beckett would never understand that sort of ecumenism, and so, they minded their pennies as carefully as they minced their words.

'Gallant Count Plunkett gave his years and his son for the cause; but his grandfather gave half of his family to the reformers, to a religion founded on the bollocks of Henry VIII. Like MacNeice's folk, they could have bought a Catholic's all for a fiver. They never did, but the chance was there all the same, and chance is a very fine thing. MacNeice had told Parable that he would have been happy had his family defected for a bowl of soup, but his shame, and that of his father, was that there had never been the need.

'Carson didn't count because his people were Italian Catholics to begin with, and not properly under the jurisdiction of Dublin criticism. Oh, Ned claimed Dublin citizenship but really he was nothing more than a Catholic carpetbagger in search of a bag.

'The Tones and the Emmets now, they were a different case altogether; they had elected to be where the gallows was at: they spread the French disease at a time that the only known cure for it was the scaffold. We owe the prods a lot; not a generation passed but some of them, somewhere, stuck a Presbyterian tongue out at the crown: and the same crown stuck those same tongues, together with their heads, on the railings of Dublin Castle. And, after the Penal Days, the prods were badly needed because the Catholic hierarchy, after being appointed felon-setters, wouldn't be caught dead among the poor.

'Of course Sam didn't see Dublin until he got to Paris and then the very sight of his native city caused him to produce the only anti-Protestant play ever written by an Irishman; *Waiting for Godot* pours scorn on the narrow-minded ministers who hid the real Ireland away from a Protestant child.

'Bertie Rodgers saw Ireland only as a gem in Britannia's Imperial crown; he knew morality but could not sublimate the curse of the codpiece:

> Turn down the candid lamp
> And draw the equal quilt
> Over our naked guilt.

'Lovely language from a minister of religion who might well have been a priest but for the Reformation.

'MacNeice was a different kettle of fish altogether. He had gone from Carrickfergus to Dublin via Oxford, because it was the thing the sons of high church dignitaries did. In the olden days the neighbours would have prayed for his mother to become the father of a bishop, but his mother married one.

'In the heel of the hunt, Louis found Oxford to be more of an island than Ireland – out of the bog and into the hole. When he did meet Dublin he feared it was too late; the very meaning of this brash, boastful basin broke his heart. He wrote that it could never be his town, that he wasn't reared in the place; that she would not "have me alive or dead", but she "holds my mind with her seedy elegance". And he went on, in line after beautiful line, begging Anna Livia Plurabelle to make friends with him.'

Parable talked to his friends, who were mostly dead, for they were the only ones to whom he listened. They were the only ones with whom he had anything in common, and they were more alive than anybody he could see, dead and all as they were.

'Was it really a question of intellectual propriety, Kavanagh? Or were you taking the piss? It was said, over and over again that you hated the citizens; that you were suspicious of their easy recall. Did you really say that Proust wouldn't have stood a chance with them? Did you seriously believe that the Dubliner will say anything to clothe the nakedness of silence? They never cease speaking well of you, now that you're dead. It's as if – to paraphrase the Quare Fella, who they are shortly to canonise – that they are doing you a favour.'

Mallarkey's story of Kavanagh was better than most – he had never written anything, so he had no axe to grind. He says he was standing at the bar of Davy Byrne's and watching the world pass by in the gantry mirror, when the battered head under the battered hat, appeared by Mallarkey's face, almost preceded by the rough demanding voice following on behind:

– Have yeh any money?

Without turning, Mallarkey told Kavanagh:

– I have.

– Would you loan me five shillings for a meal?

– I would not.

– Why would a man with money refuse another man five shillings for a meal?

– Because I've only got sixpence.

Kavanagh never spoke to Mallarkey again. It wasn't his fault, for you can take the man from the bog, dry him off, and find yourself with a handful of dust. The poet might well have seen the funny side of it, but the hungry man was not amused. Parable knew the score; writers like Kavanagh and MacDiarmid and Sydney Goodsir Smith didn't enter the scene as poets, they came into the world as human beings, whether it was to Davy Byrne's or the Bridge Bar.

'By the same token it wasn't all that funny when Kavanagh gave the Archbishop of Dublin, John Charles McQuaid, a thimble full of whiskey because that was what his lordship requested. It wasn't funny, it was fucking hilarious!'

Through the shutters of his mind, Parable could hear the hum of the hubbub – loud, abrasive middle-class voices; the slum life of suburbia. It was as if they had come from the same 2.5 child 1.5 car families in the four corners of Dublin to talk, all at the same time about the same things – about everything and nothing.

'Intellectual propriety. Kavanagh was right. Oh sweet and pitiful Jesus, Who was twice crucified for our sins, please note: it wasn't me, Jesus! No, Lord God, it wasn't me':

– Yeh know, Parable, after what I heard today, yeh could be right after all about where Dev was born . . .

'Ah, fuck it!'

CHAPTER SEVENTEEN

Love's Old Sweet Song

Jeannie Jones would never think of herself as a telephone person. When people rang, they usually wanted to talk to Parable. Now that her mother was dead, she seldom used the instrument socially. She returned Mary Belton's calls although she knew that she too would really be looking to speak to Parable. Jeannie knew that Charlie's wife was infatuated with P. J., but the torch she carried wasn't going to set the world on fire.

When they, her and Parable, were young, it had been different. In those early days, all P. J.'s male friends had wanted to dally with her – and most had wanted more than that. But she had always known that, if it wasn't for Parable, none of them would have given her a second look. They all wanted to have it away with Parable Jones's wife.

Nowadays it was all 'Oh, he's not there then?' Polite hellos, and it was as though the phone was red hot they couldn't put it down quickly enough. He didn't tell her now what was heard or said about what; and yet, the very obliqueness of the thing was more merciful than the silence that prevailed when he wasn't at home.

Parable was a great one for Mr Bell's machine; he could 'see' the faces of the voices, and he was always funny. His personality was ideal for the medium, since conversation with Parable Jones was, more often than not, a one-sided affair.

When Jeannie heard him say: 'Wasn't that a good one, wha'?' she knew that the person at the other end was still laughing at some witticism or story made by her husband to somebody, somewhere else. On these occasions she told the caller – in her mind:

– Aye, he's a laugh a minute; but, if you want to know him come and live with him. Better still, share a bed with him! Aye that'd keep yeh busy.

And yet it had not always been Parable's fault. They had both made mistakes. After the marriage she had fallen in love with him so deeply that she wanted to live every moment with him. She began to resent the time he spent away from her and, in the end, the love had simply evaporated, leaving nothing but selfish, pointless possessiveness.

As her looks began to fade she began to love Parable more. She refused to share him with his friends and used his work as a barrier. Only now did she realise with sadness why he kept repeating that story about Dylan and the notice on his BBC door, 'PLEASE DISTURB'. Her father warned her:

– If you don't stop suffocating your husband, as true as Christ you're going to lose him, Jeannie, just as me and your mother lost each other.

Her father's outburst had shocked her because she had never thought about parents loving, making love or hating each other. But it didn't change her attitude to Parable Jones.

She insisted on him staying at home, getting on with his work, being settled. Wild oats were only to be sowed by the wild young. Her husband thought otherwise; settling wasn't for him. There was nothing good about that night into which she wanted to ease him. Parable was par for the course; he would stay the pace, for he knew that old age was not inevitable – however long it might take to live life on the edge of the grave. Aye, he would defy vulgar death, or die in the attempt.

Jeannie knew that her possessiveness had been poisoning their relationship for years. She knew that she was driving him into the arms of another woman; she knew who the woman was, because she knew the woman. She detested Sally-Anne O'Reilly with a loathing that she found impossible to fully consummate. She didn't take communion now because the priest refused to give her absolution until such time as she had at least promised to try to purge her heart of the sin of hate.

In the beginning she clung to religion because she knew that thoughts of God annoyed Parable Jones. Soon it became a habit and she found herself drawn to the dreadful unlived-in churches. She could sit for hours in commune with a vengeful God, and sometimes punishing her knees so that the sense of relief when she sat back in the pew was wonderful.

When Parable had called her a religious masochist nut she had resented the remark; now she knew that there was more truth in his conviction than she had been prepared to allow. She had long ago made her own rack, and, because it was her peculiar creation, she had convinced herself that she must lie on it.

Mary Belton had been appalled at her interference with her husband's work the other morning. She hadn't even meant to tell her anything about it, but she just couldn't keep it to herself.

Parable would call that sort of thing 'self expiation' but she knew she didn't do it in any spirit of atonement; she spoke about these things because she wanted people to know that the all powerful Parable Jones didn't scare her – not even slightly.

Of course the incident was unforgivable. She knew the terror that buff envelopes held for him; and yet she couldn't hold herself back: she was simply constrained to do what she had done. She couldn't stop herself. It was the same with the well-timed tantrums, the snide remarks, when all Parable was guilty of, was trying to be nice. She knew what she was going to say, got some perverse momentary enjoyment from saying it, and then bitterly regretted having opened her mouth.

Oh, God, the terrible wanton waste! Time was when she would have disguised every worry, concealed every debt: shielded her husband. But she could only vaguely remember when that time was. She had become a shrew – and without a great deal of help from anybody else.

Even her preview of what was going to happen was more rehearsal than precognition. Parable would get into a temper. Because he had never been able to strike another human being, he would attack something inanimate – usually something that was dear to him. He would destroy his writing implements or tear up his work. Once, when she had taken out her bad temper on him, he had just placed a finished manuscript in the kitchen stove and stoked it with the poker as her father wept while he watched it burn.

There was a terrible mixture of pride and envy in her dealings with her husband. The world loved Parable Jones, and the world, in turn, was loved by him. Even with a competitor as remote as the world, Jeannie didn't want to share her husband. Adverse criticism of his work was still a dagger to her heart. She could nurse a vendetta for a reviewer such as he never could: invariably his reaction was:

– If he thinks he can write half as well as he believes I should, then the fucker should be a millionaire.

No doubt that Jeannie's main difficulty was her inability to articulate her feelings. She was aware of the needs of her husband, but her sympathy was a religious emotion totally lacking in empathy. Oh, she could enter into his personality; she could experience his feelings: but only as part of Parable. He wouldn't have anybody as near to him as that; he needed to get away from himself occasionally, and he couldn't escape if there was already somebody occupying his hiding place.

She could appreciate the needs of his gregarious nature; he must meet as many people as he needs to meet. She even understood when he said he wanted every person he met. She could even accept his separate public life; but there was no way she could assent to her alienation. Sometimes she felt like screaming:

– If a wife is not entitled to as many faults as a mistress, is she not allowed even one bloody mistake? I've made mine, Parable! What about a bit of that forgiveness that you keep for the world? I slept with you before ever humanity did!

But, then, how could she stand in a public house, with him, a public figure, while he held forth? 'An unnecessary nun' he had called her:

– Jeannie will neither shit nor get off the pot, he said onetime in an untypical display of vulgarity. And yet he understood this terribly shy woman, and who she had been. He had married her because she had been outgoing; but his awareness had given her new and different values. She had become ambitious for him:

– This is fucking death, said Parable, the only ambition any writer should ever encourage is the aspiration to know himself completely.

P. J. had introduced her to a world that was new. A world she had known about in a shadowy sort of way. He had shown her how to read meaningfully, with understanding. Interpretation had been so important to him, and then to her. In time, literature was no longer a closed book. Sadly, every action has its reaction. She had reacted to her husband and told Father Jesmond their secrets: the priest could not divulge her confessions, and that was the worst thing of all, she and Father Jesmond shared intimacies that should never have left the bedroom.

Why the hell had she not let her man hang as he grew? She just hadn't wanted him to be another word-spinner. Real writers, like Joyce and Tolstoy, are treated with respect. Parable Jones was like Larry McHale's dog, everybody knew him and expected to go a step of the road with him. When she heard about how he had made people laugh she had called him a stage Irishman. The boozers' benefactor! The cheap jibe and the ready guffaw; like Dylan and the Quare Fella, honest rage was dissipated in outrage. Jeannie knew that there was no place in real literature for such buffoonery; she knew because Parable Jones had told her so. It went through her heart whenever somebody remarked:

– God, Mrs Jones, wasn't Parable a scream in the paper this morning? How does he manage to be so funny day after day? God, yeh must lead a charmed life!

Nobody would have said things like that about Stendhal or Proust. What sort of a bloody writer is it that's recognised by his laugh? The trouble with Parable Jones was that he wanted to be known as everything but what he was. Strange, lonely, extrovert, introvert, Parable Jones, the boy who had been described by MacDiarmid as a 'shy introspective youth'. But why want to be somebody or everybody else – anybody but the one you were? Tolstoy and Joyce would hardly have wished to change places; wouldn't have wanted to be each other or the man next door. And, what was so clever about two individuals winning such immortality that either the word was God or God was the word? Parable Jones said that he had made up his mind years ago:

– I don't want to be either a count in St Petersburg or a cunt in Sandycove. But why should you know about it, Jeannie, when I'm only barely aware of it myself? Indeed, I would have known nothing about it had I not been forced to think about it. 'It', Jeannie, the most important word in the English language; so impersonal, so indefinite as to be a book in itself. 'Yes' and 'The' may be all right for some folk, but can you flaunt them, Jeannie? Answer me that, me lovely unnecessary nun!

With something of a start, Jeannie realised that the phone was ringing. Wearily, and with not a little trepidation, she picked up the instrument, and put the hearing piece to her ear. It was Mary Belton. Her husband had not come home. No, Parable was still out. Yes, maybe they were together. She supposed it was a good thing to know that, wherever they were, they were just drinking. Oh, aye, it was a great comfort in this world of AIDS to know that your husband didn't jump into bed with every willing woman. Yes, Mary, I always blame the woman, too. Very degrading for the wife. Oh indeed, show me one and I'll show you a hussy. Yes, a drop too much, was many a good man's complaint . . . and it's the poor heart that never rejoices. Oh, you could say that again, Mary, we are very lucky. Jump for joy and put out more flags.

Mary Belton had a bee in her bonnet. She wished her husband wouldn't be so up-front with publishers; after all, they were the ones with the last say. If they just made up their minds a thing might never see the light of day. But you know what Charlie is like; just full of his dignity! And, as Mary had always said, 'It takes a lot of dignity to keep food on the table, a fire in the grate, and a roof over your head':

– Of course my Charlie will always take the hard road to the Klondike. You might as well kill him as placate him! Only the other day, hadn't he told Harry McGill, 'One change in one word of one line of one paragraph of my book . . . one comma, I told him, Mary, and you, Harry, can shove your contract up your fucking arse!' God, Jeannie, aren't writers a cruel cross for wives like us to bear?

As Jeannie put the phone down, she had to breathe deeply to suppress her seething anger:

– Well, of all the bloody cheek! Imagine! Comparing the likes of Charlie Belton with Parable Jones!

CHAPTER EIGHTEEN

The Second Policeman

– Ah give us a bleedin' chance, Tom, said the taxi-driver. Yeh surely don't expect me to take them like that? For fuck sake! Parable can't even talk, and his girl-friend . . . well . . . if arses could speak, and if me own little mother hadn't been a woman . . .

– See you . . . tried P. J. . . . if I could shpeak I'd tell you what to do with your fuckin' charichot of fire . . .

Charlie Belton diplomatically removed himself to within earshot of the contenders, and stood in the company of Geordie Hinnie, published poet. The cabbie and Tom and Mousey agreed that Paralytic Jones should lie in the window seat and, when he had slept most of his drunkenness off, the taxi would return:

– I'm not trying to be awkward, Tom, but if either of them was to be sick – you've no idea how long it takes to get the smell of vomit out of a cab.

Mousey said, as they laid Parable to rest beside his love:

– Understood, Squire, but yeh will come back, all right?

– No problem, Mousey, just give it an hour or so.

– I'll hold you to that, now, said Mousey, and the taxi-man knew he would.

As Paramour Jones and Sally-Anne lay back to belly in the window-seat, the bravura of a hundred drunks made dents in their dreams. In the half-real world, Mousey Duggan was trying to ward off the intimidating advances of a new member of the Garda shekooneys who had taken over, now that Detective Matthews was drunk and gone home and his shift over. The Second Policeman was of the prevailing praetorian persuasion, that crooks must not alone be done – they must not be seen to be done.

Parable was neither drunk enough to sleep nor sober enough to stay awake. Closed eyes didn't shut down his mind, and the sound of Geordie Hinnie holding forth on James Joyce, was a warning that language was going to be the loser for those who were dumb but not deaf – the curse of not having had enough but too much to drink.

Geordie was into Joyce's use of song in *Ulysses* and *Finnegans Wake*. 'Thematic, don't you know . . . when the jejune jesuit is talking about the bloom being on the rye, he is using "Annie Laurie" to make another comment on Leopold Bloom . . .'

Parallel Jones told himself that 'Annie Laurie' was a vile song, 'Imagine anybody writing the line, "Maxwelton braes are bonny!" All the beautiful place names that there are in Scotland from which to choose, and they have to pick that North-British shit; small wonder that in *Finnegans Wake* Shemus Augustine refers to "knee Bareniece Maxwelton"':

– 'Talk about Irish names of places', said Geordie Hinnie, when Joyce used that phrase he was more than criticising the book by his kinsman, P. W. Joyce . . .

– No relation, protested Parabellum Jones' mind, but his voice made no sound.

– Musical leitmotiv, don't yeh know?

'Aye, don't yeh see that now. Keep yer mind still, Geordie Hinnie, for Leopold Bloom was the only man who was never put out of Davy Byrne's for being drunk; Poldy Bloom and Father Kurt Fahrt – oh, aye, and Esther Mac An Uisce, maiden mother to Proinsias.'

It was Paradox Jones who had christened Gearoid O'Cuinnagain in the nickname of Geordie Hinnie, because he had gone to Newcastle to read his poetry at poor defenceless miners who had never done him a minute's harm; only they couldn't pronounce the name Gearoid. It stuck for ever more, and he deserved it for he had done worse to those poor creatures of the dark than Rob Roy McGregor could have inflicted in a second geratology.

It was to his lasting regret that Geordie had not written a baker's dozen. But still, even with the one twelve he was very national, don't yeh know; but hardly up to his imitation of Kavanagh's pilgrimage to Christ, despite the impediments and impedimenta of the Church.

Now he was anxious, before the millennium, to run out to the smelly river and rhyme reams of streams of paeans of praise about Buck Mulligan's Saviour:

– Pollution? I could tell you about pollution! Someday, whispered Anner to Isaac, you will butt me no butts, when you learn that, in his maiden name of Gogarty, the Buck himself gave me a couple of swans, and they have been filling me with shit ever since.

Isaac told Annie:

– I'm as old as original sin. Before Parnell there was me, don't yeh see? I didn't have to wait for a second-hand Corkman to come to Dublin and make me famous. Because a man is born in a stable does it follow that he must have a big nose?

– Nonsense, Isaac. You are angry because JaJ invented Parnell before getting round to you. Since he created me literally as well, I know a little about his character. You might say that I know that my creator liveth.

– I've had my own hour of glory too, remember.

– In which book did you bide, by the bye?

– Well, of course I've been mentioned in all, or most of them, but my big scene was in *Finnegans Wake* . . . He called me saire Izard.

– But sure the dogs in the street are in that mish-mash, everybody from 'Skin-the-Goat' to Major Shaw.

– Yes, but I'm one of the chosen ones; on page 227 he calls me 'MacIsaac', and that must show some proper regard.

– For God's sake, Izzy, catch yourself on; he also speaks on page 297 about Wilde's mother and on page 27 he says, 'I've an eye on queer Behan and old Kate and the butter, trust me.' To be quite honest I think he doesn't have the most complimentary things to say about you at all.

– And what about yourself, may I ask?

– Me? Everybody knows how highly he thinks of me . . . sure there's hardly a book of his that wouldn't fall to pieces if I wasn't holding it together! No, Isaac, I am his real leitmotiv; nothing runs through Joyce like Anna Livia Plurabelle; though Gogarty said that drink did, and made the author 'curl up like a tobacco spit'.

– The same Jemser doesn't think all that highly of you, then . . .

– Who doesn't? Where?

– He doesn't, in *Finnegans Wake.*

– No? So?

– On page 273, he describes you as 'Hanah Levy, shrewd shroplifter and nievre anore skidoos with her spoileds'.

– Is that so? Well I never got that far in his competition, besides which, I don't give a fuck, because I'm a Wicklow woman meself . . .

What you must remember, Geordie Hinnie was saying, is that Joyce deliberately set out to metamorphose into Purnell's literary doppelganger.

Paramount Jones asked himself if anybody had ever heard such shit:

– Did anybody ever hear such shit? Dear Geordie Hinney will now prove . . .

– By the use of Stendhal's mirrors . . .

– By the telling of rosary beads . . .

– And pictures of the Pope and/or J. F. K. . . .

– Plus the signed confessions of Madame Blavatsky . . .

– Who has really been in drag all this time . . .

– That *Dubliners*, *Portrait of the Artist as a Young Man* (and dog) were, like *Exiles*, all written by ould doublyn dactyll himself . . .

– When he wasn't operating on Michael Collins.

– But where, asked Mrs Leonard Woolf, does that leave *Finnegans Wake*?

There were many cries of, 'Answer the question!' from the crossbenches, and, after several shouts for order, the Sigismund of Parliamentary Jones, in papal blue, insisted:

– Feeling very Jung and Freudened . . .

– Are you saying that Oliver St John Gogarty wrote *Finnegans Wake* as well?

– Oliver St John Gogarty never wrote anything well, but, like all other Dubliners, he 'talked' a better book . . .

– 'Talked' a better book?

– He came from the ancient tradition of the Seannaice, in which the use of paper was totally personalised and sanitary . . .

Most people would have let such a statement go for what it was worth, but dreams like drunkenness must be misunderstood; for they have nothing but beginnings, middles, and ends, that happen out of sequence, and especially when most recent Freudos are stuffing the faces of the dreamers with dog foods before retiring.

Paracrostic Jones hated Alice B., who said *a rose is a rose is a rose* that will cut the fucking hand off yeh if yeh grab it the wrong way, or the head off yeh if yeh happen to be carrying yer own cross in Jerusalem. In Oxford they called Miss Stein a pedant because few people there can pronounce the word 'peasant', there being many a lisp between cup and lip.

'Of course, then, I'm not saying that peasants cannot come from all walks of life, indeed our own Noll wrote that:

> . . . a bold peasantry, their country's pride
> When once destroy'd, can never be supplied.

'Jesus, Noll, just say the word and we'll supply as many as yeh want; we'll clear out the whole of Kildare Street for yeh.

'But, to get back to the question at issue; it's the long spoon you need when supping with the bould peasantry, but don't give them two or they will play a bloody tune on them! God bless their crossroads mentality, they will dance Jim Crow whenever there's a Kennedy in Wexford or a Reagan in the town of the small potato.

'Long before Heinrich Heine said, *First the books and then the people*, the English were scorching the arses off our peasantry.' And Pandecta Jones said that this was a terrible thing, but why didn't the silly bastards take a bowl of soup? Oh, the broth is far more substantial than transubstantiation, and the ould wafers go off after a bit. 'That's not to say but a chap would have been better off with the bread and wine; the dehydrated Jesus is for the birds and spacemen, who are always nearer their God anyway.

'And, by the same token, who wrote the laws but poets? Sir John Perot's blueprint for Goebbels, made ready for the Nazis as far back as 1580 was actually composed by Edmund Spenser:

> All carroughs, bards, rhymers, and common idle men and

> women within the province making rhymes, to be spoiled of all their goods and chattels and to be put in the next stocks, there to remain till they shall find sufficient surety to leave that wicked trade of life.

'Aye, decreed Ned Spenser, getting rid of the Irish opposition. Of course that was only part of it; a closer examination will reveal that the poet was a sort of literate Chapman Pincher:

> Irish laws, customs, and religion, must be reformed on the English model. But, subjugation must precede reform. Vacillation has been the curse of the government. Let them now bring over ten thousand foot and one thousand horse; place these in six convenient garrisons, give the rebels twenty days in which to surrender, and then hunt down relentlessly all who stand out.

'Looking back over those four hundred years, Ned, I can't help thinking that they were the long twenty days. And yet, it was the good God that was in His heavens then; a good-natured, good-humoured God who saw to it that the first house to be burned down was the one given to one Fairy Queen by another, in consideration of a hack's contribution to sixteenth-century genocide. Aye, Ned, that year of 1588 when Kilcolman was razed to the ground, is still remembered round County Cork, as a gay time. The pity of it that John Reidy is not around to inaugurate an annual fag day in remembrance.

'Nor yet would God deny the help He received from Hugh O'Neill who chased the unworthy poet all the way back to England where he died with the Irish still on his heels and Harry Sidney in his bed. What was it, Ned, you said the *Faerie Queene* would teach us?'

– To fashion a gentleman or noble person in vertuous and gentle discipline.

Paromiac Jones, laughing to himself, thought:

'By Christ but those English wallahs know how to get rid of the literary opposition!

'Put all the poets in the stocks if they kept making nuisances of themselves; and, of course, if they persisted, put them in jail: or, better still, shoot the fuckers.

'Jazes, there's many a word-spinner I'd love to beat to death with balls of his own shite, but Spenser was a fairly stern critic, when all's said and done.

'Isn't it quite extraordinary how some poets will take the odd sinecure of revolution when it doesn't mean putting themselves in any physical danger? There was the bould Edmund when the brilliant Elisabeth decided to repair the damage imposed on her realm by her profligate father. Stood shoulder to shoulder, or knelt grovel to haught with her as is the wont; but he got out of the kitchen fucking rapid when those crazy Paddies came at him with their poetic axes.

'Yeats too, who couldn't find time off to post a letter in Easter Week, accepted a job in the Senate without any hesitation when the smoke had cleared. He and Gogarty, who had always rejected any change in the status quo.'

Parnassian Jones felt that, if he could think with any real feeling, maybe he would blot out the cadences of Geordie Hinnie's up and down lilt that made his voice a cross between Austin Clarke, John Betjeman, Gertrude Stein, Thomas Stearns Eliot, and Willie Yeats trying to make *The Lake Isle of Innisfree* sound mediocre.

He told himself that there was no accounting for folk who could create literature in the head and make music by the mouth.

'The only language they can read is ogham, and, to keep this folk-culture pure, it is said that they have sworn never to learn how to write it. A society with such a flagrant disregard for paper and pianos, could not expect but to come second-best to a country able and ready to produce Anne Hathaway testers.

'Was her husband too, a tin of fruit? Did he really compare his boy-friend to a summer's day? Did Willie actually keep his best bed so as to coin a phrase, or that his fancy-man might lie in it? Does it really matter?

'God! there was hope for Ireland in the old days; Sir Henry Sidney – who constantly took the blame for Spenser's worst work – thought that the Welsh were 'among the most easily governable peoples in Christendom'. But, when it came to the Irish – God help us!'

> I cannot find that they make conscience of sin, and I doubt whether they christen their children or no; for neither I find a place where it should be done, nor any person able to instruct them in the rules of a Christian.

'Isn't that bloody marvellous! Where the hell did we go wrong? Still and all, if Harry Sidney and Ned Spenser thought that the Irish didn't have their bellies full of Christianity, all I can say is that they should have had a mass said for themselves.

'Religion and the Irish? Chicken and the egg. Same old dream that leaves not a wrack behind – unless it's the moist sort, and then it's mostly on the leg . . . Enzyme or gene? Silly old bio-bodies. Everybody knows that Finnegan and his moleskins worked along with the others on the building of Jack's house; otherwise there would have been no Celtic DNA.'

– He didn't believe in the immortality of the soul.

– Who didn't?

– Edmund Spenser didn't.

– Who said that?

– I did.

– And who the hell are you?

– I'm God.

– And where are you speaking from?

– Everywhere.

– Ah, for jazes sake . . .

– Honestly.

On the edge of Parallax Jones' dream, the pub was heaving. And outside the pub was God. And He was responsible for the stream of consciousness that insisted on insinuating itself into Parable's mindless thought. God never left Parable alone. Maybe it was an illusion that could be slipped into a manuscript envelope and posted to Newton. But, if everything was as heavy as it was supposed to be, how the hell do we ever get our feet off the ground? Gravity was the stuff of nightmares; when the victim is stuck tight to the bed without even a voice to scream for help.

'Leave us alone, God, for Christ's sake. Don't you ever sleep. Oh God, you do go on about physics, chemistry or holy Sabellus! but don't split your infinity in front of me. I'm just not up to it. I must have gotten a bad pint somewhere.'

And yet God is there. And God is good, and that must be right for everybody says so. Just outside now, in the lane behind the pub, the Second Policeman is being assisted by solicitous Mousey, who is holding in his right-hand coat sleeve what he chooses to call his avenging blade:

– Go ahead, mate, throw up, there's nobody to see you here.

– And you'll not forget, Mousey, that you and me have a deal. You give me the information that I want and I'll leave you alone. You'll fix me up?

– Sure that's what I'm here for, friend, you leave me with no alternative but to fix you up.

A small plop in the river, a giant drop for the Second Policeman, and Annie asked Isaac:

– Is that Mousey Duggan's dagger I see before me?

CHAPTER NINETEEN

Sparras Can't Sing

The clergy fasted, every Friday; on fresh salmon. That was why, as a young man, Tom Reivey had wanted to join the priesthood. He felt he could sacrifice without undue suffering. He would be giving up nothing, in matter of fact, for, if he was poor, his next of kin was poorer. His kindred kinship being his uncle, Padraig Dwyer, and Padraig's wife, Assumpta.

All things being equal, his vocation was short-lived. It didn't last much longer than learning how it is that only the progeny of politicians and publicans are allowed the hardships of the uncertain clime and the anadromous vertebrate. Aye, the pity of it all; none but the ordained working class are to be sent to the sunspots of the world, to Africa and India: to the fleshpots of Ethiopia and the Sudan.

Tom decided that he was not good enough for such penitential exile; so, instead of becoming a Catholic curate, he became a grocer's curate, trained by Vintner and Tea Merchant, Cornelius Madigan.

Diligence, like virtue, brings its own reward. Having scrimped and saved, for years, from Corny's till, and having got very good odds from the Pru about his wife failing to complete the course, Tom soon had enough money to purchase his own little place. Very soon, uncle Paul and auntie Assumpta were able to boast to the neighbours, how 'the nephew is a self-made man in Dublin'.

Loudly, the estate agent had praised the features of the Bridge Bar. Tom was to 'look at its situation next to Collins Military Barracks, not a stone's-throw from the Garda Siochana Training depot in the Phoenix Park, and, within an ass's bawl of the Dublin

Fruit and Vegetable Market where citizens could imbibe legally from seven o'clock each morning'. He was to think about 'the amount of drink that thirsty soldiers might consume'. He was to 'keep in mind the value of the volume of the passing trade'.

Some folk said that the rust-red hair wore from the top of his head, because of Tom's habit of running a distracted hand through his curls every time a passing customer went by. And, between the estate agent and the truth, there was no love lost; Fionn himself couldn't have thrown a stone from Tom's pub to the new Garda Training Depot in Templemore; the army brass hats had put the Bridge Bar out of bounds at about the same time that the previous publican had stopped kicking back, and the pub had never been designated a 'market' bona fide.

In desperation, Tom had bought stolen whiskey from some of Mousey Duggan's friends, and, following in the age-old tradition of honour among thieves, they shopped Tom when the police caught up with them. That was how Reivey became an innkeeper without a licence. He was about the most expendable publican that ever owned a pub: a jockey without a horse; a gigolo minus his balls.

But, it's a true saying, 'God never opens one door but there's a terrible draught'. If his Uncle Padraig and his aunt Assumpta were without a good name and poor indeed, they had one possession for which men have hungered and thirsted – a licence to sell wines, beers, and spirits.

Padraig and Assumpta were going about their respective awful businesses of plumbing and praying, when Mr Reivey's *cri de coeur* came on the lips of the postman:

– Tis from your nephew, Tom, in Dublin. He needs yis in the capital, quicker than if yis were travellin' on a hare's back, for the jackeens have taken his licence from him because he's not one of their own. He says that they're a fairly scrotum-tightening lot, and is sorely in need of the men of the west.

Without ever rising from her knees in front of the statue of the Virgin of the village idiot, Assumpta confided to Mary:

– Blessed Mother, was it not the terrible waisht of me father's money, that me poor mother spent learnin' me the readin', when there are so many well educated postmen in the County of Miraculous Mayo?

And indeed Mayo is famous throughout incredulity for the village of the Virgin; if Lourdes is the nearest thing the Gauls have to Disneyland, Knock is the closest the Gaels are likely to get to Lourdes. The Irish fantasia was inaugurated in 1879 when fifteen villagers thought that they saw Our Lady. Did they see the Madonna? Sure they did! How come? No mystery. No big deal. There are people in the West of Ireland who can see things without ever looking.

What's supernatural about miracles to the people of Mayo? One hundred years after the Virgin sauntered among the clouds of Croagh Patrick, something even more incredible happened; 'Lucky' Lucan was seen at his old family seat in Castlebar. The whole of Scotland Yard wasn't looking for him, and with great success; but it was small beer to the Sisters of Mercy, who nowadays use his old home as their convent. The nuns saw him, and they're all TT.

It would be nothing short of astonishing if, in the county of the finest Irish moonshine, the paralytic natives were less than paranormal; and, consequently, virgins are not all that uncommon: drinkers have their priorities as Assumpta Dwyer was well aware.

Her husband was the only communist plumber in the whole of Knock. The other chap, William Smyth-Smith, was a Protestant whose day had been over ever since the other Lucan went sane at the Battle of Balaklava and ordered his brother-in-law, Lord Cardigan, to carry out Raglan's kamikaze attack on the Russian guns. Since leaving the general locality of the Phoenix Park, the Lucans had a penchant for dying away from home – Patrick Sarsfield Lucan in France, Jonathan Lucan in Mafeking, and there was now every likelihood that 'Lucky' Lucan would expire anywhere else but Broadmoor.

Thanks be to God, not everybody is like Padraig Dwyer; not everybody thinks that way about the West. Father Malachie Horan thought that the whole place was sacred to the memory of the Mother of God. Indeed he was sure that Mayo might well come into the forefront of religious phenomena, if only a 'family' group could be seen. It would be a star attraction to have Joseph and Mary: her cousin, Elizabeth: Jesus and His brother James: their cousin, John the Baptist, and them all smiling on Ireland from the top of Nephin.

But Malachie Horan was concerned with beginnings, not conclusions. He behaved in the same lax way when the nuns commissioned Padraig Dwyer to convert their central heating. The simple priest should have forgotten, if only in the interests of ecumenism, that Smyth-Smith was not of the true faith. No way should a drunken commie have been allowed to affront the Sisters. But, whatever he wasn't, Padraig Dwyer was a lapsed Catholic, and, as he told Mother Concepta:

– Sure a Protestant is a lapsed nuthin'.

If Father Malachie, or Monsignor as he was known to our betters, had one fault, it was that he was religious mad, but he wasn't a bitter Catholic. Had Father Malachie known how things were, don't yeh think that he would have done a deal with Smyth-Smith about one conversion for another, and then the two of them could have given that commie bum the bum's rush?

But Father Horan was busy. His vision of a Knock International Airport gave him little time for the contemplating of anything so ephemeral as communism or plumbing. And yet, no man is to be blamed for his preoccupations. In a village that lives on a belief in spectres projected on mountain-top mists, the question of flight is of relative importance. Malachie Horan must have been aware that, some day, like that other intrepid climber of holy shrines, who took Mount Sinai in his stride, the time might come when mortal men might well be taken up to heaven in a whirlwind. True, a jumbo jet might never get us as high as Elijah, but, with a little help from God and His Blessed Mother, a few decades of the rosary, and faith in our own Aer Lingus, might not the poor reach the Upper Circle?

And, was this not the Day of the Rabblement? Of James Joyce? Of Eamon de Valera? The Long Fella had put the former Archbishop of Dublin in his place; he had stomped all over his grace. Would his successors do the same to Malachie Horan? It would be different now when Dublin met the mad monsignor. Bog meets bog.

They had laughed at da Vinci and the Wright brothers; they had jeered Cockrell and Barnes Wallis. How they fell about the place when Malachie Horan told them that it was his intention to build runways in the belief that they would attract aeroplanes. The Maya Indians had built them to attract Gods, but they were a superstitious lot of bastards.

Of course the good father was dead right; if the illusion is to succeed, build the runways: something solid, on to which passing aeroplanes may be brought to earth. Stand by your runways and pray! Then the mass hypnosis. Everybody knows that hallucinations are catching, and that is why the first and last rule of aerodynamics, is, 'what goes up must come down'. Fill up with faith and wait for your aircraft, for now, having built something on which they may land, you have demonstrated a real belief in the power of prayer. We must be grateful to Father Malachie Horan for giving Europe the first Irish Bermuda Triangle.

Throughout the first quarter of 82 Knock was at fever pitch. During his first visit to the village in 79, his Holiness had nudged and winked that, regardless of what he might be wont to say in public, at heart he was an Irish republican Catholic. And what Pole wasn't? Or Italian, for the matter of that? Ever since J. F. K., the most extraordinary folk were claiming allegiance. Indeed, rumour had it that Klaus Barbie in Brazil and Kurt Waldheim in Austria were singing 'Mother Machree' to the tune of 'Tannenbaum'.

Of course, at this time of the year, Knock is excited enough anyway. From May to October is the kneeling season, when the world and his wife prays its hunkered way up the rugged 2,510 feet of Croagh Patrick to be nearer their God to Him.

Since 79, the Sisters did the pilgrimage twice each day because the Holy Father had not stayed with them on his last visit. They would be the last to admit it, but they felt that the Protestants were right; the Pontiff had refused their offer of hospitality because he didn't want the redundant balls frozen off him. At great expense, and in severe trepidation, they employed Padraig Dwyer to heat the convent.

Today, siting in the convent boiler-room, Padraig was as drunk as a prime minister's husband. Pipe after pipe after pipe he had brought from all parts of the building, until they converged in the middle of this catacomb, all waiting to be joined with the gleaming new oil heater that was standing, like a proud organ, waiting for its flues and reeds.

In the midst of the pipes he sat, like Orpheus in the underworld, a Muse waiting to gush forth. However, unlike the Orphic mentions of Plato and Euripides, he was down here to escape from a live wife, not to restore a dead one. The proletarian plumber was all set, in fact, for a Rabelaisian recreation.

Dangling his grandfather's 'hunter' by its chain he saw that it was nearly noon. In a very little while, the Angelus would ring, and then the nuns, led by Reverend Mother, would troop into the refectory. The Angelus bell was synonymous with lunch at twelve and tea at six.

In the refectory, the radiators, awaiting connection, stood idly around the walls; the female pipes peeping through the broken plaster, expectant. Mother Concepta came in at the head of her nannies, and was warmed in the thought that soon, the presently cold heaters would emit a radiance to wrap a plump popish Pole whenever he chose to return to the shrine of the Madonna.

Having said the Angelus, it was time for grace. The nuns had scarcely finished, when, without warning, there issued forth in stereophonic concert, from all parts of the refectory, such a stream of ribaldry that would have brought a blush to the cheeks of Chaucer – Padraig Dwyer's one-man show had begun. He sang everything from 'The Eunuch and the Unicorn' to 'The Cobbler Who Cobbled for Sport'.

Reverend Mother had ordered her charges to cover their holy ears and close their minds, when, just then, the bishop entered. Dwyer stopped singing and started to pose rhetorical riddles:

– Nuns are opened and closed at both ends. A conundrum is a priest with a nun under him . . .

– I see, said the bishop, that you decided against Smyth-Smith? I never use Dwyer these days. He tends to repeat himself, don't you think?

– Your Lordship chooses a Protestant? asked Mother Concepta. Then, rising from her seat, she bade her nuns eat, while she and the bishop circumambulated the refectory in religious disputation:

– I must say, Reverend Mother, that the Protestant belief in the work ethic, is more genuine than amongst many of our own people.

– But, your Lordship . . .

– Protestants take their work seriously, as if their very lives depend on it.

– But, your Lordship, what about their black legions? their hatred of Our Lady?

– And, furthermore, Reverend Mother, they have no sense of humour – a blessing in these days of free love, free-fall comedy, and piped religion.

Poor Mother Concepta! The bishop was a completely male chauvinist pig, who had no intention of allowing any Catholic in skirts to get under the hem of his cassock. The amazons were making attacks on the priestly pulpits of the Protestants, but, if his lordship had his way, the only thing without balls to climb his altar would be the chapel cat.

To make matters worse for the unfortunate nun, Dwyer started to sing again. In strident voice he pronounced every syllable of every word of 'The Ball of Kirriemuir', until Mother Concepta, beside herself with rage and hate, screamed into a radiator pipe:

– Stop it, I tell you! You filthy, filthy man! Do not sully more this board at which the Holy Father almost ate!

But, there was no reasoning with Padraig Dwyer. He gave the concert a lecture on the spiritual values of a papacy that had declined through the Medicis, Borgias and English pretenders. He made loose rhymes cheaply: 'Borgiastic: orgiastic: chasuble elastic and risible monastic . . .' In point of fact, he proved himself to be what everybody in Knock knew him to be: a dirty old man.

Mother Concepta's class anger showed in her hatred for the singer. What's so clever about being a plumber anyway? But it was the questions his songs asked. She knew that Dwyer was right; if she had known that Muzorewa was a Protestant liberal, and Mugabe a Catholic communist, which one would she have supported?

In the old days, life had been more simple. You gave a penny in school for the black babies, and that was that. Somewhere in darkest Africa, but never near enough to cause embarrassment in front of the neighbours, was your very own piccaninny that never grew any older than your childhood. You certainly never expected the front door to open, and a big blackman to come through, singing 'Mammy'.

She prayed to the Blessed Virgin for patience for herself and a heart attack for the heating engineer. But something, probably the lustiness of Dwyer's singing rather than any loss of faith, told her that the perverse plumber had never been in better health:

> The Ball, the Ball, the Ball, the Ball,
> The Ball of Kirriemuir,
> Four and twenty foreskins
> Were thrown about the floor . . .

His Lordship told himself:

– So, that's the way that that verse goes.

Aloud he informed the Reverend Mother:

– The man is a menace. He will have to go; even Christian charity has its limits.

A Catholic solution was arrived at. The diocese would foot the bill for Padraig and Assumpta Dwyer's transportation to Dublin, and, in the interests of Christian ecumenism, the plumbing would be finished by William Smyth-Smith.

– Protestants, Reverend Mother, do not stumble, because they do not drink. Their faith is the work ethic, and that is how they guard against the sparrow's fall – the bird that they chose to replace the holy dove. But this choice has one great advantage; sparrows, Mother Concepta, cannot sing.

CHAPTER TWENTY

Interlude

Just then, in the lane behind the Bridge Bar, the same schoolkids who had propositioned Charlie Belton, were practising the greed to which the government hoped they would become addicted, going through the pockets of the Second Policeman, and grabbing whatever they could:

– Jazes, his prick is like a fuckin' rock! Strange last rites, but God and finders keepers, had decreed that the Second Shekooney be the victim of mugger or muggers unknown.

And that is the best answer to the sceptics; Supergod had His likes and dislikes in this world, and, if He makes a mistake in the beginning, He has all eternity to put it right – having created an arsehole of a policeman, He used the strong arm of a good Catholic to make amends.

Not that Mousey had any idea that he had been chosen to play a part in the Great Design. If the truth be told, the only regard Mousey ever paid to Godalmighty was when the door of the flowery dell closed and he was banged up for the night:

– Jesus, God, is this the best you can offer?

Meanwhile, back in celestitude, the Deity Itself gave a Billy Graham smile as it flew over the Bridge Bar, on its way home to Belfast:

– God help us, He told Himself, but the jackeens are a lousy lot, the way they only have faith in Me when it suits them. And that Parable Jones – the things he thinks! If he believed in Me half as much as he believes in himself . . . but, thank God for the prods, for it's their simple faith that keeps Me going . . . for a long time after the split I thought that they'd be terribly left-wing, but, when Cromwell and

Luther shit on the tridentines and turned the peasants over . . . I knew I was secure. Thank God for the Mormons and the Osmonds, for Cliff Richard and the Children of Light, for the KKK, the IRA, the UDA, the UFOs, the Ayatollahs and the PLO.

He savoured the dedication of Ian Kyle Paisley and Billy Graham, and then remembered that He owed a kick in the arse to Noel Coward who was in celestial solitary at the moment for taking the piss out of The Son:

– 'Limbo' the English call it, but I know damned well that it's the nearest thing to hell anybody can experience who hasn't been on bread and water for a while.

Not knowing he was for the high jump, Coward had blotted his copy-book something terrible when commenting on a Billy Graham rally back in 1957:

> In the evening we watched Billy Graham on television . . . He called for converts, for people who were willing to dedicate themselves to Jesus . . . and they began to shuffle self-consciously down the aisles of the Madison Garden . . . Not very many answered the call and I noticed a rather nasty look in his eye and my heart ached for Mrs Billy Graham after the show was over.

– Cynical bastard, said God, but I have the fucker by the hasp of the arse now.

– And yet maybe Coward is right; Billy Graham has said that I use my angels as secret agents. And he goes on to say that I told Abraham that I wanted to burn his son! What sort of a schmuck does he take Me for?

Thinking how odd it was that the Catholics always thought of Him as a pape, God took his leave of Parable and Sally-Anne. He held a sneaking regard for P. J.'s sense of humour, but He knew that the very existence of monotheism depended on the Protestant faith.

He would have loved to have filled Parable's dreams with bands of lambeg-beating Orangemen, but even God doesn't have all that much clout in a place like Dublin. Instead He directed some mendicant folksingers to Wolfe Tone Quay, whispered 'Fuck yeh' in

Parable's ear, and got great satisfaction. With a wistful glance in the direction of the Bridge Bar, He stepped on to a passing cloud nine, and it turned left at the Five Lamps for Belfast.

It was a rotten trick to play on a man who was really an agnostic like Himself; but, be that as it may, only through faith could a good God get the respect He needed to exist on another man's beliefs. Still and all, there was no getting away from it, Parable Jones was a likeable, comical fucker, when all was said and done. He was on the very point of turning the folk singers in the direction of the National Library, but He suddenly remembered that the place was closed and, anyway, the itinerant musicians couldn't read:

– Ah fuck Parable Jones! Let him put up with that awful caterwauling for one evening, I can never get away from the primitive bastards.

Tom Reivey couldn't believe his ears when they started! Banjos, base-fiddles, balalaikas, bones and bowrans: fiddles, mouth-organs, washboards, mandolins, guitars, sitars and pissarts.

They were playing into people's faces, as if under the impression that the general public hears with its eyes. They sang into their own pockets, up their own sleeves, and under their arms. Their dervish-like stance was too wild to be merely frenetic. They didn't seem to stop for anything, even drink; indeed, judging by the amount of pints that were accumulating in front of these meconic minstrels, it might seem, to the casual observer, that gargle-gathering was the object of the exercise.

Tom had almost scratched a hole in the top of his head:

– Where in the nameajazes did they come from, Mousey?

– I'm damned if I know, Tom . . . they weren't there a few minits ago, I could nearly swear to that . . . did you see where they came from, Bobo?

– Folk singers don't need to come from anywhere, Mousey, they are an aberrant apparition insinuated into the ineluctable modality of the audible of innocent bystanders.

– People practising their Joyce again? said Geordie Hinnie.

– Talking about musicians, said Mousey Duggan, who didn't like uninvited interruptions. But there's no persistence like the perseverance that comes from the insistent pedant:

– It's just that I thought your friend was confusing one thing with another.

– Why should he? asked Tom.

– Lots of very bright people have got the wrong end of the stick. For example, even Myles thought that the ineluctable modality of the Dubliner was silence, exile and cunning. Nothing could be farther from the truth.

– Don't patronise Bobo, mister!

– That would be the last thing on my mind, Tom.

– What the hell then d'ye mean when yeh talk about 'bright people'?

– No insult intended, Tom, I do assure you . . . really I was thinking about educated people.

– Educated people? Yeh mean college boys? Sure Bobo here did five years with Brendan Behan, Neil Gould, and Mairtin Cadhain in the Curragh! Can you think of any university that could match the nick?

– I think you don't understand what I mean, Tom.

– Maybe not, but I recognise a bollocks when I come across one.

– No offence meant, Tom, to either you or Mr Bobo . . . all right, sir?

Bobo ignored Geordie Hinnie's outstretched hand:

– Mister, I've been patronised by experts; an arsehole like you wouldn't even get under me skin.

The published poet sneaked back into his soliloquy and Tom returned to the question of the ignorant ethnics:

– Did yeh notice the malevolent look they get around the eyes if they think that you're not listening to them . . . maybe it would be as well to throw them the odd appreciative grin.

Mousey said:

– Be even better to throw them the odd grenade.

– I always live, said Bobo, apropos the folkys, in the hope that when one of them opens a violin case, it will contain nothing more lethal than a Thompson sub-machine gun or a Kalashnikov rifle . . . who's the big fella standin' over Parable, I wonder?

Tom couldn't say, but thought he had the head and disfigured body of a policeman. Mousey asked:

– Who are you, mac . . . what are yeh doin' standin' over our friend?
– 'Who am I', is it? I am Charles Parnell Belton . . . who the hell are you when you're at home?
– I'm Michael Duggan, mister, and I advise yeh not to try anything quare with Parable . . . he's not into that class of thing.
– So you're the redoubtable 'Mousey'? Delighted to meet you, sir. Parable is an old friend and neighbour and he never stops talking about you.

Tom Reivey welcomed Belton to the Bridge Bar, stood him a large whiskey, and advised:

– There are certain guardians of the peace, Mr Belton, who do not wish you well, and it would be a dereliction of my duty as a host, not to warn you . . .
– What in the name of God could the Garda have against me, Mr Reivey . . . I don't pay my taxes like everybody else, and, since I have no car, I never drink and drive.
– Are you presently writing a biography of the late Eamon de Valera?
– Well, I don't think that's a state secret, Mr Reivey . . . nor is it a project to which anybody might take exception.
– You'd be surprised at what some folk object to, Mr Belton.
– Well, my publisher will be pleased that my work evokes such interest.
– Don't laugh it off, Mr Belton . . . the shekooneys may not have the sophistication of Mrs Thatcher when it comes to banning what they don't like, but many a man has wound up mortally censored before now.
– I don't suppose you have any idea of which particular Garda was showing an interest in me?

Mousey said:

– A big ignorant culchie called Detective Matthews.
– *Matthews*? I didn't know he was a gendarme.
– Once a policeman, always a policeman, said Bobo.

Tom advised him to be on his guard and Parable told himself:

– Be on your guard against the Garda! That's damned good! But, how in the name of hell, I wonder, did Charlie Belton get into my dream?

CHAPTER TWENTY-ONE

A Handful of Dust

At the 'Hospice of the Next World', the Second Policeman was pronounced dead. After a cursory examination, obstructed by a nun in silk stockings who was determined to scream an act of contrition into the deceased's left ear, Dr Sean T. O'Kelly said:

– All the signs are that he has suffered a massive heart attack.

Sister Mary Ann McGilligan was fit to be tied:

– You mean he won't have heard my Act of Contrition?

– It's highly unlikely that he would have heard the cannon section of the 1812 played in a cupboard by the massed bands of the Grenadier Guards.

– Well, I can only hope that he was a better example of manhood than most of the men I have encountered, and that he was at least prepared for his last hours.

Johnny Carey, hospital porter extraordinaire, who had been having a kip under a sheet on a slab, rose, and said:

– Amen! *Omnem crede diem tibi diluxisse supremum.*

Sister Mary Ann stared at the working-class wretch who had the temerity to do her thoughts into Latin, and swore to herself that Johnny Carey would have to go. Dr O'Kelly, ignoring the porter's linguistic impertinence, said curtly:

– Get this body prepared for chapel, and, in future, speak only in English and when you're spoken to. I hate you Gaelic Leaguers.

– It was Latin.

– Nonsense! How would a hospital porter know Latin?

– I learned it at mass and benediction.

– Then it's a good job the Latin was stopped.

Having said which, he wrote the established cause of death on a label, slipped it into the plastic card attached to the trolley, and left the mortuary along with Sister Mary Ann McGilligan.

Carey filled a white enamel pail with a mixture of water and formaldehyde and proceeded to sponge down the naked remains. He noticed a blob of dried blood under a fold of skin beneath the dead man's right oxter. On wiping over the clot, he was not surprised to come across the neat incision made by Mousey Duggan's blade:

– Heart attack my fucking arse!

He had the hand-piece of the wall-phone to his ear, and was about to commit his findings to the registrar's office, when his eye caught the deceased's name on Dr O'Kelly's card on the end of the trolley:

– Garda Sergeant Sean Gantly . . . well, well. So that's what a heart attack looks like nowadays.

He put the phone back on to the hook, carefully dried the corpse, and, with difficulty, shrouded it in the regulation brown habit. He stuck cotton wool in every orifice and placed a pair of rosary beads in the breasted hands. Then looking up at the mortuary clock, he realised it was lunchtime.

Johnny's overcoat was hanging on the handle of one of the refrigerated lockers and he took the *Sporting Chronicle* from his left hand overcoat pocket and a packet of tomato sandwiches from the right. He should have placed the Second Policeman naked on a tray and slid him into the wall, but he didn't fancy making him up for chapel in the evening, besides which, he liked a bit of company for lunch. He spread the sporting paper over Sergeant Gantly's legs, and studied form while he munched on his pieces; occasionally throwing the odd remark to the Second Policeman:

– *Auspicium melioris aevi.* That's an old Latin saying, which, in rough translation means, 'Promise of a better age' . . . But you don't stand a chance, Sergeant, not where you're bound, for you're the livin' contradiction of me father's maxim, 'The only good polisman is a dead one'.

After some time he made up his mind what horses to bet; then he put a left-over sandwich back into its plastic bag, promising it to himself with a pint when the racing was finished. Taking off his white coat, he hung it on a locker door and changed into his overcoat:

– If I put a move on I might be able to get to that bettin' shop in Capel Street for the two o'clock.

The horses were just behind the stalls and before he had time to write the slip they were 'under orders'. Carey shouted to Tom Brennan, the settler:

– Gimme a couple of quid on that thing of Eddery's in the first, Tom.

– Himself, or the brother? asked Tom.

– Himself, said Carey.

– D'ye have a whisper for it? asked Sean Daly behind Carey's back.

– Ah, jazes, it's yerself, Sean! No, I just like the look of it; according to the paper it won twice the last time out.

– Is that so? It must be a fuckin' miracle horse then, to be beatin' itself . . .

– Yeh know what I mean.

Paddy Eddery was lying very handy in the stretch and he skated home, to the cheers of the punters.

– Christ! said the poet, you've knocked it off there!

– Well, I suppose I'll get a few quid back if the price is not too short.

– Are yeh joking? It was twenty-five to bloody one!

– With Eddery on its back? Jazes, I hope yer right!

But that's what Tom Brennan figured, and he handed five ten pound notes to Johnny Carey, who, in turn, refusing to look another gift horse in the mouth, put the money in his back pocket and encouraged Daly, without need of much persuasion, to join him in Slattery's pub.

– And what, asked Carey, while they were waiting for their pints to settle, has yeh around these parts, if it's no secret?

Daly took a thirsty slug from the new stout, before answering:

– Trying to pull the divil by the tail. You know they can advertise money as long as they like, but there's not a bank in Dublin would lend a nickel to a bloke who needed it.

– Stop me if I'm tellin' tales out of school but I thought I heard Parable saying that you got an advance on your new book from Harry McGill?

– Don't mention that vile bastard! I was hardly out of his sight when he stopped the fuckin' cheque.

– Jazes, he's a right whore altogether!

– But, the next time I come across him I'll stop his fuckin' breath . . . so I will.

As Carey looked at the seething monster of a rhymester, he felt a shiver – as if somebody was walking over Harry McGill's grave:

– And the bank didn't come across?

Daly shrugged his shoulders and threw his hands apart:

– Did they fuck! It was a new fella, and I really thought I stood a chance, but, when he asked about collateral, and I said that I was a poet with a new book coming out, he fell back in his chair and didn't stop laughing until I was halfway along Ormonde Quay – it's a wonder you didn't hear the cunt when you were coming here.

– Aye, banks are not very kind to those in need.

– They seem to hate poor people more than bank robbers . . . if one is to judge by that shower of thieves who got stuck into Guinness's.

For a moment they contemplated the real owners of James Gate brewery, before agreeing that a man might get a seat on the stock exchange, but it would take a helluva lot more to put him into the untouchables of theft, the aristocracy:

– Not one of the old school was charged, said Johnny Carey, while Sean Daly smiled:

– Surely you don't think that 'Lucky' Lucan was a one off? Still, if I had a mite of the interest on their smallest investment . . .

Carey looked at the big poet and knew that behind the broad smile was a very worried man:

– Yeh don't mind me askin', Sean, but, how much would get you out of trouble?

Daly smiled sadly and told him:

– Hold on to your winnings, old son, it's a few quid more than that I'm needing.

– How much? persisted Carey.

– Christ man, I was hoping the bank would stand me three hundred quid!

– I'll lend it to you, said the hospital porter.

Daly could hardly believe his ears:

– You'll lend me three hundred pounds?

Carey nodded.

– I have it, so you might as well be using it.

Daly didn't know what to say.

– I don't know when I could repay you.

– No hurry. The missus left me a little, and I've been able to put a few quid by. Just give it back to me when you can, OK?

Carey made out a cheque in Daly's name, folded it, and handed it to the big, grateful poet. Sean was the picture of embarrassment, and it was all he could do to retain a weak smile:

– I dunno what to say! True as God I didn't know what I was going to tell the wife. Jesus Christ, but you're a decent bloody man . . . an unworthy thought struck him, but, before he could shame himself, the hospital porter assured him:

– That cheque is as good as pound-notes, ould son, don't you worry.

Grateful tears filled Daly's eyes:

– Would yeh think very badly of me if I went off just now . . . she'll be worried, because she knows what I've been trying to do, and she'll fear the worst when I don't come home quickly.

Carey reassured him.

– I'd think damned badly of you if yeh didn't leave, Sean.

– Straight up?

– I only wish I had my hairpin to go home to. Away with you, for Christ's sake!

Johnny Carey didn't stay long in Slattery's after Daly. Then to Capel Street and left into Ormonde Quay Lower, Bachelors Walk, Eden Quay, Custom House Quay, and to North Wall where he thought to have a drink in the Eagle Bar.

Along the other end of the river, in the opposite direction, ten hours earlier, Tom Reivey was telling the resurrected Parable Jones about the demise of the Second Policeman:

– Outside the back door there! And the size of the chisslers that were goin' through his pockets! Yeh should have seen them kids, Burke and Hare could have taught them nothin'!

– I can't make out who yeh mean at all, Tom: 'Second Policeman'? Who the hell was the first?

– Matthews, said Mousey, the big Mayo bastard – the 'Second Policeman' takes over when the other fella gets too drunk.

– And he was here while I was in? How the hell did I not see him?

– Sure Christ, man, it would have taken you all your time to see a hole on a colander.

– And he died from a heart attack, Mousey?

– A massive heart attack. I was about the first on the scene and I tried to give him the kiss of life, but it wasn't any good.

Parable looked at Mousey's rotten teeth and told himself that it was probably the kiss of life that killed the Second Policeman. Aloud he said:

– Jazes, Mousey, but yeh must have a strong stomach to kiss a policeman.

– Yeh know the ould song, Parable, 'If I can help somebody . . .'

And behind Parable Jones' back the hairy folksingers sang, 'If I can help somebody as I go on my way, then my living will not be in vain . . .' Without turning, Parable Jones asked Tom Reivey:

– What the fuck is that?

CHAPTER TWENTY-TWO

The Dead

How a dead policeman, any more than a live one, could merit a second thought, was beyond Sally-Anne Millington's comprehension. Theirs is not an occupation spoken of in decent society. Policemen did not frequent bridge parties or pubs that kept proper hours. You wouldn't be visiting them in hospital or bidding them the time of day except at night when the bastards stepped out of the shadows to terrify lone women. As a child she had walked home after a birthday party, from Rathgar. She was followed along Highfield Road by a man, his steps quickening as she walked faster; then, with relief, she saw a member of the Gardai in a doorway, big and powerful and safe in his great coat. In fear and trembling it was with relief that she told him of the man following her, all he had said was:

– And what makes you think you're any safer with me, honey? She had never walked abroad at night, alone, since.

But, police apart, she was sick and tired of the dead and talk of the dead. And, indeed, to a child of the 'Pope' O'Reilly, after a youth spent frolicking in graveyards, humour is less than funny when it is necromantic.

Worse still when her father and that boring old fart of a hospital porter, Johnny what's his name, got together.

Anyway, it was four o'clock in the morning, she had to be in work by nine, and there was no sign that the Bridge Bar was ready to give up the ghost.

Her mind was alert in the after drink; she was on a boozer's high, and randy. She hadn't been laid for what seemed like ages, and, now that Parable was on another talking jag, it seemed as if the only thing she was going to cuddle up to was the vibrator. Listening to P. J.

holding forth, Sally-Anne knew that she would always be attracted to his constantly fresh way of looking at things . . . if only she could have gotten his intellect between her legs.

The young ones were wonderful and awful, and, when they tried to act sophisticated, Sally-Anne felt like screaming:

– Shut yer fucking mouth! It's your clever big cock I'm after, not your stupid little mind!

She looked over at Parable who was now on about Kafka, and she knew that he wouldn't be riding to hounds for a while yet. Sally-Anne sipped a left-over whiskey and was nauseated by the taste of her own bad breath. How she longed to get home for even an hour's kip, but Parable was in full flow:

– Kafka believed that God did not want him to write; said that literature was a reward for service to the devil.

– Kafka was a . . . began Geordie Hinnie, before being cut off by Parable, in his prime:

– Kafka was a fucking nut! A nut who had great things to say. When he stops talking about 'descending to the dark powers' and tells us that 'The writer is the scapegoat of mankind because he allows man to enjoy a sin without guilt', Kafka is bloody brilliant!

Sally-Anne told herself that Parable's mind was preoccupied with the sin of sin which he saw as one person deliberately offending against another. Jesus, it was hard being his mistress! How bloody frustrating. Maybe it was the same for men. She must ask Jack. But then he was probably the man of the marriage. Christ Almighty, she hoped so. Surely he wasn't a big Jessie? Though, on the other hand, when she remembered how much she enjoyed it, maybe he was having the best of both worlds.

She wondered how much of Jack's life was natural, and how much was a turn-off from her and her problems. The main hitch had been his desire for a family. She hadn't wanted kids, because motherhood wouldn't allow her to work, and independence meant a great deal to Sally-Anne. So her whole existence was dominated by the mensuration of menstruation.

She wanted Parable because he wanted the same things as her; he wanted to come without any comeback, and he wanted a woman who could stand her round. He had no hang-ups about contraception, though he wouldn't have conspired at a miscarriage – much as he loved saying that Jessie Helms is the one great argument in favour of abortion:

– Kafka, Parable was saying, told us that life was too short for humanity to have separate worlds that cannot make themselves understood by one another.

– That doesn't mean that he was obsessed with death . . .

– Only in so far as death is part of life. He doesn't want any separateness . . .

– You mean 'separation', suggested Geordie, rather clumsily.

– I mean no such thing! In the story of Hunter Gracchus, for example, Kafka says, 'My death barge lost its way – a wrong turn of the rudder, a moment's inattention on the part of the guide, a distraction because of the breathtaking loveliness of my native land . . .' That shows that Kafka doesn't see death as separate from life.

Sally-Anne admired Parable at this stage, but she knew that one or two more halves would reduce him to the equal of Geordie Hinnie, and that she didn't want to happen.

– Tom, she begged, give that cab of yours another ring, please.

Parable turned on her:

– I hope I'm not the one you have in mind for your taxi!

– For God's sake, Paddy, it'll be comin' out through your ears.

Parable couldn't resist playing to the gallery:

– Well, that'll be a change, what? For it's already coming out through at least two other places I can think of . . .

Charlie Belton was simply trying to make peace:

– Don't let him think that you're acting like his wife, Sally-Anne.

She said straight into his face.

– Just you get one thing straight, I'm not his wife! I'm his fucking mistress! I'm not the one he sleeps with; I'm the one he stays awake with: and I'm certainly not the poor cow who washes the shit off his underpants.

Charlie was tempted to respond, but the angry look in Sally-Anne's eye made him think better of it. On the pretext of going to the jacks, he went home. Parable had forgotten his anger with Sally-Anne because the published poet remarked on how Kafka had dissociated himself from both Judaism and Christianity. Apropos of which, Geordie Hinnie asked:

– Is it appropriate, then, to wish a Jew a 'Happy Christmas'?

– More so, I should think, said Parable, than to wish him a 'Happy Easter'.

With a screeching of brakes, the taxi arrived and Parable, in mid-sentence, was bundled into the back seat by Tom, Bobo, and Mousey Duggan. Sally-Anne jumped in beside the driver who asked:

– Where to, love?

– Rathmines Road . . . corner of Church Avenue, Sally-Anne answered, and slept, seated, until aroused by the taxi-man.

The house in Rathmines was big and ugly with a preservation order on it. Despite conservation, it had seen better days. They stood, Parable leaning on the taxi-driver and Sally-Anne banging on the grinning door-knocker. The sound seemed to carry for mile after mile in the early morning silence of the late-rising Rathmines. The driver asked quietly:

– Have yeh no key, at all?

– D'ye think, mac, that if I had a key, I'd be knockin' hell out of my father's front door.

– I only thought . . .

– My father won't keep us long because he's probably working already or he'll have to get up for a piss.

The taxi-man had not previously heard a resident of Rathmines, and certainly not the female of the species, swear before. He had no intention of having heard one now. He decided to ignore the aberration:

– There's nothing like being up with the lark, I always think.

After an eternity, the door was opened to them by a tall hunched man, who might have been any age between palaeolithic and neolithic. He carried in one hand a lump hammer, and, in the other, a cold chisel. His white frock coat was covered in a fine dust, and, on the brim of the crown of his wide Panama hat, he boasted the legend, 'I. N. R. I.':

– You and Parable are early, daughter.

Involuntarily the driver muttered, almost beneath his breath:

– Early? In the middle of the bloody night! But the 'Pope' O'Reilly could hear the mating call of the Brobdingnagian unicorn, so, after the manner of the famous poet, the sculptor cast a cold eye on the horseman, while addressing Sally-Anne:

– I wish that the working class wouldn't feel that they have to behave like the gobshites their bosses take them for!

To the driver he said:

– How, in the name of the long suffering jazes, can it be the middle of the night when it's the middle of the morning?

The working class, according to the media, boasts more than its fair share of fools, but the cabbie was not such a gobshite as to argue with any man holding crazy ideas and a two-pound lump hammer. With the merest suggestion of a bow to Sally-Anne, he grabbed a fiver from her outstretched hand, replaced it with a single pound coin, fled back to his taxi, and into the direction from whence he had come. The 'Pope' O'Reilly, staring in the wake of his celerity, said:

– D'ye know, child, I have a spare sundial that'd do that fella fine, or maybe he's not that advanced yet . . . but sure, every cripple has his own way of walkin' . . . let's get your cripple inside.

Sally-Anne went off to bed; Parable grunted: the 'Pope' smiled as he half dragged the semi-conscious writer into his studio, and said:

– Well, ould son, it seems it's me for the hammer and chisel, and you for the couch. Ah, how sharper than the serpent's tooth it is to have a daughter who doesn't give a fuck!

– You can say that again, Holy Father.

The 'Pope' O'Reilly looked around the room at his masterpieces, and was content. There were angels on crosses, and crosses without angels; magnificent marble wreaths with flowers that bloomed only on gravestones and with inscriptions about the deceased that would have been libellous had the dead been alive.

He knew that his fellow rock chasers didn't look kindly on what he was doing; but he had known in his first week at art school that he wasn't going to be a Rodin or an Epstein. Because he liked the feel of stone he opted for the outside life of Henry Moore and settled for what he could get. There is nothing much more outdoor than a graveyard.

The 'Pope' O'Reilly stood on a small platform in front of a huge block of grey granite. He made a few chalk marks here and there, eyed them against the light on three sides, and began to tap gently the cold chisel with the hammer. The reiteration of the incessant beat echoed in Parable's mind, and, gradually, its senselessness sent him to sleep.

CHAPTER TWENTY-THREE

All for Hecuba

At Bryden MacWilliams' examination before the Grand Order of the Knights of Columbanus, the heretic refused to plead to the charges laid against him. Instead, he agreed with Joyce that the Irish Catholic Church was '. . . the scullery-maid of Christendom' and incessantly iterated the hymns of benediction, in relentless reiteration:

O salutaris hostia,
Quae caeli pandis ostium;
Bella premunt hostilia,
Da robur, fer, auxilium.

Some common members of the lodge told him to shut his stupid mouth; the lay Provincial asked if he would be so good as to give ear to the complaints made in relation to his conduct:

– I'll take no part in your trial, I will not dignify this court martial with recognition.

– It's not a court martial . . . it's not a trial at all.

– Very well: your accusations. The very Dublin saint, in whose name this order was founded, was himself indicted before a Synod of French bishops because he was more religious than them. Hail Columbanus!

– This is a hearing, not an indictment. We simply wish to know why you will not obey the wishes of the Holy Father.

– I am loyal to Vatican II!

– But you are not loyal to the Church.

– Who said that? I am more loyal to the Church than the present Vatican Council!

– Then why are you writing an anti-Catholic work?

– My book will provide solace for countless millions.

– Aye, of Orangemen!

But he would not relent his Latin benediction, despite ribald repartee, that included derogatory remarks such as:

– *Paisley's proselytiser*, and

– *Monkey nuts for monkeys!* (A reference to the common belief among Northern Irish popeheads that Protestants receive monkey gland injections in an attempt to make them as good in bed as Catholics):

Uni Trinoque Domino
Sit sempiterna gloria,
Qui vitam sine termino
Nobis donet in patria.

As frequently as they liked they could call him a 'Lefebvre Leper'; it rolled off Bryden MacWilliams' back like Thames dew off the hanging corpse of Roberto Calvi:

Tantum ergo, Sacramentum
Veneremur cernui:
Et antiquum documentum
Novo cedat ritui . . .

It was on to that last simple line that Father Jesmond latched:

– See, hoist with your own petard! '*Novo cedat ritui*' actually means, 'the newer rite is here'!

– And, what about it? asked Bryden.

– Don't you see that the very benediction means that the Church is always open to change?

– Dammit all, man, the whole idea of the Latin mass was so that the service would remain a mystery to the entire congregation. It isn't right that simple folk should comprehend the sacrament.

Then the Council went into closed session at which it was decided that Brother MacWilliams should be shorn of his sash. Bryden, ignoring their deliberations, intoned the entire benediction in Latin until he was tapped on the shoulder by a member of the newly formed 'Irish Intelligence-Gathering Unit' who asked simply, but firmly:

– Care to come along with me, sir?

Outside Sacred Heart House there awaited two cars and five plain-clothes members of the Garda Siochana. As Bryden MacWilliams was being shoved into the lead car, he screamed at a passing Johnny Carey:

– I'm being arrested by the secret police, tell my sister Julia to let my publishers in London know.

– I'll do that, Bryden, shouted Johnny Carey, but Det. Sergeant Matthews, of the Irish Intelligence-Gathering Unit, ordered his minions:

– We'll have that commie fucker as well!

And with little ceremony, and less circumspection, they bundled Carey into the second of the two cars.

The evening sun was shimmering on the handless face of Tom Reivey's gutless clock, inside the glass case of which, he displayed the motto, 'NO TICK'.

The time was, however, well recorded along the Liffey, by a campanology of chimes, from a benison of bells, booming a Catholic benediction on Protestants, Jews, Muslims, Hindus, agnostics, atheists and anti-Christs alike. Joseph Wilmot, thespian, corrected his turnip, clicked back its nickel cover, and told himself that it was twenty minutes before six p.m.

Joe had been home for a fast feed, a quick kip, and a read of the actor's bible, *The Stage*. Sleep starvation had not been the actor's biggest worry recently; he was, in the euphemism of his trade, *resting*. He liked the Bridge Bar in the adolescence of the day, for the young soldiers came and were easily impressed.

And, too, Reivey, like some urban vampire, eschewed the sun. The running of the pub before lighting-up time was in the hands of his uncle and aunt, Padraig and Assumpta Dwyer, who, because they only did the day-job, hadn't yet gotten over the country tradition of offering hospitality to those in need. Many a cheque rejected by Reivey at night, stared obstinately at him from the evening till.

An innocence of rookies, recently released from training at the Curragh Camp, and now seconded to Collins Barracks which is situated just over the wall from the Bridge Bar, listened, fascinated, to dulcet tones such as they previously believed belonged to the mystery of the silver screen. Oh, yes forsooth! Far from plays and players had the would-be warriors been reared, and farther yet from the world of elocution and illusion, while tented on the plains of Kildare, they had lived in the land of sheep, shite and soldiers.

The actor was in his element, and the defenders of the Gael thought him the cleverest man they had ever met – which he probably was since they would not be aware that the cleverest men in the world wrote his scripts.

Wilmot was on about matters military, and the boy-soldiers clung to his every word, never even hearing the cynical remarks of Padraig Dwyer and the few old-sweat NCOs who muttered on the periphery:

– Ould soldier, ould shite; young soldier, gobshite.

But, for the young and easily led, there is no way that the tales of Troy were to go a-begging, especially from the lips of Joe Wilmot, a consummate actor who hears only the sound of applause:

– The Trojan horse was more than a symbol; it was a warning to humanity. 'Beware of gifts bearing Greeks' is not all that it seems. Those who remember the guile of El Greco, while forgetting the slain, do not appreciate the significance of the parable.

When the young men heard how Hector's mother had put out the eyes of Polymestor, and murdered his two sons in revenge over the death of Polydorus, they agreed unanimously that 'Mrs Hecuba' was:

– Fuckin' right!

They also felt that Euripides was:

– One real war correspondent!

Lysistrata didn't grab them because 'war is a man's game', and the threat of being denied sex by Mrs Thatcher was a sanction with which most could abide:

– The poor ould *Belgrano* never stood a chance. Like shootin' fish in a fuckin' barrel.

On the edge of the vulgar expletive, the evening bell to remind Catholics of the incarnation once more, rang in Halston Street Chapel, only beating Adam and Eve's by a short head, and Radio Eireann by a nose.

At the far end of the counter, Assumpta Dwyer laid aside her knitting, turned up the wireless to deafening decibels, and screamed politely at the customers:

– We'll have no drinkin', talkin' politics, thinkin' impure thoughts, or usin' bad language, durin' the Angelus. And, as the bared, bowed heads bent to pray, Padraig Dwyer donned the protest cap he kept behind the bar for such occasions, and told everybody:

– She'll be servin' yis with indulgences soon!

But everybody knew Padraig; otherwise they would have kicked the bejazes out of him in honour of Our Blessed Mother.

Wilmot, as you probably are aware, is well-known for his immaculate sense of timing, so, if he is going to be upstaged by Jesus, he can make humility appear to be another curtain call. Indeed, no less a man than Parable Jones has said that Joe could steal the show from MacLiammoir with his reading of the Phoenix Park bye-laws. He can say nothing with the consummate ease of an Ayckbourn or a Stoppard and has moved audiences to tears with a rendition of *Krapp's Last Tape*.

When the supplications had ceased, and came the post-prayer pregnant pause; taking in as many vacant visages as possible, Wilmot remarked:

– There's a certain validity in every truth . . .

The listeners were not too sure of what he meant, if anything; but, people who are prepared to pray at the peal of a bell, or willing to wait on the wonts of a woeful woman, are hardly likely to dispute opinions expressed in the accent of the old school tie:

– We actors made the world safe for our fellow citizens. Indeed, one of our illustrious fellows took the monarchs and their minions, and laid bare the hypocrisy of kings and queens on the stage of their own politics! It was the Bard himself, who showed us that there was never an absolute ruler, but that person was either mad, bad or sad. The madness of Hamlet, the sadness of Lear, the innocent guilt of Othello, and the badness of Lady Macbeth . . .

As they listened in awed ignorance, Wilmot demanded of a very young private:

– Think on it! What does Desdemona mean to you?

– Des who? asked the startled youth in an ignorance that the actor didn't comprehend. Wilmot decided that the boy was being a 'smart ass', and, in scarifying tongue, he admonished him:

– You and your likes deserve to be left where Jesus left the Jews, or where He told His only brother, James, to await His return – outside the tomb.

A sergeant-cook trading food for drink, took a pint from Padraig Dwyer and exception to Joe Wilmot:

– Are you tellin' us, mister, that the Blessed Virgin had more than one child?

The actor cleared his throat, wiped his nose with a green handkerchief, stood in stiff theatrical pose and said:

– I am!

– And, was Joseph the father?

– No. The father of James was Alphaeus.

Padraig Dwyer was intrigued:

– Have you any idea what you're saying, Joe? D'ye know what that makes of the Virgin Mary?

The mad laughing eyes of Dwyer caused the actor to reflect on his perilous position. Unless a miracle happened, he could see, in the drink-pious faces of his audience, the instrument of his impending doom. Salvation came from the most unlikely quarter; Assumpta Dwyer, anxious not to have questioned that in which she unquestioningly believed, asked:

– But, both of the children would have been by Immaculate Conception, Mr Wilmot?

The half-drowned actor clung to the straw of her Catholic contradiction:

– Is there another way, madam, that Our Blessed Lady's Womb might be inseminated and remain unstained?

Padraig Dwyer was lost in admiration. He whispered in the relieved thespian's ear:

– Begod, Joseph, only a bloody lion could have extricated himself from the cage of those all-forgiving Christians! Only a lion like yourself!

CHAPTER TWENTY-FOUR

Little Things Mean a Lot

Mary Belton could hear the lavatory bowl flushing. Charlie would now wash his hands. He would brush his teeth and gargle gratingly. He would belch loudly and fart discreetly as if the particular orifice decided etiquette. His wife, meanwhile, had lit the grill to prepare his punishment – thick pork sausages and rashers of greasy bacon. The nearly-fried eggs – *fetus interruptus*.

It was with the greatest reluctance that Charlie took leave of the lavatory. He clung, desperately, for support to last night's copy of the *Evening Press* that he had bought on his way past the Ballast Office. Then he had been, happily, three sheets in the wind. For an instant, the taxi-driver had thought him not drunk but daft, for, having entered the cab, he had craned his neck to stare at the Ballast Office parapet. The hackney man had felt disposed to ask at what he was looking:

– According to *Ulysses*, there was a timepiece placed on the top of the Ballast Office so that it could have been read with binoculars from across O'Connell Bridge . . .

– Yer talking about the book and not the Greek?

– Well, I doubt if Homer was into watches . . . he certainly never saw the Ballast Office.

– Would it not have been simpler for Joyce to carry his on a chain?

– It wasn't Joyce's watch. It was a sort of advertisment for a firm of jewellers . . . d'ye like Joyce?

– I suppose I can take him or leave him; on the one hand he gets graveyards a bad name, but, on the other, he creates so much necessary literary confusion.

– How d'ye mean?

– Well, every guy that ever learned to read, says that he understands *Ulysses* and *Finnegans Wake* no bother . . .

– And you don't think they do?

– Many of them have never even read Joyce.

– Chancers, you mean?

– Not them all. Joyce is a bit like AIDS, yeh can't help picking him up. There has been so much word of mouth about his work that folk can't avoid knowing something, but most people have either never read the man, or else they have read him wrongly.

– *Most* seems to be somewhat of an exaggeration.

– Well, at the time they were opening Gogarty's Martello Tower as a Joyce museum, I ran an American professor out to Sandycove . . .

– The Yanks know their Joyce.

– Do they fuck! As Parable Jones says, 'they know as little as everybody else, but they treasure it more'.

– Did Parable say that?

– Either him or his ghost . . . anyway I took this guy by way of the Vico Road, and at once he said, 'So that's the relevance of the reference to "vicus of recirculation" in *Finnegans Wake*.' Imagine, a bloody professor, and he'd never heard about the Italian philosopher Vico!

Uneasily, Belton replied:

– Imagine.

And, even when they reached Belton's house the driver wouldn't leave the question alone:

– The whole bloody book is founded on a philological premise of Giambattista Vico, sure every stupid bastard knows that . . .

– Oh indeed, the dogs in the street.

The cab had stopped and Belton was a hostage; the back door had child-locks and no way was the driver going to let Charlie out until he had made his point:

– Take the whole question of life according to Vico; who as you know preceded Marx and his theory of dialectical materialism in which the world is in a constant state of change, by a hundred years . . .

– Oh indeed.

– To Vico it was logical to use science to unite the study of history and the social sciences through philology and philosophy as a demonstration of general truth . . .

– Sure what else!

– Dialectical materialism and the Viconian Cycle are, in themselves, an explanation of eternal life on the one hand and a contradiction of Christian dogma, on the other . . .

– That's fascinating . . . but the wife will be waiting up and . . .

– D'ye know that nearly every little river and stream in the world is mentioned in *Finnegans Wake*.

– I wouldn't doubt you . . .

– It has to do with the nature of confluence . . . all the rivers running everywhere into the sea from whence all life originated . . . but, we had better not get into that or we'll be here all night . . .

Charlie remembered thinking to himself that maybe Dublin taxi-drivers should be in some other trade. This morning he was certain that they should. His head was bursting and he was sure that it was because of conversation concentrated at a victim in a confined space. Mary was talking:

– You were rightly scuttered last night.

– I had a few jars.

– And a few jars took you all that time? It's a wonder you came home at all!

– Is it a capital offence now for a man to stand in a bar with a few friends?

– I'm surprised that you didn't bring them home with you . . . to see us in the workhouse all the sooner.

– Ah, sure it's the poor heart that never rejoices and we'll be a long time dead.

He put a cajoling arm around her, but she shook herself free:

– Jesus, Mary and Joseph! The smell of stale drink and vomit! How you live inside yourself the morning after, is a puzzle to me. You've spent all that you borrowed, I suppose?

Charlie's abiding dislike was unpleasantness. He'd go to hell for good manners. He was a firm believer in consideration for others, but the 'morning-after' Mary seemed to provoke his most irritable comments:

– If you're not afraid of contacting AIDS or something, put your hand in my inside jacket pocket and you'll find every penny intact, in my wallet. To quote that great Englishman of French letters, 'not a penny more: not a penny less'.

Mary fingered the soft calf leather of Charlie's wallet. It had been made by her nephew, Tom, who had had plenty of time for that when interned by Mr de Valera. It was a vulgar piece, really: carved Celtic scrolls and the little prayer under the ugly 'freedom fighter', *Let me carry a sword for Ireland, Lord*. Parable had been less than impressed:

– Swords, eh? Against MIs: Gustaves: and Kalashnikovs? If Ireland doesn't mind, I think I'll wait to hear the result on the radio.

Mary was relieved to find a roll of notes, but her voice couldn't resist the bitter word:

– And who did you borrow from, or cash a cheque with? You must have stung somebody because you're more often at a public house counter than most barmen.

– Well, if that doesn't beat Banagher! There's no way a chap could win with you, is there? I could turn me arse into an umbrella and still get my fucking feet wet!

– Less of the histrionics, Charlie. All I'm asking is where did yeh get the money to drink all day yesterday? I need to know so that I know who to repay, when the time comes.

Charlie sat in the easy chair by the gas cooker and contemplated the floor. He had one shoe on, and the other he held in his right hand. His stomach was daring him to bend. Instead, he looked up; the suggestion of a glint in otherwise dead eyes:

– I was the guest of that honourable body of men, the Dublin Bookmakers Association. In other words, I had two five to one shots, an eleven to four, an even money, and if the other cripple hadn't been arrested for loitering, I would not yet be back to this place that people think there is no place like, and those people may be fucking well right!

The phone rang. Mary answered Jeannie Jones' *Hello*:

– Parable? No . . . he hasn't been here in I don't know how

long . . . No, he's not out with Charlie; he's here beside me . . . Out all night? My fella? Not bloody likely! I'd cut the legs from under him . . . Ah for God's sake, Jeannie, why apologise? Not at all . . . not the slightest bother.

She put the phone down. Charlie was angry:

– Why the hell did you have to say that? I bet you've landed poor ould Parable right in the shit! How d'ye know he wasn't going to tell her that he was out with me?

– He's not out with you. You know where he is. His wife knows where he is. I know where he is . . .

– Don't take it so personally.

– Who's taking it personally? Why the hell should I care where he is?

– You could've fooled me, then.

– It's just the vulgarity of the situation that offends me. Serves him right if he's caught. Its disgusting so it is, a man of nearly sixty going out with a young girl. The 'Pope' O'Reilly should know how obscene it is.

– Obscene?

– Certainly obscene; Parable is at least twice Sally-Anne's age. What can he see in her?

– That I should be so lucky, said Charlie as he banged the hall-door behind him.

Belton made his way towards town, agreeing with everybody that it was a fine morning thank God that was holding the promise of a nice, soft day. The sight of the ragged news vendor, outside the chapel, reminded him that he hadn't lifted his *Irish Times* from the hallway. The tabloid *Irish Press* would be better for the top deck of the bus anyway; not too much to distract a person's mind from other things, and the print big enough to please a man's vanity.

The newsagent was busy mouthing the responses to the mass that was being diffused on the tannoy system ringing the chapel front. The fucker was terrified that he might die from the affects of impure thought, or lose any customers.

Charlie's stomach was at him, his patience was fraught and his temper frayed. And yet, he tried to rationalise his feelings – was he angry with the news vendor or with himself?

It is a terrible state in the affairs of man, the morning after the night before. The much vaunted consciousness of Shaw is no longer dulled. Perception is at its peak. Man can descry the suggestion of communication in a sea of verbiage. To drink a little more at this stage would carry a chap, into jig-time; after which it's the DTs. And yet the present crystal clarity is almost too much.

The news-monger was occupying God's room, but Charlie didn't want to think of Theo in His space or he in Theo's. Nor did he want to become preoccupied with thoughts of Jeannie in Parable Jones' shape of things to come. He just had no intention of thinking of God as if He and Parable Jones were the only thoughts worth thinking. God and Parable Jones are not the only concern of mankind. Nobody is as big as that; nobody ever had been; not even de Valera or his Catholic friend, Charles de Gaulle:

– You wanted the *Press* sir? Sorry about that, but this is the month's mind for the mother . . . buried four weeks ago today . . .

– Oh, I am sorry to hear that.

He handed the newspaper to Belton, counted the change into his hand, saying as he did so:

– She had a fair innin's, sir, but thanks all the same.

Charlie mused that it was funny how death and disaster brings people together, and he was thinking how Parable Jones might have used that interim, when his soliloquy was disturbed by a tap on the shoulder accompanied by the request:

– Would you care to come along with me, sir?

CHAPTER TWENTY-FIVE

Mac The Knife

Kevin Duggan, known to his friends as Rocky, kissed his son, Damien, and watched until he crossed safely over Church Street on his way to school. Just then, Rocky waved to his brother, Michael, who approached from the opposite direction. The brothers stood together at the doorway until Damien was lost to view, having turned into North Brunswick Street.

In the kitchen, Kevin breakfasted on rasher sandwiches and tea. From the gas cooker, Mousey picked up an aluminium teapot that was gently simmering as it sat on a low jet:

– This long made?

– It'll support your weight, anyway. Been stewin' there for half an hour, at least.

– That's the way I like it.

He poured himself a helping of tea into a big earthenware mug, and, dosing it with sugar and milk, he sat to the table, stirring the copper-coloured beverage as he collected his thoughts:

– Did yeh go to work last night?

– What do you think?

– Try Nassau Street?

Kevin beamed with delight. He placed his half-eaten sandwich on the arm of his chair, stood upright, and, from under his seat cushion, removed a canvas portmanteau, plump. Emptying the contents of the bag on the table, he watched his brother's face for an expected reaction. Mousey gave a long low whistle as there poured forth a veritable treasure trove. There were leather wallets, billfolds, purses and pouches of every description – all bulging fit to burst. Mousey was astonished:

– Jesus, Mary and Joseph! Is there anybody in Dublin left with a deuce?

Rocky basked in the glow of his brother's satisfaction:

– These millenniums are bloody great! They should make them an annual thing.

– They only come every thousand years.

– More's the pity. Christ! the tourists that are packing the city and the places they keep their bread, they shouldn't be let out without guide dogs . . .

– Did ye work it with Annie?

– No better woman for the dip and dump. She came towards me as I bumped each mark. But it was a bloody sin the way they were inviting us to clip them. God, she's a gem of a girl!

– I always had the idea that you'd marry well; but Annie is the quality: no doubt about that. She's not home yet?

– She shouldn't be long. Just down to Halston Street: she likes to say a little prayer to St Anthony.

– I thought he was the guy who found things for people?

– Well, she couldn't dispute that.

Mousey sorted the currency into countries and denominations. Then he counted it and made a note on several bank bags he had brought with him. He wasn't too sure about the exchange rate for lire and drachmas, but he was happy that, with the state of the dollar, there wasn't too much American about:

– Even as shaky as it is, we won't get the full whack because the banks are such robbin' bastards! Still, it's good to see that the dollar has settled down to nearly two for one; it's been over-valued for bloody years.

– Christ, not half! Last year during the rugby international season me and Annie thought we were workin' for nothin'.

They agreed that it evened things out, now that the punt was down in favour of the dollar; it meant that the Yankee visitors were getting a squarer deal. Mousey said:

– Parable was tellin' me that, when he was a kid, there were four dollars to the pound . . . only Englishmen were worth pluckin'.

Kevin thought for a while before saying:

– How is it that the likes of him talks to the likes of us?

– Well, most fellas in his game are not like the rest of the hoi polloi. Parable is interested in other people and their occupations.

– He knows what we do then?

– Oh yeah.

– All of it?

– Of course! He knows that you handle the dippin' and I look after the livestock.

– He must be an understandin' bloke.

– Oh indeed. Only recently I was apologisin' for me profession, and he said, 'Don't mention it, Mousey, sure the only difference between you and Mrs Thatcher's father is the fuckin' shop. Made me feel good that, knowing that me and a prime minister came from the same background. By the way, he says that he'd be interested in a word processor if one was to fall off a lorry . . .

– What's a word processor?

– How the fuck would I know . . . a sort of highclass typewriter, I think . . . just read the labels.

– George Colley says he's a nut.

– Who's a nut?

– Parable Jones.

– And who the fuck is George Colley to say if a guy is a nut? George Colley couldn't read a book, let alone write one.

– He makes up whole books? Jazes, that's somethin'.

– He's writin' one just now about Dublin in the millennium . . . but don't mention it to anybody, he doesn't trust other writers, only me.

– Jazes, that's some compliment, to say that the only one he would trust not to steal from him is a fuckin' thief . . .

– Well, he obviously knows who'll keep a secret . . .

– And he's not cracked?

– Oh, I'm not sayin' that . . . he's certainly well to the Kildare side . . . but then most clever people are a bit round the bend. Joe Wilmot says that there's only a hair's breadth dividing genius from insanity . . .

– Who's Joe Wilmot?

– Joe is an actor and he is a fuckin' nut. Parable asked him which side of the line he thought he himself was on.

– And, would he talk about ordinary things, this Parable Jones?

– Ordinary things? He can talk about anything under the sun. And he makes everything interesting because of the way he has of looking at the world.

– Everything?

– Even the Bible. There he was on one day about some geezer called Moab.

– Moab? Are yeh sure he didn't mean Noah?

– There's more things in the Bible besides water and the fuckin' Ark. This Moab had a crowd of horny daughters who got him pissed out of his mind one night and tricked him into ridin' them . . .

– For fuck sake! He's not sayin' that the Bible is about things like that?

– No, but there's things like that in it.

– Moab? He even sounds like a dirty ould bastard! To do that to his own daughters!

– It wasn't his fault; the daughters got him so steamboats that he didn't know what the fuck he was doin'.

– Well, that's a likely fuckin' story. Jazes, he was a cute old cunt. But that couldn't be in the Bible . . .

– It certainly is; every line and chapter.

– No wonder the Church doesn't want us to read it . . . I wonder how yeh'd get a copy . . .

– Buy one, of course.

– Yeh mean it's not banned?

– The Bible? How the fuck could anybody ban the Bible – there'd be a religious revolution!

– Jazes, if the Pope ever reads it!

– He has read it, that's why he doesn't want to let the rest of us get our hands on it.

– And, has yer man got a really dirty mind, then?

– Parable? I've known him one helluva long time and I've never heard him tell a dirty story.

– Doesn't even swear?

– Oh, he can lord mayor with the best, but not half as much as most; he has more words you see, to talk with. Then he doesn't speak of swearin'; he talks about using the vernacular.

– That means a language that's common to particular folk, right?

– Yeah. Christ, you're clued in!

– It was a question on one of them quiz shows the other mornin'.

– Very educational, them things. Well, Parable says that the rich have their vernacular swearing where they use words like 'damn' and 'bloody', but that of the poor is different from person to person . . .

– Different?

– Well, really holy poor people, or the ones with good jobs in Guinness', say feck instead of fuck and bejapers instead of bejazes . . . Parable says that they are really offensive because their swearing is intentional and well thought out.

– Jazes, he's a clever cunt, isn't he? Where did you meet him – at the Bridge?

– Long before that. I knew him up in the shovel.

– In Mountjoy! Was he a lag?

– Yeah, only he was doin' time for politics.

– George Colley was right so, he is a fuckin' nut!

– Well, I'll tell yeh somethin' for nothin'. When a lot of our fraternity were in the nick, and the Irish-Irelanders were too grand to speak to us, it was Parable Jones who crossed the exercise yard to ask if he could be of any help.

– His own crowd wouldn't have liked that.

– Well, Parable told us that we were unreasonable to expect folk like them to mix with folk like us. They could blow up hundreds, or steal millions. We were penny-ante . . .

– It must have been a real education.

– The only one I ever got . . . he even taught me how to read . . . and I wasn't the only one. But the other crowd!

– Yeah, I always heard that the IRA were a stuck-up shower of shit.

– Not Parable. Sure when our poor mother passed on, I knew less than nuthin'. Parable it was who learned me . . .

– What d'ye mean 'passed on'? Yeh always told me that she went to Manchester with her fancy man . . .

– Well, it's a nicer way to say it, in case the kids or the nuns were around. Anyway, have you ever been in Manchester?

– I'm glad yeh told me about Parable, but it's strange that yeh never mentioned before that yeh knew him up in the 'Joy'.

– Not 'knew' him, Rocky. I didn't say that I knew him. I said he taught me how to read . . . me and a lot of others.

– And what did he get out of it?

– Not a light! Said that he was a prisoner like everybody else. Saw nobody any different. Said that legal terrorists were as dangerous as illegal ones, and that if yeh were bombed by the state or the IRA neither you nor anybody else would ever be able to tell the difference.

– Jazes! He's a dangerous cunt if I ever heard of one . . . he needed lockin' up.

– Yeah, I know that. Thinkin' like his threatens everything decent people stand for. Still, he's an old mate . . . and I won't hear a word said against him.

Mousey put the English currency into his outside greatcoat pockets. He handed the dollars and the other foreign currency to his brother:

– When Annie gets back from the chapel tell her to put her glads on and take this bit of gear up to Charlie Ainscough. Make sure it's all counted because you can't trust investment brokers. Tell Ainscough to put it into Manchester Ship. I have a red hot tip for that. Anything else?

– Not that I can think of at the moment . . .

– Oh, yeah, I knew there was somethin'. The credit cards? How much battery acid will yeh need?

– None.

– Have yeh some left?

– No.

– And how are yeh goin' to get the owners' names off? Yeh can't use them as they are or you and Annie will be nicked.

– I told Annie to burn them.

– Are yeh out of yer tiny bleedin' mind?

– There was this programme on telly the other night. It was all about a new electronic machine that shows up the slightest alteration on a card or a cheque . . . It's too risky for us, Michael, with the kids and all. No way could me and Annie do porridge now.

– We'll be worse off than the nurses soon. How the hell do they expect a man to make a crust with their new machines for this and new machines for that? Still, they'll never bring them into the stock exchange, and I suppose that must be somethin'.

Mousey put an arm around his brother and hugged him roughly. He went through the hall-door with just a winked farewell to Rocky and turned left into North King Street. He hadn't thought the death of the Second Policeman worth discussing. Policemen were dying every minute of the day, every day of the week. Indeed, in the other end of the country, dead policemen were almost a way of life.

CHAPTER TWENTY-SIX

No Religion for a Gentleman

It was the midday sun, more than the hammering, that woke Parable Jones. The sun was reflected by a green block of Connemara marble straight into his eyes. For an instant he thought about Joyce distinguishing between refraction and reflection, but really: there's a time and place for *Ulysses*. He stretched out his left leg, feeling for his wife, encountered only the back of the couch, and realised where he was. Parable raised himself slightly so that his head was out of the line of the second-hand sun.

Opening his eyes, he saw dangled above him examples of Michael Aidan O'Reilly's craft. Christs on crosses, Christless crosses and crossless Christs, suspended from the ceiling on a dependence of wires. There were impossible cherubs supporting impossible scrolls bearing impossible verse. These were not the winged creatures that traditionally supported Jehovah. Indeed, the closer Parable peered, the more certain was he that their human faces owed more to photography than inspiration:

– Jesus! That one is the image of Sergeant Bilko . . . and there's the bald fella from the Three Stooges . . . is that Snozzle and W. C. Fields in angel drag?

It was pure theatre. The 'Pope' O'Reilly was not mourning anybody – least of all the dead. And P. J. told himself that he couldn't blame him. Death was the most obscene end ever devised to life. It was a shabby, disgusting affair, and He, who claimed to have thought of it, should have had a better sense of humour. The melancholy mourners, the preying preachers, the overtaking undertakers, all added up to a dejected, depressing, doleful despondency inimical to good taste. Parable told himself that he would rather die than be mourned.

By now he was wide awake but he didn't want that state to be understood abroad just yet. He needed to contemplate his being. The back view of the 'Pope' O'Reilly was of an earnest, leaning-forward craftsman indenting a chalk mark. The chip chip of the chisel and the tap tap of the hammer spoke a language understood by the sculptor and the marble. To anybody else, such rhythm was noise.

P. J. sat up on his elbows, stretched his body in self-indulgent luxury, and asked the sculptor's back:

– Where the hell do you find your customers, Michael – in the music hall?

– Good morning to you, Patrick Joseph Henry Pearse Jones. The answer to your impertinent query is that my customers find *me*, dead and all as they are. I cater for ingratitude and spite, mainly. For widows who detested their husbands and widowers who hated their wives . . .

– Aye, but how do they get to know about you? Where do you get them from?

– Ah yes, there's the rub! Or, in the unlikeliness of the language that the Galway people do not know – from where do I get my customers. Did you read that letter in the *Grudian* the other day about grammar?

– Prepositions and things . . .

– Indeed! You know, Patrick, my child, it's more than prefixes, suffixes and such, that are the worry of the middle classes. One eejit wrote to say that, thirty years ago, C. P. Scott wrote an ugly sentence, so as to avoid using a split infinitive.

– You don't say? Imagine anybody remembering a split infinitive after thirty years!

– Imagine anybody with so little to think about than remembering a split infinitive after thirty seconds!

– You think it's all nonsense?

– Well, it all depends on what you mean to say . . . we were always taught that a phrase must be so placed in a sentence that it does the work it was intended to do.

– 'The old gentleman left happy women', and not 'the old gentleman left women happy'?

– Well, maybe Winston, in his literary innocence, had it right. Johnson wrote about using the language of Shakespeare and Milton, but they didn't write the same words as Sam.

– No?

– He was the man mainly responsible for driving Shaw around the bend.

– You think so?

– I know so, sir! Johnson was more responsible than anybody else for the existence of unpronounceable words. Yes, sir, he put the *ache* into Shakespeare's 'aking hart'.

– That old Milton was a curious cove.

– Curiouser and curiouser, old son.

– You know he more or less admitted that his was a twisted nature?

– He wouldn't be pleading guilty to a lie, I'm thinking . . . not after his sponsorship of Cromwell.

– Yes, he wrote, 'Only in destroying I find ease to my relentless thoughts . . .'

– That sounds like a Miltonic truth! But soft, what sound through yonder wireless breaks. It is the north, and Jesus is the cloud!

Radio Eireann diverted its early morning listeners with the views of a Dublin Protestant paper:

– 'Having spoken to many people about their experiences of "inter-church" marriages, we feel that young Church of Ireland people should approach the possibility of wedding a Roman Catholic with extreme caution.' So says the editorial in the April edition of the Church of Ireland youth magazine, *Links*, which has a detailed feature article on 'mixed' marriages.

– It details the case histories of two marriages between Catholics and members of the Church of Ireland in the Republic, which were fraught with difficulties caused mainly by the Catholic Church . . .

Parable put a hand to his sore head and begged:

– No, Michael, I couldn't bear Christianity at this hour of the morning. Jesus, but your Christians are worse than the Jews and the Muslims . . .

– You're right, my lovely son, religion is not my idea of opium, I must admit.

– It's the tiresome bigotry . . .

– Yes, and the southern Protestant crowd are worse because they're so articulate . . . I mean all you need do with Paisley and McGuinness and Robinson is throw them a few bananas, but the crowd in Dublin have the words, don't you know.

– That's because they're surrounded by Catholics . . . in the North the R. C.'s are as thick as bricks because they're in a sea of Protestants!

– Christ, Paddy, I never thought of that now! But, at that rate the national question will never be solved, because, by the law of diminishing returns, one crowd will always be as stupid as the other until Urbi et Orbi becomes a reality on the Shankill Road.

– God forbid, Michael, that we lose our belief in atheism.

With a swift blow from his lump hammer, the 'Pope' O'Reilly knocked the little radio to the floor and beat on it until not even a whimper was heard:

– I can no longer stand it, Paddy, me and Joan of Arc and the Playboy of the Western World are destroyed by the voices . . .

– Why the hell did you do that, Michael? Why break a perfectly good radio?

– But, was it? I think that it was got at.

He lowered his voice, and, looking all round the studio, he whispered to Parable:

– You have no idea of the shit that has been coming through those airways at me . . . and not just Rodeo Eireann.

– No?

– Even the trustworthy old Beeb is broadcasting instant religion. Time was, Pat, in the reign of Randy Reith, when the God slot was at a proper time.

– Is there such a thing as a 'proper time' for religion?

– John Reith said that the *Epilogue* must be put on at the end of the day, when the world was asleep . . .

– And be read by somebody dressed like Dracula . . .

– Don't knock it, lad. Look what we have now. D'ye know that there was a Baptist minister on the BBC the other morning, objecting to a lottery in aid of the National Health Service.

– Well, that's understandable, the Baptists are against all forms of gambling, aren't they?

– But, how did he couch his objections?

– I'm sure I don't know.

– He said, 'A lottery calls for faith in the unlikely existence of a supernatural lucky number!'

– If they were not also opposed to stained glass windows, I'd say that a statement like that must border on blasphemy.

– And so nasty with it . . .

– Ah but sure, one person's bigotry is another person's bad manners.

– Lord, Paddy, if only my crucifix had reared our daughter properly, I'd have offered Sally-Anne in the sacrifice of marriage in exchange for you.

– Do you not mean 'sacrament'?

– After carrying my cross I know what I mean, believe me.

– Remember, Michael, what Jung said, 'If there is anything we would change in a child, it may be better to see first if there is not something we might change in ourselves'.

– I rescind my regret! Only a trite shite would quote Jung. Christ, the poverty of philosophy is in the pronouncements of philosophers, right enough! Shaw said that parents should only beat children in anger and he was never a father. Jung never married!

– Sorry about that, Michael, put the lapse down to the youth of the day.

– Ah, sure, living in a country like this, every man is entitled to use one cliché in a sentence . . . what the hell is that?

From the ground floor is heard the most fearful knocking, and Parable said:

– There's somebody in a bloody big hurry and, if you don't open the hall-door, you're going to have to fork out for a new pair of hinges.

The 'Pope' beamed:

– Maybe it's some distracted widower wanting a widow-weight?

– A 'widow-weight'?

– That's what I call the heaviest of my gravestones. Well, I suppose we must reveal the aperture to find out what's on the other side of the hole.

Parable listened to the departing steps of the 'Pope' descending the stairs and thought that for a man as tall and as old he was light and confident on his pins. The hall-door opened and the outside world entered, motor-cars throbbing, milk-bottles clattering and shouts out of context. But the foremost sound was the unmistakable voice of Detective-Sergeant George Matthews, who told the 'Pope':

– You took yer bloody time . . .

– Before the 'Pope' could make reply, Matthews and six stout policemen in plain clothes uniform rushed past him and opened all the doors on the ground floor. Finding their search fruitless, they came to ascend the stairs on the bottom step of which the 'Pope' O'Reilly stood, his trusty lump hammer in menacing mien:

– I may be an old man, but I'll crack some of you muggers' skulls before I'm robbed or raped!

Matthews stared at the white-coated patriarch in disbelief:

– What the hell are you talking about, we're not muggers, we're the police.

– And what's your authority for breaking into my home? Show me your warrant, if you have one.

– Yerra jazes, mister, sure ever since the Prevention of Terrorism Act, warrants are a thing of the past. We can go where we choose now, without let or hindrance.

– That means we're now living in a police state.

– It does, thank God . . .

CHAPTER TWENTY-SEVEN

The Last Post

Sally-Anne Millington had left the office early. Her head wasn't too good from the night before and her job wasn't too secure now that Jeannie Jones had declared to all and sundry that she was no better than a prostitute. Jesus! The whole of Molesworth Street must have been listening; indeed she could nearly swear that she heard windows being raised in Leinster House.

Now she had a pain in her arse listening to the customers of the Bridge Bar wondering if after young Bobby Kennedy's altercation in the north, what chances there might be for peace, if the Pope made another visit for the millennium.

– Maybe the Queen would send for Ian Paisley and tell him to have more respect for the ancient religion of her fathers. Mrs Thatcher might kiss the ring and promise His Holiness to bring the fourth green field back into the emerald pasture.

– Aye, and if me aunt had balls, she'd be my uncle.

She was drinking iced gin and tonic with not too much ice and very little tonic. She was looking at Assumpta Dwyer knitting row upon row of something never ending – either a long scarf for Padraig or an entry for the *Guinness Book of Records*. She was listening to talk between Mousey Duggan and Det. Sergeant George Matthews. The latter sat back in his chair and swore, 'that they':

– Took her away screamin'. As crazy as a cow in calf, Mousey.

– Mad? A nun?

– Sister Mary Ann McGilligan. She went around the Hospice breaking every statue of St Anthony that she could lay her hands on.

– Is that so? Is he out of fashion now?

– Who?

– St Anthony. You know the way the Pope dropped St Christopher?

– I don't think so.

– My poor mother used to swear by St Anthony. A great man for the poor, she used to say.

– That's why I think Sister Mary Ann hated him. He became a sort of fixation with her. Said he was a renegade to conservative church politics. Swore that he hated the rich.

– Then she really is crazy! Sure wasn't Our Lord poor?

– For Christ sake, Mousey, don't make statements like that or there's no way I can protect yeh.

– And where will they put her now? Do they have a special booby hatch for nuns?

– I couldn't really say. They have a puzzle factory for potty priests, but I've never heard of one for nuns.

– It's all sex, yeh know. That's the cause of that.

– D'ye think so?

– Oh, nothin' surer! If she doesn't get the hi diddle diddle, cat in the middle, the cow is bound to jump over the moon . . . that's what Parable says anyway. He thinks that priests and nuns are no different to the rest of us, the sex has to go somewhere; if it doesn't get out in the ordinary place it comes through the head.

Across the table, Matthews inclined his mouth to Mousey's left ear, and whispered:

– Do yerself a favour, Mousey, and forget about Parable Jones.

– How d'ye mean?

Matthews put the point of his index finger to the bulb of his nose and whispered:

– Just markin' yer card, friend, a closed mouth catches no flies . . .

Sally-Anne quietly wondering if her lover would come in today, ordered a large gin. Padraig said kindly, if a little drunkenly:

– Why not have a small one on the house, love, just to be goin' on with.

Sally's eyes flashed:

– Don't tell me that I came to the Sacred Heart Temperance

Society by mistake, Padraig. You're not such a great ad for sobriety . . .

No sooner said than she regretted her outburst. As Padraig put the drink in front of her, she took his hand across the counter in apology:

– I'm sorry, Padraig. You're the last one I should be angry with. I just dropped in on the off-chance that Parable might be here.

– He seldom puts in an appearance at this hour, but, sure, a good man is worth waitin' for, child.

Sergeant Matthews laughed, and whispered to Mousey:

– She'll have a long bloody wait.

– How d'ye mean?

– Enough said, ould son . . .

As Mousey pondered the mysteries of the police, a young man asked in a northern accent if Assumpta would object to him leaving his suitcase in the corner until he came back from Sean Heuston Station. Everybody laughed, and shouted, in typical Irish originality:

– As long as it's not full of bloody gelignite.

Padraig had one too many, for a publican, and had started to ply Mousey, Matthews and Sally-Anne with free drink. Worse than that – in the eyes of his wife – he was talking politics. As Mousey started to sing 'Thora', Assumpta screamed at her husband:

– Cut them politics from the conversation! I've told yeh before that there's to be no politics talked in me nephew's pub!

– It's economics I'm discussin', yeh silly bog bitch!

– It sounds like politics to me, so it does.

– Well, it's not, so there!

And Mousey trilled:

– 'Speak, speak, speak to me Thora . . .'

And Joe Wilmot asked Padraig:

– Is it the 'futures' market that you are talking about?

– The very thing! a racket that guarantees high prices for the consumer, high profits for the stock exchange, high risks for the small farmer, and high unemployment for the country.

Assumpta counted her stitches like beads marking a decade of the rosary, and screamed:

– Them is politics yer on about. Everybody knows that unemployment is caused by politics.

– 'Light of my life, saint of my saints . . .'

And, all the time he sang, Mousey was trying to manoeuvre the suitcase under his chair with his foot. Wilmot was saying:

– There's nothing new about the 'futures' market, Padraig.

– No?

– 'Saint of my saints, angel of love to me . . .'

Mousey was convinced that there was good gear in the bag. In a moment he'd slip to the jacks – nobody would ever notice a man goin' to the lavatory with a suitcase, and, if they did, fuck 'em. Wilmot quoted:

– 'Here's a farmer, that hanged himself on the expectation of plenty', is a line, Padraig, from Macbeth. What does that tell you?

Before Padraig could respond, Sally-Anne interjected, drunkenly:

– That farmers were always a moaning shower of fuckers!

– It shows that the year was a bad one for wheat prices. And it proves that even four hundred years ago, folk in agriculture were betting on the future . . .

Joe knew that he shouldn't have mentioned the 'Scotch' play, but he couldn't resist the opportunity to shine. Mousey had gotten to the big finale: 'Light of my life, saint of my saints, angel of love to me, angel of love to . . .' When he and the chair, and Sergeant Matthews and the table, went flying through the pub ceiling . . .

Parable Jones, Bryden MacWilliams, Sean Daly, Charlie Belton and Bobo Martin, were walking, two by two, around the exercise yard in Mountjoy Prison, when they heard the explosion. Charlie had been telling P. J. about the taxi-driver's account of Vico, and Parable had been gilding the Italian lily:

– Vico, through folk tales and poetry, was into the power of the imagination, the strength of which was manifest in folk poetry, especially that of Homer. That's why Joyce was so fascinated by him.

The exercise yard was like the ring within another ring described by Wilde in *The Ballad of Reading Gaol*. Parable's group consisted only of the six persons mentioned, but, walking around them, yet quite removed, were the dignified terrorists of stiff step and martial mien; who suspected comrades, and murdered strangers. Every now and then, out of the corner of his eye, Parable noticed Bobo, looking long and longingly at the patriots, and P. J. knew that it was only a question of time before he reverted to type.

After the bang, the conjectures. The explosion came from somewhere near the Phoenix Park so it was assumed that the Magazine Fort had erupted. Soon enough the news spread, for it is said that prisoners get to know about things almost before they happen. The Bridge Bar had been blown up by the Ulster Volunteer Force. There were twelve soldiers killed, and a member of the Garda Siochana who had been there in the line of duty. A well-known Dublin criminal and an unidentified woman.

Parable said that Tom Reivey had sold somebody a bad pint; privately he consoled himself with the knowledge that Sally-Anne would have been at work.

Looking at the mindless republican terrorists circumambulating the yard in stoic silence he was able to contemplate the minds of the Protestant terrorists who had bombed a dirty Dublin drinking hole. This heroic attack would go down in the annals of terrorism, down, down, until the other crowd bombed some shit-house on the Shankill Road:

– But, surely not even the crazy northerners believed that Dublin had any time for anywhere else? Bombing was necessary in some places – for the mean little houses in the Falls and Shankill Roads, and the mean little minds of Newry and Portadown. But, Dublin! Jesus, Christ, Almighty! To save the country, Patrick Henry Pearse had offered his life as hostage for the city.

The landing screw and the yard screw were getting cold and restless, as they watched from the prison steps. Had they been overseeing ordinary lags, they would have locked them up when the exercise period turned sharp. But they were terrified of the 'politicals'. They harboured a grudging respect for the terrorists who, like them, believed in military discipline.

They hated Parable Jones and his hairy intellectual friends, and would constantly tax their minds thinking up ways to annoy them. Only this morning after reception, a chief screw had shown Parable the cell where two of Jordan Hutch's young protégés had committed suicide. P. J. remembered the incident well; the two students had been praised as promising poets by Jordan Hutch, but, after he and his friends had stolen their virginity, Jordan had assumed his Dorian Gray persona and left them severely alone, having told them that they had no literary talent. The chief screw had laughed as he said:

– Wasn't it queer dat two queers couldn't write, Jones?

And Parable had replied:

– Surely you, chief, would be in a better position to understand the intellectual abilities of your sex than me?

But now he knew that there was somebody coming to the inside of the exercise yard door because, within the prison, he could hear the shouts of:

– One on to you, sir!

– One on to me, sir!

Then the prison door opened and a lag appeared bearing a note which he handed to the landing screw. The two jailers read the note with an increasing sense of fun, purpose and satisfaction, looking all the time from the paper to Parable, and back. Then the landing screw told the yard screw:

– This is the moment I have been waiting for. Wait'll you see that fucker's face.

Then he called:

– Jones! Jones, over here, please!

He handed Parable the note and the two prison officers were astonished when P. J. jumped down the steps to his comrades and told them:

– Bryden! Charlie! We're made up! We'll want no more! Our books have been banned!

Charlie asked:

– The three of them?

And, when Parable nodded, Bryden enquired:

– Mine as well?

– The three of them, said Parable.

Bobo knew that it was time to rejoin his warrior comrades, Carey thought it was time he took up writing, and Daly said it was time to give up poetry:

– Would you believe that no Irish poet has been banned since Brian Merriman wrote *The Midnight Court*?

– More shame to the fucking poets, said Parable Jones.